What Would Ginger Rogers Do?

What Would Ginger Rogers Do?

CAITLIN RAYNES

buried
river
press

ISBN 978-1-910208-24-3

Buried River Press
Clerkenwell House
Clerkenwell Green
London EC1R 0HT

www.halebooks.com

Buried River Press is an imprint of Robert Hale Ltd

2 4 6 8 10 9 7 5 3 1

Typeset in Palatino
Printed and bound in Great Britain by
CPI Antony Rowe, Chippenham and Eastbourne

This book is for
Cami Ostman and Pamela Malpas
Merci mille fois, mes chères amies

Chapter One

'*Jingle Book Jingle Book Jingle All the Way!* It came to me in a dream,' she said. 'Don't you see how perfect that is?'

'*Jingle Book.* Interesting,' I observed, though I took a sip of scalding coffee so I wouldn't have to say more. Miss Carter's brilliant marketing ideas always came to her in dreams, or in flashes of inspiration while she walked through meadows, or strolling stormy beaches while eagles soared overhead. Or, sometimes she just ripped them off from other bookstores and took the credit. 'How do you see this working in the store? I mean, actually on the shelves?' I asked.

'Well, Tosca,' she replied, her sharp little teeth gleaming, 'that's your job, isn't it? Isn't that why I made you Events and Publicity? That's your forte, isn't it? You put my *idea* into *action!*'

So I put it into action, knowing full well that if the idea succeeded, the success was hers; any failures were on me. I created a banner for the front window of Carter & Co. Books: *Jingle Book Jingle Book Jingle All the Way.* I hand-made little paper ornaments in the shape of books, brick-red construction paper to look like old leather, and wrote the titles in gold ink. Through each I threaded a red piece of yarn with a little bell on it, and hung them all over the store. Fiction, non-fiction, staff pick shelves, the Children's Corner, Cookbooks, Travel. Every time so much as a draft rattled through the store (frequently) there was a festive little cacophony of *Jingle All the Way*.

And with all those little bells ringing, you do sort of get into the spirit, *ho ho ho* and *'tis the season*, even if in the book trade this has been the year of living dangerously, whether you wanted to or not. The book trade needs the holidays—truly, whimperingly needs. A third of booksellers' annual sales are in December. Shoppers get more desperate as the days dwindle down to the 25th. Books look better and better; a book is forever, as we are fond of saying. In Christmas seasons past, our business was so lively Miss Carter would hire high school kids to sit in the drafty storeroom at the back and gift wrap. But not this year. This year was grim. This year Jessie, Sally, Wendell and I not only had to sell the books, we had to wrap them too. Still, no matter the economic climate, Miss Carter's annual Christmas party was a famous tradition on the island, a Fezziwiggian event not to be missed.

The night of the party, Jessie and I were the last two in the shop. By the time we got the last customer out, front locked, the computers, fans, and lights turned off, the heat turned down, and left by the back – it was seven o'clock. We shivered under the small awning sheltering the loading dock while I locked up. We splashed down the alley together under a light snowfall, and ran the three blocks to my place, second floor of the old Seafarer's Union.

The Seafarer's Union as an organization was a distant memory, back when Friday Harbor was supported by fishing rather than tourists, but the sturdy brick building, Edward Hopperish, with long narrow windows and a steep staircase, remained. A firm of lawyers had the first floor. The second floor was carved up into apartments; mine was the corner one with lots of windows. We clamored up the stairwell that was filled with the smell of someone else's cooking.

My apartment is perfect for one person; uncurtained windows let light into the living room where there is a whole wall for a desk and bookshelves, a TV and a Playstation. Beside the door my bike hangs on the wall like a piece of art. Across from it, and hanging above the couch, is a beautifully framed 1905 Art Nouveau poster of the famous opera singer, Emma Calvé in *Tosca* (birthday present from my parents). The ironing board in the corner by the kitchenette is not a work of art. It didn't have to be. Housekeeping is not my forte, and I live alone.

'It's freezing in here,' said Jessie as she dashed for the bathroom. 'Can you turn up the heat?'

'We're not going to be here that long. It's a pit stop. We have to get to Miss Carter's Christmas party, or all the really good hors d'oeuvres will be gone.'

Jessie went into the bathroom and I collapsed briefly on the couch, pulling my phone out of my bag. *Don't 4get the fish Xmas Eve.* Text from my sister Norma. Norma can't help being a nag, it's in her bone marrow (mine too, probably since we're both related to Aunt Clara). Voice mail from Aunt Clara: 'Don't forget the fish.' Voice from Aida: 'Would you please choose a nice cookbook for me to give to Jim's sister? Make it moronically easy with a lot of pictures. She couldn't cook her way out of a candy wrapper. Thanks, Prune. See you soon.' Voice from Kate Zilich, high school art teacher, and fellow member of the chorus of Community Theatre's *The*

Music Man. 'Hey, Tosca, the population of eligible men year round on this island just doubled. I've heard that a certain math teacher is getting dee-vor-iced. TTFN.'

I knew who she's talking about, and I knew why he was getting a divorce. Everyone knows everything on an island. I texted her back: *TBNT. Newly divorced men R trainwrex. 76 trmbones 2U2 XXOO.*

Lastly, a voice mail from my sister Carmen. 'Hey Prune, just a heads up, Chris will be back for Christmas dinner since you and he were such a great hit at Thanksgiving.'

'Were we?' I ask no one, sliding the phone back in my bag. My sisters all married young; two of the three were knocked up when they said I Do. I am unmarried, and every holiday family gathering, the proverbial Nice Young Man is as much a fixture as the cranberry relish. I'm *thirty*, for God's sake, and they still called him the Nice Young Man. This past Thanksgiving, my nephew Charlie and his wife (yes, I have a married nephew older than I am) brought Chris Egan. Chris Egan brought a very nice bottle of Italian wine. Before the turkey had gone all the way round the table, my mother and Aunt Clara had managed to extract from him that he worked at *Microsoft* (as though the word itself trailed clouds of glory), that he had gone to Johns Hopkins, and that he was raised Catholic. Perhaps Chris Egan did not hear the collective expectant sigh from the Tonnino women, but I did. My movie date with him the day after Thanksgiving filled my mother with such dewy hope that I hadn't the heart to dispel it. Chris is nice, even attractive in that pale, freckled Irish way, but nerdy, and I felt no chemistry with him. I told my sister Carmen this, and she remarked that nice but nerdy might describe me as well. I resented this. I am artsy, stylishly retro and full of panache, which is one of my favorite words. I like the way it tastes.

Despite the hand-wringing of my mom, my Aunt Clara, my sisters Norma, Aida and Carmen, I feel no imperative, biological or otherwise to marry. I've seen enough of marriage among my sisters to recognize the eternal compromising that eventually whittles both parties down till they look and sound like each other, neutered in other words, by the time they're middle-aged. I don't want to live like that. (Though I must say, my parents, Frank and Donna, have not paled into one big marital lump.) Still, in the words of the old Oingo Boingo song, I like my stupid life just the way it is. I have flingettes often, well, often enough for a feeling of tonic anticipation. That's what I enjoy; I am not into domestic partnerships. When I come home at night there is no sulky man looking for a blowjob before I cook dinner as he watches the thrilling NBA playoffs.

On the contrary, I go out! I have lots of friends, island-wide. My job, Events and Publicity, is both demanding and socially fulfilling. I represent the bookstore on the Tourist Board, and I lead the monthly in-store Book Club too. I serve as Vice-President of the Bike San Juan Cycling Club, a post which, mercifully, had no duties, and seasonally I am an island eagle-counter. Now and then, when they do a musical with a big chorus, I join the community theatre. I have yoga class twice a week, and I was the best student in my tango class last spring, though sadly, the class ended; the teacher realized that no way was she going to convince Northwest women to give up their jeans and athletic shoes, and put on a skirt and high heels even once week. I didn't need convinc-ing; I love high heels, fancy scarves and shawls, skirts that respond to a breeze. Winters in the Puget Sound of course require jeans and boots, but I draw the line at flannel. No flannel for *moi*, thank you, and I intend to go to the Christmas party tonight looking stunning.

'Hurry up, Jessie,' I called out. 'I need to pee!'

I meandered into the bedroom which, as usual, was a mess. The bathroom, unfortunately, is off the bedroom (one reason I seldom had guests). Jessie is my best friend, and she doesn't care that the bed is unmade, clothes scattered, the laundry basket overflowing, dust on the bureau, and books in piles of three and four falling over by the bed. The walls are papered in vintage movie posters, Ginger Rogers and Fred Astaire posters, *Top Hat* and *Shall We Dance* and *The Gay Divorcee*. My favorite poster was above my bed, a framed, Ginger and Fred gliding against a spare, elegant background to *Let's Face the Music and Dance*.

I peeled off my work clothes and hanging on the closet door, found the elegant skirt, black silk blouse and red-fringed shawl I'd bought months ago (in a shop I discovered via quirky new book, *Vintage Seattle*). I put on my stilettos, knowing I wouldn't have to walk far in the snow because Miss Carter always has valet parking for the party. I regarded myself critically in the long mirror, and made a vow to lose ten pounds and get my brows waxed before Christmas. Make it five pounds. Five I could do. I gave my hair a quick up-sweep, and pawed through the earring box to find the perfect pair.

'Jessie, hurry!'

Then I heard little gulping cries from the bathroom, barely repressed sobs. I went to the bathroom door, knocked, and said, 'Forget Murph. He's a bastard.'

'Is not.'

'Okay, then, he was a fool to leave you. A fool. He never deserved you.'

There was a pause, then a low, trembling voice, 'I'm thirty-three years old, Tosca. I want to be married. How will I find someone else? Why did he leave me for her?'

'Men are fools, Jessie,' I said, echoing what we'd all been telling her since Thanksgiving when her cat died and her fiancé moved out of their house (which he had built on his own property). Personally, I thought the cat was the greater loss. It was the old/new story: on Facebook, Murph found his old high school girlfriend who now had two kids and an abusive ex. They became Facebook friends, and presto! Four months later Murph quit his job, left Jessie, and went to the mainland, Bremerton, where he moved in with this woman and her kids. Facebook, if you ask me, is fine if you are into high school cliques, or checking up on your teenagers, or if you're middle-aged, like Murph and trying to recapture your youth. But otherwise? I am in the minority – and naturally, I used Facebook daily professionally – but personally, I prefer to keep books and faces separate.

When Murph abandoned Jessie, everyone at work was supportive, as you would be for any friend. To no avail, I should add. Jessie couldn't seem to wean herself from misery. Still, you'd had to have a heart of stone not to feel for Jessie's pain. I changed the tone of my voice.

'Look, Jessie, just wait till summer! Men everywhere! Come on, soon as the boating season opens, San Juan Island is crawling with tourists, good looking, well-heeled men with boats, and plenty of time and money. They're everywhere. Think of it that way.'

'I'm not like you. I'm not looking for a summer flingette.'

'Hey, some of my affairs lasted into the autumn, and then I lost interest.'

'Or they did.'

'Same difference.'

'Seven years with Murph,' she sniffed, 'how can I date again? I've forgotten how to date.'

'No one forgets how to date, Jessie. You just have to dust it off,' I said, ignoring the impulse to quote the lyrics from *Dust Yourself Off*. 'Like riding a bike,' I offered cheerfully.

'I want commitment, Tosca. I want to be loved. Who will love me? Who will live with me? It's all right for you, being alone. You like it.'

'Who says I like it?'

'If you didn't like it, you wouldn't do it. You're attractive. Murph always thought you were cute.'

'Great. Just whose opinion I value.'

'You're afraid of commitment. You haven't had a relationship that lasted more than a year since Vince. Admit it, you like hooking up and moving on.'

'Oh, Jessie, don't go all Dr. Phil on me now. We have to leave.'

'Vince broke your heart, and you're still not over it.'

This was complete shit, but I knew better than to argue with her when she was like this. Once Jessie launched on the subject of commitment, she was frigging relentless.

She finally opened the bathroom door, dabbing her eyes with a towel. Jessie was tall, with narrow shoulders and narrow hips, and long sandy-colored hair that fell straight around her face, making her seem somehow taller and narrower than she was. She let me have the bathroom and she went to the bureau mirror to put on her eye make-up.

When I came out she had fresh make-up, but she still looked pathetic. 'Honest, Jessie, everything'll look good again in June.'

Her lip trembled.

'May, then. Boating season opens in May.'

'Oh God, you and your men with sailboats! Why don't you just get your own boat?'

'I don't want my own boat. I like to let someone else have the expense and the worry and the upkeep, and all the time it takes. I like the *picture* of myself on a sailboat.' I stood beside her in the mirror and lifted my chin. 'I like to think of myself – alluring, sexy, while the sunshine glitters on the waters of the Sound and the handsome man at the tiller is dying to find a secluded cove so he can make love to me on deck.' I smiled, and put on mascara. 'I'm a romantic.'

'Is that why you're not married?'

'Oh God, Jessie! You sound like my mother or my sister or my Aunt Clara. They'd have me mumbling the Old Maid's Prayer.' I rolled my eyes heavenward, 'O Lord, send me a man! Get it? Any man. Not for me, *mon amie!*'

'You never compromise, do you?'

In reply, I gave a very Gallic shrug. I was a renowned Francophile.

'You want to know how low I've sunk, Tosca?' As if to prove it, Jessie sank down on the unmade bed. 'You know what my life has come to, how I have compromised?'

I didn't, but she looked so pitiful, I put my hand on her shoulder.

'It was me and the spin cycle last night.'

'The what?'

'You know, like that temp, Carly told us a couple of years ago? Carly knew how to get along without a man.'

'I hardly remember Carly. She only worked here one summer.'

'She told us how she bonded with her washer. On the spin cycle. How you could sit on the machine during the spin cycle, and it was every bit as good as a man if you—'

'I go to Laund-o-Rama, Jessie, so I've never tried it.'

'It works. I never thought I would be reduced to the spin cycle, but I miss Murph so much.'

I hadn't the heart to remind her that Murph's less-than-awesome erectile performance was a constant refrain in our girl-conversations. 'Re-shuffle your deck, girlfriend! Ask yourself, what would Ginger Rogers do?' I pointed to the big framed poster above the bed, glamorous Ginger and elegant Fred. 'Ginger could, if she so chose, slay a man with the arch of her pencilled eyebrows.' I arched my eyebrows to prove it. 'Do you think Ginger Rogers would sit around moping after a man who mistreated her? Hell no. Ginger Rogers would put on her best, her most gorgeous, frothy gown, her silk stockings and high heels, tell the doorman to hail a cab, and off she'd be to someplace where the music was hot, and the men were hotter.'

'Oh, Tosca,' Jessie laughed in spite of herself.

'She'd sashay in, greet the barman by name and order a sidecar.'

'What's a sidecar again?'

'A sophisticated drink from the Thirties – Cointreau, brandy, lime juice and sugar round the rim. She would take long strolls through the room, like this.' I did my practiced imitation of Ginger's stride, full of insolent economy. 'And regard every man there with a cool, assessive eye. She might say to herself, perhaps I will sleep with that man.' I pointed to the suave, tuxedoed mythical man looking handsome beside the laundry basket.

'They didn't do that in the Thirties.'

'Don't kid yourself. Ginger and Fred could get more sex in one little glance, one dip, one sway across the dance floor than all the grappling on *Game of Thrones*.'

'Yes, yes. I know. You've made me watch those old films with you a hundred times. But Tosca, they're so fake!'

'They're not fake, they're fantasy. And anyway,' I tangoed toward the door frame and leaned against it, one arm up, caressing the jamb. 'You see this handsome man? This man oozing sex appeal? I will sleep with him.' A twirl toward the bed where I fell with abandon, turning to my pillow. 'You see this shirtless hunk? I will sleep with him too.'

'They call that slut, Tosca.'

'No, Jessie,' I said, getting up, smoothing my skirt, and shaking my head, 'they call it erotic independence.'

'I don't want erotic independence. I want to be married.'

I ignore this. 'Anyway, it's not about actually Doing It with lots of men, it's about knowing that you could. Women like Ginger Rogers are proud of their experience. They're sassy and sophisticated. They move through the world with confidence. They don't wait around to be plucked like a flower, or visited like a flame, happy for any old moth who comes up to them.'

Jessie turned to the mirror and applied her lipstick. 'Why can't you just be a fan of Jennifer Lawrence like everyone else, Tosca? You set too much store by Ginger Rogers, and all those ridiculous old musicals, those old Thirties films. No one lives like that. No one ever lived like that.'

'So ... we should just sit around and weep in our beer over faithless men?'

'You wept over Vince.'

'Did not. All right,' I conceded in response to her rolled eyes. 'I did.'

'Besides Tosca, look in the mirror. Ginger Rogers was a gorgeous blonde beauty. Are you?'

I walk over to the mirror. I'm taller than all the other Tonninos, but there's no doubt I got my mother's aquiline nose, my father's mouth, and the Tonnino mass of dark curly hair. My eyes, however, are my own. One brown and one green. I'm not a beauty, but I say in my defense, 'Never mind beauty. I prefer mystique. Ginger Rogers has mystique.'

'Oh, Tosca, you are impossibly artsy-fartsy. Let's go to the party.'

I was always the artsy daughter. Much to my father's delight, I had musical ability, and he had visions, I'm sure, of a musician, even an opera singer in the family. I played soprano sax till I was about twenty, and I took dance lessons forever, and I had a bit of talent, I suppose, but I never had the drive or discipline or commitment. Reading and writing seemed easier, and I always loved books, so, naturally, I was an English major in college, with a minor in French. I might have majored in French, but that required too many language classes. I didn't want to translate for a living; I wanted to live *la vie en rose*. The minor in French satisfied my infatuation with all things French: Edith Piaf, Henri Cartier-Bresson, Cezanne, Matisse, Proust, Baudelaire, Balzac, Flaubert, and Julia Child, who, I knew wasn't French, but her cookbook was as close as I was ever likely to get to Framboise Flambée. I spent a semester in Paris in my junior year where I took a French lover – who, honestly wasn't that great – and learned to smoke.

I quit cigarettes on my return to the States. But at least I could say I've had a Gauloises and a French lover.

On my return to Seattle University, a roommate dragged me to a Seattle International Film Festival celebration of classic Thirties films. This was my first introduction to Ginger Rogers, Bette Davis, Katherine Hepburn, all those savvy women, broad shouldered broads who stride in trousers, who assess the world around them with an unsentimental gaze, who can pile more meaning into the innocuous phrase, *Oh brother,* than your average Oscar winner can in a string of F-bombs. These were women for whom the erotic is always spiced with the elusive. In those classic films with Fred Astaire, Fred always pursued Ginger, knowing for a fact he was in love. Not Ginger. No easy capitulation for her. Ginger was smart, talented, choosy, and independent, a glamorous woman, a working woman. That Christmas, my parents and Aunt Clara got me the Astaire/Rogers DVD set, and sat through all the films with me, the farcical plots redeemed by the glorious dancing.

I knew I'd never dance like Ginger Rogers but discovering her helped me say a firm No, Thanks to my family's expectations once I graduated. These can be briefly summed up thus: I would date while I went to Seattle University, a Catholic institution, until I married a Catholic. I could marry quietly, or I could have a great big wedding like Carmen. (I was her flower girl.) Once married, I would set about having children, incurring a mortgage, and doing holidays year after frigging year with the same people, and I would come to love it. To see it as a positive value. To pass it along to my children who would in turn.... In short, the dreary, monotonous familial rut, shackled nonstop to people who share your

DNA. That's why Vince appealed to me as a lover. Vince wanted to have adventures on the *Invincible*, his sailboat. I too wanted to have adventures. I wanted to live making waves, or at least ripples, to tap dance, or tango, to embrace the unconventional. I'd rather vibrate with desire than tremble with guilt. I look at the world with Ginger Rogers's default expression: direct, sexy, and a little defiant.

Ginger Rogers came to stand for that whole cadre of Thirties heroines who had careers and ambitions, actresses who portrayed real women, not simpering girls. They could and did fall in love, care for men, yes, but they were first and foremost true to themselves. What would Ginger Rogers do? That's what I ask myself in any social or romantic dilemma. She sometimes replies inside my head, her voice cool, sly, sophisticated.

Chapter Two

THE WOODS WERE snowy, dark and deep, as the saying goes, and the road to False Bay was slick and narrow, but my trusty Subaru did not slide as we zipped between sloping fields and meadows basted with neat fences, and sparkling under a full moon. Miss Carter's house at the end of her private road was brilliant with light and cheer. Designed by a famous Seattle architect, it was very modern, all soaring ceilings and vast windows. Before that she had lived for many years in a much less showy place on this same property which had been in her family since Prohibition. Miss Carter's grandfather was a rich bootlegger who escaped your usual bootlegger's fate by moving to Vancouver and operating out of there. San Juan Island – at that time the most Westerly point in America – was a nice little stopover for the transport of illegal Canadian whiskey. On the bounty of these ninety proof riches, the Carter family bought vast tracts of island waterfront property, especially tracts that had secret coves. After Prohibition ended, Miss Carter's grandfather held on to the land, but put his ill-gotten gains into aircraft plants.

On his bootlegging largesse and Seattle's aircraft industry, Edith Carter grew up wealthy, well-traveled, educated at the best schools. After Bryn Mawr she went to the Sorbonne in Paris where she too, no doubt, learned to smoke and took a French lover. Miss Carter had more than one kind of love affair in Paris. She fell in love with the legend of Shakespeare and Co., the famous Left Bank bookshop on the rue de l'Odéon, that mecca, preserve, and home to great literary talents, Joyce, Hemingway, Gertrude Stein. Miss Carter's dream was to follow in the footsteps of Sylvia Beach, the American owner of this Parisian bookshop. In short, to serve Literature. When Miss Carter says the word, Literature, the capital is implicit. The ambience of Carter & Co. Books is decidedly Bohemian Paris chic, complete with a sliding library ladder on the back wall. Edith Carter's life has echoed Sylvia Beach's in other ways as well. Miss Carter and her stout companion Nan are as traditional a marriage as you'd care to see. Nan dotes on Edith, keeps a magnificent house, and has nothing to do with the store. Portly Nan, with her short helmet of hair, looks like Gertrude Stein. Miss Carter, as she has aged, has come to look more and more like Alice B. Toklas, small, ugly, with great dark eyes, and a sharp nose. And like Miss Toklas, she favored strange hats. And, like Miss Toklas, anyone who called her Edith got instantly corrected.

Miss Carter was the only Islander whose parties required valet parking. I handed the guy the keys to my car as if I didn't recognize him as the checker at Island Grocery, and he treated me as if I drove a Mercedes and not a Subaru Outback. Music and laughter tumbled out of the house, onto the porch. We knocked, Nan answered, and reminded us that Miss Carter liked cell phones off before you entered.

'Mine's already off,' said Jessie glumly. 'Who'd call?'

'Now come on, Jessie. Cheer up.' I said. 'Who knows, maybe there'll be someone new here.'

'Oh, there's someone new,' said Nan, rolling her eyes, and handing our coats to a hired lackey. 'Wait'll you girls see him. You girls will say, *Yum yum, don't wrap it up, I'll eat it here.* Follow me.'

An enormous noble fir tree nearly scraped the cathedral ceiling. Everything was done up with festive panache, wreaths and ribbons and swags of greenery and bright poinsettias across the mantel, draping the stairwell, mistletoe dangling from the chandelier, the whole essence of seasonal extravagance. Overpowering, really, almost oppressive. The place was awash with laughter and voices; waiters from Island Caterers wearing crisp white shirts and black trousers moved among the crowd of perhaps sixty people with champagne, canapés and cocktail napkins. A string quartet of high school students wafted Christmas music from the sunroom. Miss Carter's party was an island tradition, cocktails and elegant hors d'oeuvres from six to eight, dinner at eight, gift baskets for all her guests as they leave. Every Friday Harbor boutique, café and restaurant owner was there, and they all needed serious cheering up; an island economy depended on tourists, and we'd had a brutal summer. Other guests included lots of other island luminaries from the boating and banking and real estate world, and they were depressed too in this economy. Oddly, the artists and authors, also plentifully represented, were not that depressed; they were used to hard times, and after all, the food and drink here were free.

Jessie and I each took a glass of champagne, and an artful bruschetta and milled among the guests, most of whom we knew, some we saw all the time. Our manager

Wendell, for instance, and Sally from the bookstore, their spouses, as well as Thelma, the book-keeper, even Martha who mopped and cleaned the bookstore twice a week. Surrounding Miss Carter was a coterie of local writers, a few islanders like Frances McTeer, and many from the mainland, Bainbridge and Seattle, Anacortes. She basked in their admiration which was absolutely deserved. She was the patron saint of local writers. She always touted their books, and they got an automatic ten per cent discount in the store, just for being writers.

Miss Carter saw us from a distance, left the writers and greeted us with Continental affection. 'Ah, Jessie! Tosca! The Girls.' Miss Carter inserted herself between us. There clung to her something of the well-bred, wide-eyed debutante she once was. Miss Carter wore a shimmery red blouse that caught the light and a taffeta green skirt, and her thin legs wobbled on high heels. Give her that, old as she was, she was still in high heels.

'Look who's here, everyone!' Her hand firmly at our elbows, Miss Carter steered us through to the living room with its vast windows opening on a picturesque snowy preserve. In front of the Christmas tree, she tapped a tall man on the shoulder. He was talking to Statler and Waldorf who nodded to us.

'Girls,' she said, 'I don't believe you've met Ethan James.'

He was prettier than anyone in the room. *Yum yum*, Nan's phrase echoed in my head. He had blindingly white teeth, salon-streaked dark hair, and a golden tan, and he was so beautifully clean-shaven I fought the urge to move in closer just to smell his cologne. He was well-dressed too, not at all Northwest flannel-and-fleece, but very Abercrombie and Fitch. I glanced at Jessie to see if she'd taken all this in, and she had. *WTF? This guy at*

Edith Carter's Christmas party? He too looked like debutante or starlet fodder, one of those unisexy, vaguely menacing, metro models you see in slick *New Yorker* or *Vanity Fair* ads, certainly not an island man. His handshake was firm, but fast. He did not cling.

'Ethan is the grandson of my old Bryn Mawr roommate, Marjorie Dorn. Class of '56,' said Miss Carter. 'Marjorie was married to a partner at Goldman Sachs, though Ethan's grandfather died in 2006, so he certainly can't be blamed for all that nasty unpleasantness a few years back! Ethan is totally East Coast, poor dear.'

'Never been west of Philly,' said Ethan with a small lift of his glass.

'You have a wonderful experience before you, here in the Northwest, Ethan,' Miss Carter rattled on, extolling the Northwest beaches, mountains, amber waves of grain, concluding, finally, 'Here in the Northwest, we have men to match my mountains.'

'What?'

'A wonderful Irving Stone book. Have you read it?'

Jessie and I exchanged glances. No one reads Irving Stone or Georgette Heyer any more, except Miss Carter who adores historical fiction, as does Sally. Together they kept the flames burning for long-dead historical novelists. Jessie and I each grabbed another glass of champagne from a passing waiter's tray.

'Do you have anything stronger?' Ethan addressed the waiter.

'Stronger?' said the waiter.

'Stronger.' repeated Miss Carter.

'Yeah, you know, like Scotch. I'd like a Scotch. Single malt if possible.'

The waiter looked to Miss Carter who told him to ask Nan where to find the Scotch.

'Well, now you've met our little bookstore family, Ethan,' she went on, 'Wendell and Sally, of course. And Jessie who is an invaluable asset, and Tosca who is our Events and Publicity person. I wanted to call her position Community Outreach, but Tosca felt it sounded too much like a social worker. Still, it is outreach of a sort. And we are a community. Tosca also runs the bookstore Book Club, and holds monthly meetings in our store. We're thinking of branching out, aren't we, Tosca? Perhaps having a Political Book Club, a Teen Readers Book Club, a Cookbook Book Club.'

She smiled at me and I smiled back. *She* might be thinking of branching out, but I'm not. I'm on salary – a decision I regretted agreeing to. The work kept piling on, but the salary stayed the same.

'Tosca does a wonderful job lining up first rate authors to come to our little bookstore for readings.'

I murmured something inane in reply. I've never had an A-list author come to San Juan Island. Seattle – Third Place Books, University Bookstore, Elliot Bay Books – always got big name authors on their book tours. No nationally prominent authors, or their PR people, would willingly make the two hour drive from Seattle to Anacortes, to line up for the ferry (another hour) and the two hour ferry ride (and a return trip of course) to come to Carter & Co and talk to fifteen people, and sell maybe ten books, max.

'Tosca is *très charmant*,' said Miss Carter, invoking our shared Francophilia. 'How could she not be with a name like Tosca? She and her sisters are all named after operas. Now, let me see if I've got this right. There's Tosca and Aida and Carmen and Norma. Tosca's the youngest.'

'My father loves opera. What can I say?'

'You're lucky you didn't get named Madame Butterfly,' said Ethan.

'And Jessie,' Miss Carter put her arm around Jessie and offered a little hug, 'Jessie is suffering under a loss and we all have to be extremely kind to her. At Thanksgiving Jessie's fiancé moved out and her cat died.'

'The cat was put down,' said Jessie.

'Maybe you should have had the boyfriend put down.' Ethan's smile stayed in place, unmoving as the wreath above the fireplace.

'We have our own in-house bookstore cat whom you'll meet, Ethan,' Miss Carter went on, oblivious. 'Every bookstore needs a cat for ambience. Our Mr Hyde is very spoiled, and very naughty. He walks in beauty like the night,' Miss Carter added, though her gaze rested on Ethan. 'He'll be joining us next week.'

'Mr Hyde?' I asked.

'No. Ethan. He's new to our staff.'

'Like working there?' Jessie asked.

'Ethan's going to join Carter & Co.,' she said with a smile. 'He can start with the gift wrapping, and then you can train him.'

'In the middle of the holiday rush?' I strangled on my champagne.

'Well, trial by fire, they always say.'

'They do,' echoed Ethan. The waiter brought him a Scotch with ice.

Jessie and I silently cried out: *Is she out of her fucking mind? Foisting a newbie on us in the middle of the Christmas season?*

But just then Wendell, the store manager, wandered by, and clearly, Wendell had already got the bad news. He looked grim. Wendell was bald, probably pushing sixty, past the point of vanity, though he combed his hair across his pate. He had blue eyes behind big specs, and like the rest of us who lived on the island year round, he was putty-colored pale. He was corpulent, and his many chins fold over his collar which is always cinched by a bow tie, today, seasonally red and green.

'We look forward to having you join us, Ethan,' said Wendell.

Patently false. Jessie and I just kept our eyes on our glasses.

'Bookselling is a team sport,' Wendell went on in his professorial manner. 'We each bring our gifts to the team, and share them on behalf of our customers. Miss Carter loves British mysteries and historical fiction. Jessie is especially fluent with self-help, fitness, outdoor adventure and travel books. Sally loves historical fiction, young adult novels, and women's literature. Tosca is an eclectic reader, fiction, classics, memoir. I tend to like sterner stuff, history biography, politics. What are your reading passions?'

Miss Carter patted Ethan's arm. 'He has a degree in English from Dartmouth. Now, don't be modest. It's true.'

'It's true, but I'm not much of a reader, really. I'm a cyclist. And I play chess. But those aren't things you read about. Those are things you have to actually do.'

There was a moment's weird silence, then Wendell said, 'If you're not a passionate reader, how can you work in a bookstore?'

'You don't need to be passionate about food to work in a grocery store,' said Ethan. 'You need to know where the vegetables are. In a bookstore, you need to know where fiction is, and where non-fiction is, what's the difference, and how much it costs. You're passing goods through the economy. That's all.'

He made it sound like shit through a goose. I watched Miss Carter's face for one of those little tell-tale tremors. Miss Carter believes a bookstore is a Thing Apart from ordinary retail, a Holy Calling. When Miss Carter, or Wendell, for that matter, bring customers together with books they have loved, you'd think they had somehow effected True Love and were watching the happy couple walk down the aisle

'Oh, these Dartmouth men!' Miss Carter laughed. 'They have a reputation for being very blasé and very naughty. Even back when Marjorie and I were at Bryn Mawr, you had to beware of a Dartmouth man. You never know what they'll say. When you put a good book into the hands of a reader,' stated Miss Carter, speaking to Ethan alone, 'you give them a gift. You further the cause of Literature, of art, you connect a reader and a writer across time and miles. Look at what Sylvia Beach did for James Joyce.'

'What did she do?' asked Ethan, which I thought was a pretty strange question for a Dartmouth English major.

Edith Carter's ugly face softened as she got to tell her favorite stories about the legendary booksellers of Shakespeare and Co., the rue de l'Odéon bookshop owned by the American, Sylvia Beach, who turned publisher and published Joyce's *Ulysses* when no one else would go near it, how she had lent books to Hemingway when he couldn't afford to buy, how she had nourished all sorts of authors, and musicians, French and American. Miss Carter spoke with high-pitched diction, 'I value passion on the part of people who work at Carter & Co.'

'Well,' Ethan gave a suddenly good-natured grin, 'I'll

remember that when I sell *Chicken Soup for the Soul*, or the *Guide to Bunny Suicides*. You see, I do read.'

Everyone laughed. Miss Carter said, 'Oh Ethan, you're so funny. Well, girls – and Wendell – you can show Ethan how to truly love literature, and he can show you how to be cool.'

'Cool?' asked Wendell.

'Cool,' she repeated, as if the word were a bubble she was blowing about the room.

'I am cool,' he said, his smile warmed by the Scotch.

'That's what Ethan brings to Carter & Co. You know, cool, as in *chic!*' Miss Carter gave it a very French inflection, and then she took his elbow and moved him across the room to introduce him elsewhere.

'Cool?' said Jessie.

'Ridiculous,' snorted Wendell. 'She didn't even consult me on a new hire. He starts tomorrow! The most demanding week in bookselling! This year we couldn't afford gift-wrappers at minimum wage, and now she's taking on new staff? The store can't support it.'

'Look,' I said, 'she must know what she's doing.'

Jessie gave a surreptitious giggle. 'You always think her ideas suck.'

'Well Jingle Books worked well,' I said, not wanting Jessie to get started on the many times I had indeed questioned Miss Carter's marketing genius, like her decision a couple of years ago to move some bookshelves away from the big front window, take down the café curtains, and set up two wing chairs and a chess table. Really, it looked just like Masterpiece Theatre set, especially with the bookshelves for backdrop, and the house cat, Mr Hyde, sleeping nearby. Miss Carter thought it was brilliant, that it provided us with *Thee-ahter!* in her phrase, and so it stayed. However, truthfully, the wing chairs and chess set took up a lot of retail space, and seriously cut down on our inventory and selection.

At dinner, everyone was seated at about a dozen round tables stretching from the dining room to the sunroom. Each table had a bottle of red and a bottle of white wine, nestled at the center amid greenery, fir boughs so fresh you could smell their sap rising. The man sitting next to me, Statler, was drinking altogether more than was good for him. On his other side, his wife chided and nibbled, nibbled and chided. Statler ignored her, glancing enviously at another table where his crony, Waldorf was engaged in a lively conversation with Ethan. Statler and Waldorf aren't their real names. I forget their real names. I started calling them Statler and Waldorf after the two crotchety old farts on *The Muppet Show* who sit in the balcony and rain down abuse on poor Kermit. Like those two, these guys are critical, white-haired, mustachioed gents, Republican retirees, who took up residence in the wing chairs right after the Masterpiece Theatre set went up. They played chess in our bookstore every morning except Sundays. Their chess board was sacred, though summertime tourists don't know that.

'So I hear the new man at the bookstore was a Dartmouth chess champion,' Statler said.

'I don't know anything about the new hire, except his name.' I turned my attention to Frances McTeer on my right, and asked about her book coming out this spring, the third in a series. I knew that Frances would keep me occupied for half an hour while she touted her claymore-wielding, fierce medieval Scotswomen. Frances is stout, round-shouldered, prim, with graying hair, and you would never guess to look at her, the way that weapons are brandished in her novels.

After dinner, dessert and coffee, the party wound down, and as each guest departed, Miss Carter pressed specially selected gift baskets into their hands. These were tied with red ribbons, and held items from local specialty shops, chocolates from Charlotte's Confectioners, lavender hand lotion from Lavendaria, little jars of jam from Strawberry Fields Forever and always, a book. These were mostly books Carter & Co. could not sell, that had been slightly marred, or the dust jacket a little faded, a corner, perhaps torn. As Miss Carter put the small basket in my arms, she asked if I would be good enough to drive Ethan back to Friday Harbor where he was living, in the harbor, literally, in the marina on a sailboat. I said sure. I was driving Jessie home anyway because her car was in the shop.

The valet boys brought my Subaru up to the porch, and Ethan immediately took the passenger seat, relegating Jessie to the back. Didn't even ask. This pissed me off, Jessie too, as she wordlessly got in the back seat.

'Why does your car smell like wet dog?' he asked as I pulled onto False Bay Drive.

'Does it?'

He leaned forward, breathed deep, like he was into yoga. 'Old wet dog. Everything up here smells like old wet dog.'

'Oh, you mean the damp.'

'You'll get used to it,' said Jessie, 'everyone does.'

'Only if you stick around.'

I replied, 'Didn't you just get a job here? Isn't that a reason to stick around?'

He made a grumpy noise, as though he'd shot his whole wad of sociability at the party.

'You should at least stay through the summer,' Jessie

offered pleasantly. 'Summers up here are great, especially if you sail.'

'I don't sail.'

'But I thought you lived on a boat.'

'I didn't sail it over. It's berthed here and I'm renting it from a friend. It smells damp too, and it's claustrophobic. It rocks every time I fart. I keep hitting my head whenever I go outside the cabin.'

'You'll get over that,' I said, 'but you'll find out what they mean by ship-shape when you live on a boat. Everything in its place. I used to live on a sailboat, a twenty-four footer.'

'You and who else? I mean, girls don't usually live alone on sailboats.'

'Tosca came here on a boat with her boyfriend,' Jessie said. 'They were sailing up and down the Straits of Juan de Fuca. It was very romantic.'

'We spent almost a year,' I explained, 'and we fell in love with Friday Harbor, and decided to stay here for the winter. I got the bookstore job right away. I was buying a book from Miss Carter when someone telephoned, and said they quit, just like that. I couldn't help but overhear, and I said I could do the job, and she hired me on the spot.'

'It helped that you were buying some Froggy novel,' Jessie clarified. 'Miss Carter adores the Frogs, just like Tosca.'

'Flaubert is more than a Froggy novelist. He's—'

'What's the name of your boat?' Ethan asked. 'The one you lived on.'

'Oh, long gone.'

'Great name.'

'I mean it is long gone. It was the *Invincible*. My boyfriend's name was Vince. I have an apartment in town now, but I still love sailing, being out on the Sound, the way the wind and water and canvas work together, and you know you're harnessing nature, working with nature, and making nature work for you too. Just like the ancient Phoenicians.'

Ethan scoffed. 'The ancient Phoenicians can have it, any kind of boat, including yachts. We used to cruise the Mediterranean when I was kid, my mom and one of her rich asshole husbands and all their asshole pseudo-friends spending the summer on these frigging floating palaces. What's the good of standing there on a boat, even if it is a yacht? I like to cycle, to be out on the road and moving! I'm no fan of boats. I told Edith that when I came here.'

'I wouldn't call her Edith if I were you,' I said helpfully. 'No one does.'

'Well, Marjorie does, so that's what I call her.'

'Marjorie, your grandmother? Miss Carter's college roommate?'

'My father's mother.'

'Well if you hate boats and you're not a reader, why are you here?' asked Jessie.

'What is this, *Jeopardy*?'

I glanced at Jessie in the rear view mirror. We were thinking the same thing: *Give it time.* Pretty soon, we'll know everything about Mr Ethan James. Life on an island was like that. You couldn't fart in the public library without everyone knowing what you had for lunch.

When we got to Jessie's house, I waited there, motor purring, till I saw her go in, and the lights flip on, and then pulled out onto the road toward Friday Harbor.

'Don't you have any music in this car?' he asked at last.

'Radio's broken. I just use my iPod when I travel any distance.'

'Any distance? That's a crock. I've been here a few days, riding around on my bike, and I've seen everything. Don't you get island fever? No matter where you go, you always come back to the same spot.'

'An island is no different from anywhere else. Most people live in a little circle, follow the same paths. They just don't think of it like that. I've lived here almost five years.'

'You like it then?'

'Yes. Yes, I do. I guess.'

'Not much action, though.'

'Not unless you count the tides. They're very reliable,' I laughed.

'Everybody I've talked to here, they're so bloody happy. Why is that?'

'What's wrong with happy?'

'Don't they want anything more? Don't you want anything more?'

'Of course I do. I'm learning from this job, everything I'll need to know when I have my own PR firm in Seattle, Tosca Tonnino and Associates: a suite in one of those airy, renovated brick buildings downtown with a view of the waterfront. I'll wear high heels that will snap along parqueted floors as I go to meetings with important people, rigging up media campaigns for authors, creating a whole great, gorgeous edifice of media. There! What do you think of that?'

'You have it all imagined.'

'Planned. I have it all planned. After all, with a name like Tosca, I have to do something grand, if not grand opera. This job is practice for me. I'm not going to be here forever.'

'I bet that's what they all say.'

'Who?'

'All the people who come here to live and end up coming here to die.'

Coming here to die wasn't the way I pictured my own life, and I begrudged his being such a downer. 'You didn't come here to die, I suppose.'

'I didn't come here to live either.'

'Well, why did you come here?'

'I'm between things,' he snapped, and then lapsed into a long, resentful silence.

There's something odd about the enforced intimacy, being alone in a car, driving through a snowy night with someone you scarcely know, especially someone seemingly content with the silence, the hum of the car. I could have nattered, as people do, but Ginger Rogers would not have given this grim dude any more of her time or effort, and neither did I.

I finally came into town, and eased down Spring Street toward the harbor which, under its light dusting of snow looked picturesque, a forest of prim white masts against the dark water and sky. Nearly all the boats were darkened, and a few were strung with Christmas lights. I pulled into the marina parking lot. 'Which one is yours?'

'I told you, it's not mine. I'm renting. It's the *French Letter.*'

'The *French Letter*?' I repeated, astonished.

'You know what that means?' He seemed amused.

'It's a euphemism for condom. An eighteenth century euphemism.'

'Yeah. How do you know that?'

'Duh. I'm a reader.'

'Well, I never heard of it till I rented this boat. But the

guy I'm renting from, he thought it was just way clever. He used the boat as a babe magnet, and believe me, he needed one. When he scored, he'd say, 'I'm taking out the *French Letter.*' What a dipshit. Thanks for the ride, Tosca. It's a hard name to say.'

'I'm sure you'll get used to it. We'll be working together, remember? See you tomorrow.' Dipshit.

He slammed the car door on his way out.

Oh brother.... I could all but hear Ginger Rogers, and all but see her roll her beautiful blue eyes.

Chapter Three

THE NEXT MORNING when I arrived to open the store, Ethan James was waiting for me at the loading dock with his bike, a serious bike, slender and tensile, the spokes gleaming even in the dull winter light. He wore iridescent cycling clothes in bright colors that clung to him like paint. You could see his every … well, his every every. I said, 'You can't work here dressed like that. You look like you're ready for a race.'

'I'm always ready for a race,' he said, lifting the bike which was so light, it seemed to hoist itself aloft. I opened the door and he carried the bike into the large, unheated storeroom, leaning it carefully against the wall, and used a rag to mop the condensation. He mopped it with the care a mother gives to a baby's bottom. When he finished, he unsnapped his sharp-pointed helmet that reminded me of a shiny beetle. He took off his cycling gloves, regarded them studiously for a moment, then he took his right hand glove and hurled it down the length of the storeroom. Next he wound up and threw the left. 'Look at that,' he observed, 'the right one beat the left one.'

'Dude, you are seriously hung up on competition if you have to race your gloves against each other.' I rinsed out Mr Hyde's food dish and water bowl, and dumped his kitty litter in the dumpster out back.

Ethan watched, fascinated. 'Is that part of the job description? Emptying cat shit.'

'The person who opens the store does it,' I replied coldly. I fed Mr Hyde, a great leonine tabby, who regarded the human race as mere footservants to his will.

The storeroom's two corners were reserved for stock, one side for boxes with books coming in, and one for boxes going back. (Publishers mercifully still accepted returns on books that didn't sell.) We had two wheeled carts of folding metal chairs, and long shelves holding inventory, backup we didn't have room for in the store proper. (Thanks to the Masterpiece Theatre set.) In the center there was a long table, and off to the side, a kitchenette with a hotplate, microwave, coffee-maker, a little fridge, and a sink with a sign reminding you that your mother doesn't work here: clean up after yourself. I went to the central switches and flipped on the lights, the fan, the steam heat furnace, old radiators from fifties which warmed the store itself, but there was no heat back there; it was cold and drafty in the storeroom, everywhere except the inner, enclosed office where Miss Carter and Wendell had facing desks.

'We don't open till ten, so you have time to go back to the boat and change your clothes.'

'If I'm working back here, who cares?'

'Wendell will care.'

'Show me how to gift wrap first.'

'You've never wrapped a present?'

'They don't teach you that at Dartmouth.'

'Not even for Mother's Day for your mom?'

'Spare me the sentimental crap, and show me how to do it.'

I had to demonstrate the whole frigging process: wrap the book, tie the ribbon, (we only had one kind of paper and one color ribbon) froth up the ribbon.

'Awesome.'

'And always put a yellow sticky on it with the title, so the customer will know which book is which. That's important. Store's open in thirty minutes, it's a week before Christmas, so you'd better ride back to the marina and get changed. You're needed on the job.'

He left, and I went out to the main store. This was my favorite time of day in the store. Alone. On the shelves the books often leaned into one another, as though whispering to one another, and if I were quiet, I could eavesdrop on the tales they were telling each other. Sometimes I had the feeling they were sharing some hilarious joke that I had just interrupted, as though little giggles rippled into the corners. I turned on the overhead lights and strategically placed lamps. Carter & Co. Books was warmly lit, and the general air that of Bohemian clutter, much prized by Miss Carter. We have, of course, your standard bookshelves, but also shelving courtesy old wooden milk boxes from a long-defunct island dairy. Our library tables are just that, fine, old fashioned, solid oak with lathe-turned legs (all cast off Carter family furniture). The Children's Corner is kid-friendly with bean bags on the floor, and a little rocker. The cookbook shelves could be identified because old copper pans hung from the ceiling above this aisle. Travel books are actually displayed in an old Carter family steamer trunk from the Thirties with its innards cut out and shelves built in. The whole place reeks of charm and careful attention to ambient detail.

My office, on the other hand (wedged between the shop and the storeroom) is a broom closet with windows. For my birthday, Miss Carter gave me a brass plate for the door: *Tosca Tonnino, Events and Publicity*. I have a desk, a computer, printer, file cabinet, my own phone and antique Rolodex, but I still share this space with the mop and bucket, the broom, the tubular Electrolux. Long dusty windows look out to the alley, the dumpsters, and the back of Charlotte's Confections. The PA system sits on the shelf above my desk. I flipped on the Mozartian muzak, which floats out over the store, and turned on my computer. I pulled open the shallow central drawer, checked my teeth in the hand mirror there, and smiled at the glamorous picture of Ginger in *Top Hat* taped to the bottom of the drawer. Thus fortified with confidence, I began my daily virtual stroll through the usual blogs and newsletters, Shelf Awareness, Bookseller, Bookslut, Goodreads, Barnes and Noble, Maude Newton, Powells, Buzz, Balls & Hype, and all the rest of them, the whole lovely in-the-ether edifice of books and bookselling. I also had a look at which books Amazon was flogging, those undercutting, mercenary predators. I spend time daily on Carter & Co.'s Facebook page, updating our events. I Tweeted, reminding people to come to our last pre-Christmas reading tomorrow afternoon, *The Dancing Dolphin;* author and illustrator, both locals, were coming to read in the Children's Corner. Then I quickly read *The Dancing Dolphin*.

Reading the book sounds like an obvious obligation for Events and Publicity, but lots of bookstore events people don't read the books. They just choke down the flap copy, Google the author, and then stand up, and spew out outdated bits of undigested info. Having done their duty, the Events person sits in the back, texting discreetly while the author struts and frets his little moment on the tiny stage. Trust me, it really does happen that way in lots of bookstores. Not at Carter & Co. I read the books of all authors who came here. I have standards, and a reputation to uphold. I take pride in the work itself.

And on those occasions – all too often – when authors show up here and find almost no one present, I feel personally responsible. I always get this weird bubble of regret that I must burp out, blaming the empty chairs on the weather. Good weather makes people want to be outside in the sunshine. Bad weather? Just too vile for people to leave home. Sometimes I throw in a seasonal note: the first nice day, the last nice day, the really brutal rain. I tell the authors how much I *loved* their book, and then I excuse myself, dash out and call Jessie, or Sally, and beg them to show up, and bring a couple of friends. And bless them, they do! They even dash in and exclaim, 'Oh, I'm so glad you haven't started yet. I was afraid I was late!' Their enthusiasm thaws the author's icy disappointment, and no one is any the wiser that Sally and Jessie work there. I hope when I have my own PR firm I won't have to do deal with such failures. I have Great Expectations.

At nine, Wendell and Sally showed up. We fully expected to be working our asses off today. And just as the first customers opened the door and fluttered all the little Jingle Books, I went back in the storeroom to find Ethan dressed in his Abercrombie & Fitch style, pressed shirt and all. (Island cleaners would certainly be happy he was here; I knew from experience there's no room for an ironing board on a twenty-four foot sailboat.) He sat at the long table, leafing through the *Island Times*.

'Is there any coffee?'

'There's a coffee-maker over there,' I pointed to the counter. 'Have a go at it. Put a quarter in the can beside it.'

'I mean, espresso. A latte. A macchiato.'

'There's Jumpin Java across the street, but don't bring it into the store. I mean, the front of the store. You can drink it back here.'

'It's fucking freezing back here.'

'I'll get you a space heater. That's the best I can do.'

'Do I get a lunch break?'

'One half hour. Like everyone else.'

On his half hour, Ethan came into the store to watch Statler and Waldorf play chess. He criticized their moves., telling them everything they'd been doing wrong. They did not take this well.

'I'll play the winner,' Ethan said on his way out to Jumpin Java. 'And I'll beat you too!'

When I brought some books into the backroom for gift wrapping, Ethan had his phone on speaker and he was chatting away with someone about skiing and sports scores. *Oh, brother,* let Wendell get a load of this. Wendell did and made short work of it.

Ethan didn't seem to mind the rebuke. He just said, 'Sure, dude.'

By the end of that week, Ethan had introduced himself to our customers via our website and Facebook page. He wrote his own employee profile which was scant: 'Ethan James is an avid cyclist, skier and chess player.' Nothing about books or where he was from. Miss Carter pressed him for more, something more, in her word, endearing. He changed his bio to say he had an English degree from Dartmouth, and he liked jazz. More than that he refused. He refused her respectfully, even perhaps affectionately, but he refused just the same.

As a bookseller, Ethan James was successful by his own standards: he knew where fiction was, and non-fiction, and he knew the difference. His Staff Picks shelf included *The Book of Bunny Suicides*, *Moby Dick*, *Siddhartha*, a glam new novel set in the Hamptons, and a much-lauded debut novel of addiction and rehab, *The Body Electric*. By the end of that week, Statler and Waldorf had inducted him to the Island Chess Club of mostly retirees, and he had declined the invitation of the San Juan Cycling Club, who were mostly fitness enthusiasts fighting off middle age rather than racers. He said he was a racer, not merely a rider.

But also, in a short time, Ethan James altered the chemistry of Carter & Co., subtly, but certainly. Wendell did not like him at all. That alone can turn a work environment sour. Not toxic. Just sour. Ethan never seemed to take offense when Wendell criticized him, though I had the feeling it was because in the world of Ethan James, Wendell and the rest of us mattered so little, that frankly my dear, he didn't give a damn.

Ethan's attitude toward women (I exclude Miss Carter) also had an odd effect on the rest of us. Like the husband in a conventional marriage, Ethan assumed that as a man, he would be spared all the dull stuff, like, for instance, gift wrapping. Once he was working the floor, he would tell customers, 'You know, I'm just hopeless at gift wrapping, and this gift really demands the best. You should get one of the girls to wrap it.' And the customer would come to me, or Jessie or Sally with this bright, expectant look, and what could we say? Ethan called us all The Girls, like Miss Carter did, and what was tolerable from her really nettled me when I heard it from him. Or, if we were not the Girls, he'd call us ladies. As in, 'Can I help you ladies with the heavy lifting?' (The heavy lifting was, I suppose, to compensate for his not doing the gift wrapping.) He treated us with flirtatious gallantry that acted as a balm on Jessie's wounded heart, and appealed to Sally's old-fashioned notions of manners, but he left me irritated, and cranky, though admittedly, I let him do the heavy lifting.

If his effect on the staff was negative, the customers were just the opposite. He clearly didn't think of bookselling as a business or profession, and he didn't know shit from Shinola about books, but he lavished time on the customers. He'd talk with them earnestly. He'd take time to chat, ask their names, and remember them, even the high school kids, even, astonishingly, the Old Girls whose book clubs always signed up for the latest Lucy Lamont novel. And Statler and Waldorf? Ethan galvanized those two. Ethan made a date with Statler and Waldorf for his day off. They in turn galvanized their cronies who all came to the store to watch the match, and stood there, maybe half a dozen geezers taking up retail space, and underfoot in the holiday season. Wendell complained to Miss Carter, but she only said that a bookstore should nourish the soul of the community. End of discussion. For Miss Carter, Ethan James could do no wrong. And that too, altered the chemistry here.

On the morning of the 23rd December, the busiest day of all booksellerdom, I opened the store early, at eight o'clock, and I was out front at the store's main computer when suddenly the Mozartian muzak went off, and the bookstore was suddenly shrouded in unaccustomed silence.

'Hello?' I called out warily. Then bursting overhead like the rocket's red glare, TOSCA!

I screamed.

'TOSCA!' Ethan's voice.

I marched into my own small office, and there he was, playing with the wires at the back of the radio and CD player.

'Too loud, wasn't it?'

'What the hell are you doing?'

'I had this idea, see? I thought, why not hook a PA system into the muzak? Then, whenever you want to call someone, you don't have to look for them all over the store. See, I borrowed this mike from that guy at the electronics store. Just to test it. You want someone in the store, you just come in here, flip this switch, and—'

'You can't come in here and screw around with stuff in my office. See my name on the door?'

'Sorry. But you have to admit my idea is more efficient than looking all over the store, and by the way, what do you think about playing music that's a little more energetic? A little jazz, maybe.'

'We always play classical muzak here.'

'It puts people to sleep. You want them to buy books, not nod off.'

'Please don't use my office.'

'Unless I need a vacuum cleaner, right?'

I tried to think of some Ginger Rogers smart-ass retort that would put him in his place, but I couldn't. So I gave him a look of what I hoped passed for consummate disdain rather than gastric distress. He left whistling *Jingle Bells*.

And by 3rd January, when I came back from Christmas holidays in Seattle, there was indeed an intercom. The muzak box had been moved from my office to Miss Carter's office. The muzak itself had changed. No more Mozart. Light, jazzy stuff, spilled over the store, Ellington, Armstrong, that sort of thing. More energetic. Cool.

Chapter Four

THE FISH AND I came in through the back door. The salmon (courtesy a Friday Harbor fisherman) was my contribution to the Tonnino family Christmas Eve dinner. The kitchen of my parents' big Capitol Hill home was warm and noisy, the uncurtained windows steamed up with cooking and many bodies. The women in my family dominated – in numbers, as well as every other way. My father and my sisters' husbands were fond of saying that the Tonnino women were their own force of nature; this includes Aunt Clara who has lived with us for as long as I can remember. We are a tight-knit group, full of the usual in-laws and intrigue.

My mother was happy to see me, and told me I looked terrible. That's how I knew she loved me. 'Your hair. Look at your hair, Tosca. Carmen, look at her hair. Can't you do something with it?'

Carmen dropped what she was doing, and looked at me carefully. 'You need a haircut, Prune.' (Her nickname for me, short for Prunella. How I came by that, as with most nicknames, is a long story and not worth telling.) Carmen was a hairdresser, and her salon, not coinciden-tally, was in the same building with Tonnino's Pizza. 'I could give you something chic. Your hair, what can I say, it's on your head, but it does nothing for your face.'

'I like my hair.'

'Where're our presents?' asked my youngest nephew.

'She always gives books,' Carmen's teenage daughter Maddie added, bored. 'That's all she knows.'

'Well, books are something everyone should know!' said Carmen, shooing them out to my car to bring in the gifts.

'Let's look at the fish,' said Aida. My oldest sister, an accountant, always went straight for the bottom line.

We unloaded it into the sink, and appraised its silvery self.

'Nice,' said Mom.

'Where's Dad?' I asked.

'Where do you think?' said Norma, with a sniff. 'Making pizza for people who are so busy they have to eat pizza on Christmas Eve.' She was the traditionalist.

'Maybe I'll walk down there and help him out.'

'Yes, of course, leave me here with all the work,' sighed Aunt Clara. 'No one ever says, can I help you Clara, can I—'

'Can I help you, Clara?' I asked, responding like a tuning fork to Clara's guilt-ridden entreaties.

But Carmen said, 'Go wash up, wash the ferryboat off you, and meet me in the dining room.'

When I did, she had a sandwich and a cup of tea, and she sat with me, eager to hear all my news, especially my love life.

'Give me the TV Guide version,' she said.

'Oh Carmen, you are so passé! TV Guide? Get real!'

'What should I say? Text it? Twitter? I don't need the gory details, just a general sense.'

'There's nothing to tell. No one since I broke up with the Canadian.'

'Oh, he was too old for you anyway.'

'That's what I thought.'

'Have you seen Chris since Thanksgiving?'

'No.'

'Been in touch?'

'Yes.'

'Often?'

'Now and then.'

'And?

'I'm seriously considering him for a flingette.'

Carmen laughed, 'Oh, Prune! He's not supposed to be a flingette!'

Carmen is my favorite sister. We are more like our dad than the other two, even though we are eighteen years apart. I grew up like an only child. By the time I arrived, my parents were tired and set in their ways, and they'd seen everything. They brought me up with a kind of resignation somewhere between stoicism and a shrug. They, and Aunt Clara applauded my successes and accepted my lapses with equanimity. They couldn't understand why I would spend hours playing video games, addicted to Sonic the Hedgehog; after all, none of the other girls played video games. (Guess what, clueless ones: there were no video games when the other girls were growing up!) I inherited all my sisters' bikes and toys, but I refused to wear their hand-me-down clothes. I was the youngest and most adored. And that was no doubt why I'd always had a sort of breezy (and no doubt, unearned) confidence: I expect to be admired, I expect to succeed, and I am always surprised when things turn out otherwise!

Like all my older sisters, I worked in the family pizza parlor stocking the shelves, minding the counter after school and in the summers from the age of fourteen till college. Minimum wage, of which the parents put half in a bank account, and gave me half. As a Tonnino, the unwritten rule was you'd work at the pizzeria till you got your own real job, or got married and moved out, whichever came first.

Not me. Second semester freshman year, I took off my Tonnino's apron and flung it to the floor. (I waited till after closing; believe me, I knew that much.) I announced that I was sick of smelling like pizza: I wouldn't work at Tonnino's another day. Ever. Moreover, I insisted on moving out of my parents' big Capitol Hill house. I would be renting an apartment with some girlfriends who were eager to move off campus. My parents and Aunt Clara were stunned and hurt. My parents declared they would not pay my rent when I could so easily live at home and take the bus to Seattle University. Never mind, I replied confidently, I already have another job, a campus job, that will pay for my new apartment. I declared my fundamental independence, and felt quite proud of myself. However, it was hard to be too terribly defiant when your mother was still doing your ironing and bringing it to your door. Mom had the unfortunate habit of showing up, unannounced. Naturally, there were beer cans and boys all around the place, the former half empty, the latter, half-dressed, Vince among them.

My parents never liked Vince. Among other strikes against him, the day that I brought him to the pizzeria, he asked for pineapple on his pizza. My heart sank. Not an option at Tonnino's. My father gave me a look that spoke volumes. Now that I am thirty and unmarried, the family probably regrets dissing Vince. (Though I can't imagine being married to him, the lying cheat and sneaky bastard.) Still, I expect any minute the

Tonninos will sign me up for a reality TV to interview Bachelor Number Three. They are all husband-talent scouts. When my nephew brought Chris Egan at Thanksgiving, the heavens parted, and a shaft of sunlight fell upon his head. When Chris knocked at the door for Christmas dinner, you would have thought the seraphim announced his arrival.

We all squeezed in the dining room around the adult table, which was getting more crowded by the year. Among them my sisters had nine kids, and the older kids brought their serious girlfriends or boyfriends, and Charlie has a wife. When all these kids grow up we'll have to rent the Knights of Columbus Hall for holiday meals. My sisters' husbands were here, Carmen's easygoing Mike, Aida's roly-poly Ron, Norma's fussy Raymond (all three by this time, mirroring their strong-willed wives). Unwisely, my mother had placed Chris Egan between me and Aunt Clara. Mom should know better. If anyone was going to chase Chris off, it would be Aunt Clara.

Aunt Clara was famous for her gnocchi, her ravioli, her affection for seventies cop shows, and her belief in the Evil Eye. Long-widowed, constantly complaining, sighing, saying she knew she was in the way, Aunt Clara was so dour she made Eeyore look like Shirley Temple. She would always wax on, apologizing for taking up room and space (for twenty-eight years, mind you), saying soon she'd die and relieve us. She hasn't had more than a cold since 1991. My mom just replies, (over and over) 'Clara, this house has five bedrooms and four baths, it's so big, you'd have to send up a flare to tell us you were dying.'

And it's true. Our house was built in 1905, and like the others in this neighborhood, it has an Edwardian

51

breadth, dignity and solidity. Capitol Hill got its name because once Seattle was going to be the capitol, and all these fine homes went up. Then they moved the capitol to Olympia.

On Christmas Day, as the plates were going round, Chris went on about our wonderful hospitality. He had pale, Irish coloring, freckled, blue-eyed and a thin nose. He wore nice clothes, and he had manners.

'My family's in Maryland,' he added, 'and since I don't have much time off, it doesn't seem worth it to go home for a day or two.'

'Johns Hopkins,' said Norma. 'At Thanksgiving you said your degree was from Johns Hopkins.'

Chris looked surprised. He shouldn't have been. They would've ferreted out of him the name of his childhood sweetheart, and his first pet given half the chance. I was too old to be embarrassed by any of this. And Chris was a good sport about it. He volunteered to help with the dishes, but Carmen, Aida and Norma all insisted the kitchen was too crowded with so many people, and that we should bundle up and go for a walk down to Volunteer Park. We could take the dog for her outing.

The dog, Misty, was old and wobbly and would rather poop in the back yard, and be done with it, but no, poop bag in hand, off we went. It was a pleasant enough walk in the brisk afternoon, with talk of this and that, movies and the like. To my professional (and truth be told, personal) chagrin, Chris thought physical books were a thing of the past. He had bought a Kindle in 2011 and never looked back.

'On the Kindle, I can carry hundreds of books. I can get them cheap and move along easily if they're boring.'

'Heresy,' I said, struggling to be tolerant, thinking: how could I, a bookseller, go out with a man who does all his reading on a Kindle? 'I like the smell and heft of books. The way they feel. I like the dust jackets and crisp print.'

'Yes,' he laughed, 'and you probably have hundreds of actual, physical CDs.'

'I do. I even have LPs. Mostly from my dad. You ought to see his collection in the study. Hundreds of LPs, opera, tango and Dean Martin. As soon as each of us was old enough, Dad would take us to the opera, especially after we learned to drive. Dad would always drive to the opera, but afterwards, one of us would drive home. He would get so wrung out, so emotional, he couldn't drive home.'

'Your mom loves opera too?'

I shook my head. 'My parents are a study in contrasts. My father is quick to tears, quick to laughter, unabashedly emotional, and my mother could sit dry-eyed through a double feature of *Dumbo* and *Bambi*. And yet, they are devoted to each other. I don't know how they manage it. It must be a secret, as much as Tonnino's secret sauce. All through my childhood I watched all my friends' parents' divorce, or just get stale and tired of one another. I see my sisters going through the same kinds of dreary changes with their husbands, wearing one another down, but Frank and Donna, well, they're amazing.'

'They're so old.'

I laughed. 'Every year on my birthday, my mom winks, and laughs, and says to Dad, 'Oh, Frank, you rascal, what a surprise this girl was!' And my dad winks at her. I think they still might do it,' I confided. 'I'm not kidding. Incredible.'

'They're so old, but you're so young.'

'I'm thirty.'

'I'm twenty-seven.'

'*Charmant, mon ami,* I like being the older woman. Experienced. Sophisticated.' As I uttered those words Misty did her business, and I had to pick it up with the poop bag.

A couple of nights later, Chris took me to a sci-fi movie downtown. He only liked sci-fi and big tent-pole films, the sort I found dull. I didn't think he knew what he was asking when he wanted to go for a pizza afterward. I declined. Every time I walked into someone else's pizza parlor, I felt like a spy. A really critical spy.

There was a goodnight kiss at the door – Chris's lips lingered long enough to be pleasurable – and when I came in the front hall, there was my mother, like a Dreadnought, hat, scarf, gloves.

'I was waiting for you to finish kissing,' she said. 'I didn't want to be going out while you were kissing.'

'Where are you going at this time of night? You never go out at night if you can help it. It's ten o'clock.'

'I'm going to collect your father.'

'Collect him? From Tonnino's? He's been walking back and forth every day since 1965, why do you need to drive him?'

'Because three months ago he was mugged.'

'You never told me that.'

My mother rolled her eyes. 'Your father wouldn't let me. He said you would worry. Anyway, he was all right. Shook up, that's all. But I don't let him walk home anymore. Not at night.

'Well, did you report it?'

'Yes, but to what good? Some druggie. Strung out and with a knife. A kid like that, they're everywhere nowadays. Nothing came of it. This whole neighborhood, it's changing.'

'I'll go pick him up, Mom,' I said, taking out my own keys. 'You stay home with Aunt Clara.'

I drove the few blocks between our house on East Valley just off Aloha and down to the small commercial district on Tenth Street, a route so well-known to all of us we could Braille our way there, winter or summer. I had to drive past the pizzeria to park in the alley, and I could see the lights were off, save for a few dim ones inside where the chairs (it was a small place, seats, maybe thirty, max) were all atop the tables. With various upgrades and do-overs, Tonninno's Pizza had endured here since the mid-Sixties, and part of the charm, aside from the pizza, was that quality of having endured, a plain charm, while everything else in the Capitol Hill neighborhood became quite chi-chi, or as my father liked to say, frou-frou. Carmen's salon was pretty frou-frou, as was the upscale florist and the shoe place, and espresso joint in the same building. But they were all new, or newish, and Tonninno's was a Capitol Hill institution. The secret to Tonninos's success – again, aside from the reliably great pizza complete with my father's secret sauce – was that my sociable father who had standards for the food, ran the pizzeria, and my shrewd mother who had standards for the income, ran the business.

Mom was not just a mere accountant, adding up debits and credits, she had a second sense, instincts. She insisted (so they tell me) on buying our big beautiful home even though they had to go into hock to do it. This was in the late Sixties, an era in Seattle history when there really was a billboard up that read *Will the last person leaving Seattle, please turn out the lights.* But the family business endured all setbacks till the economy rebounded, and then it prospered. Ten or so years later another opportunity presented itself to my mom, and she took out a huge loan, got a second mortgage on the house and bought the block of shops that included Tonnino's. Rents skyrocketed in the eighties, but Tonnino's was safe. She could sell that commercial block now for gizillions, but she wanted to protect the rent on Carmen's salon. If Donna Tonnino had been born in my generation, she'd be a CEO.

I drove round the back and down the alley and parked beside the dumpsters. Tonnino's had two reserved spaces, and one was for the delivery van. I went in the back door, calling out, 'Hey Dad, I've come to take you home!' so that the kids cleaning up wouldn't be alarmed. After all, I didn't know them. I'd long since quit bothering to learn their names. They came and went. I came and went, for that matter. The place was still warm from the ovens. In the summer, we sweltered in there, but in winter, it was comfortable. I found my dad in the office (a closet really) at the desk. The fluorescent overhead light and the gray computer screen were unkind to him, and he looked all of his seventy-plus years. I'd never known him without gray hair, but his hair was white now, and his face was lined.

'Why don't you retire, Dad?' I asked, as he locked up the place, and bid goodnight to the last two employees.

'And do what?'

'I don't know. Travel? Don't most people like to travel?'

'I don't want to travel.'

'Well you could....'

'I'm not going to be one of those old men with too much time and too little money.'

'But you and Mom are comfortable.'

'Oh Tosca, I'm not speaking of that kind of comfort. Let's go home. I'm tired.'

He got into my Subaru wearily. I was sorry that we had so little to say. I was almost ready to offer up that I thought Chris was a Nice Young Man, but instead he spoke.

'You read all those books you sell?'

'Not all. Lots. Some.'

'When are you gonna write one?'

'Me write a book? Why would I?'

'Why wouldn't you? You're the artistic one! You told me you'd never work the pizzeria again, you'd never smell like pepperoni and garlic, you'd never—'

'Dad, I was a kid! I said some harsh things. I'm sorry. I didn't mean to hurt your feelings.'

'You don't hurt my feelings, Tosca. I don't ask that you work in the family business. I don't ask it of your sisters, and I don't ask it of you.'

'But you're happy that Carmen's hair salon is two doors down, and that Norma's husband's law firm is on Pine,' I chided him, 'and that Aida works downtown, but she can still call up and order the pizza you named for her. I'm the only one who doesn't live nearby.'

'Don't change the subject. Where is your work for all your big dreams? You were the one who talked us into letting you have your semester abroad in France. And paying for it too! Paris! Oh, you were full of Paris! I always loved to hear you talk about some new book you'd read, or some new film, or even those old films, Fred and Ginger. I loved to hear you talk French. You lived in a way the rest of the Tonninos never have, and I thought, ah, this girl, this girl is gonna do something important. Like write a book.'

'I don't want to write a book. I want my own PR firm.'

'PR is for schemers. You're an artist. Oh, I never

forget you playing the soprano sax in the high school jazz band. And Debussy, *The Girl with the Flaxen Hair*.' He sighed.

'PR can be artistic, Dad. In PR you design campaigns, you bring things together so they enhance one another. It's not the Sistine Chapel, but it's creative work.'

'What do you create?'

'Buzz.'

'Buzz. What's that?'

'Oh, Dad. Look, it doesn't have anchovies, all right?'

He was quiet for a few minutes. 'Here's my point, your mother and me, your sisters even, our choices were made for us. My father delivered meat for a wholesaler, and Donna's father delivered restaurant linens. We went to the same Catholic grade school. What else are we gonna do when we get married, but open a pizzeria that needs meat and restaurant linens? Your sisters chose marriage. I don't complain. They married good men, pretty good, except for Norma's first husband, that lout. But she has a good man now, and I'm happy for them. But you, Tosca, you were always going your own way. Renting that apartment in college. Going off to France, coming back and telling us all this wonderful stuff we can't even imagine, always telling us the kind of exotic life you were going to live. Going off on that boat for a year with that Vince – I didn't like that Vince, or the boat, and don't get me wrong but you were always doing what no one else was gonna do. No getting tied down with a man and kids, fine! Make your own choices, but when you do that, you make the responsibility too. You see what I mean?'

'No.' I was pulling in behind our house.

He turned to me. 'One day I have to close Tonnino's.'

'Why? I thought you weren't going to retire.'

'Fourscore and ten, Tosca, I've passed mine. Retire, die, change is out there. I'll tell you this, I'm not going to sell the place, and let someone take over and ruin my reputation. They might put pineapple on the pizzas. Infamy.'

I shouldn't have been surprised at the drama. The man loved opera. 'Will you stop it? You're not going to die. You sound like Aunt Clara. You should take some more time off. That's all. Here, here's an idea. Why don't I make up a PR campaign for Tonninos? Then you'd see what I can do.'

My dad shook his head and sighed. 'Never mind, Tosca. I don't need no PR campaign.'

'What are you saying? That you wish I were a boy and would take over the business?'

'I never said that. I never wanted a boy.'

'Well, are you disappointed in me, Dad?'

'No, no, never.'

'But you think I ought to be doing … what?'

'Forget it, honey. I'm just an old dog, and you should take off your slipper and beat me.'

We both laughed. 'Just like Buster,' I said.

'Yes, just like Buster, I will never learn.'

When I was just a little kid they had a dog, Buster. He was old and spoiled, and he resented this cute little tot, *moi*. Buster, though he was long house-broken, would deliberately pee in the house to get attention. As a child I didn't like Buster, felt none of that chummy-yummy bonding with your dog so beloved of novelists and movie-makers. But Buster, as a legacy, exerted a profound influence, on our family, a legacy resonant as Mr Kane's *Rosebud*. Buster gave my whole family the phrase, 'Take off your slipper and beat him.' All the Tonninos used this phrase, as in: *I should just take off my slipper and beat myself* when you've done something stupid, or futile, simply unwise, or even silly and time-wasting. Because every time Buster would pee in the house, my mother would call out to my father, 'Frank, Frank, he's done it again. Take off your slipper and beat him, Frank.' My father, however, having spent twelve or thirteen hours on his feet at the pizzeria, didn't feel like chasing Buster around the house, slipper in hand. So he would look up from the newspaper and holler back, 'Which slipper, Donna?' Though I know it sounds pathetic, this phrase was enough to crack them up. The damn dog was never going to be punished, and all efforts to stop him were either futile or silly.

So though I didn't know what exactly my father thought was futile or silly, we let the old family phrase serve as closure, and we went in the house where my mother and Aunt Clara were watching TV. As usual when my dad came home, Mom got up from her chair, kissed his cheek, took his coat. He plopped down in a chair in front of the TV, no matter what was on. She brought him a glass of wine.

Aunt Clara likes re-runs from seventies cop shows. Invariably when Aunt Clara was watching *Hawaii Five-O*, she would turn to everyone in the room – as she did this night when my dad and I came home – roll her eyes, and exclaim, 'Why do they even try? I ask you. Why? Don't those Bad Guys know Steve McGarrett will never stop until he catches them? Why do they even try?'

We always replied with some variation on, 'Who knows, Clara?' as if sharing in the fatalistic doom and misguided hubris of Bad Guys.

Riding the ferries is one of the things I love about living

on an island. Those great white, glorious vessels glide over the waters of Puget Sound carrying their cargos of humanity, all thrust together for that brief crossing. I love the sense – false, perhaps, but intense – of communality, community, coming together that pervades the ferry on the crossing. Hundreds of people, caught up together in that one moment, and though at either end of the journey your paths would diverge and never again cross, for that crossing, you smiled and chatted, and connected. For two hours, everyone on the ferry shared experience, a feel-good association. You see them all, young lovers, Gothic teens, sprawling families, retired couples, noisy kids, buttoned-up commuters with laptops and scruffy college kids with backpacks.

On this crossing on 2 January, the Puget Sound was shrouded with fog and the chill permeated right down to your bones. Following along in the wake of the ferry, the gulls melded with the gray sky, the light snow. I always go to the top observation deck, and stand outside at the back (for as long as I can endure the cold). I watch the wake, and the gulls and the land swallowed up by the Sound, the other islands. The cold wind blows back my long hair and my long scarf. Chin high, face to the future, I always feel very like Ginger Rogers in that ferryboat scene in *Shall We Dance*. I pressed my scarf against my chin and though I wouldn't have exactly broken into song, I had the feeling that drama and romance hovered just in front of me, that fate would be both kind and exciting.

Chapter Five

MY FIRST MORNING back at work, Sally had opened, and I could hear her running the Electrolux around the Masterpiece Theatre set. Sally was fastidious and never satisfied with the way Martha, the cleaning lady, left the store. When Sally finished, she brought the vacuum back to my office, and I had to move out of the way so she could shove it under the desk.

'How did it go, having Jessie join you for Christmas?' I asked.

'T-terrible. She was such a downer,' said Sally, uncharacteristically blunt. Sally had this slight speech impediment which only endeared people to her. She had graying hair, dyed blonde, bright blue eyes, and a sunny disposition. 'My husband and I d-danced all around her trying to get her to smile, but she wouldn't c-come out of it, and my daughter brought her new b-boyfriend home from college, and h-here was Morticia Addams.'

'All is woe!' I threw up my hands à la Aunt Clara.

'I w-wish Jessie would get over that brute, Murph. He didn't deserve her in the first place, and now, she's just, well, I f-feel sorry about her break up and all, but my husband said if I invited her for New Year's he'd l-leave home and ride the ferry back and forth all n-night if he had to.'

'Did Jessie spend New Year's alone?' I shuddered a little at this thought.

'No, actually Miss Carter invited her, and she went there. With Ethan.'

'That must have been …' Words failed me.

'I guess it was just the four of them on New Year's.'

'And they'd have to stay till midnight. Whew. That sounds dismal. Did Jessie find out all about Ethan?'

Sally thought on this for a moment. 'N-not really. His grandmother M-Marjorie lives in Westport Connecticut, and his family's very rich. Of course Miss C-Carter went on and on about Marjorie, her old r-roommate.'

'Well, did Jessie find out if he had a girlfriend or not?'

'I d-don't think he does.'

'Does he have a boyfriend?'

'No, Tosca.'

'Maybe Jessie will take up with Ethan and get over her broken heart.'

'I d-don't th-think Miss Carter would much like that. I don't th-think she wants to share him with Jessie. Or anyone.'

'Share him?'

'Miss Carter adores him. It d-doesn't take Dr. Phil to see that.'

'Of course she adores him. He's the grandson she never had. Anyway, he's not Jessie's type. Too brooding. She likes blunt men like Murph. No deep currents there, just the regular tides you can count on.'

'Is he your t-type, Tosca?' Sally asked with a small wheedle in her voice.

'Only if I were reduced to the spin cycle.' I waved away her inquiring look, and went out front to unlock the doors. There, as usual, coffees in hand, were Statler and Waldorf. These old duffers, why couldn't they learn? Why did they think that one day, someone would let them in?

'No coffees, gentlemen,' I reminded them. 'Miss Carter's rules.'

'It's too cold to drink it outside,' said Statler.

I pointed across the street to Jumpin Java, and retired to my office, checking my inbox (choked with messages unread for days) and pleased to find a note from Miss Carter, directing me to two more publishers' websites that had picked up my endorsements and put them on their own pages. I like seeing my name on publishers' sites, but it meant I only ever get to cheer the book. If the book sucks no one would ever print that, would they? No bookseller would write a sucky review, for that matter. Waste of time. We are booksellers, not critics. Still, our endorsements mean more than they used to, since newspapers cut their book pages, and then, guess what, the newspapers themselves are all on life support. I say this as one who gets all her info via the net or from NPR. Miss Carter, sentimentally, subscribes to the *New York Times Book Review* for the store, but the only paper we actually sell is the *Island Times* which comes out twice a week.

Flipping through the publishers' websites on my computer, I come to Smithson/Empire, one of the best and biggest. Their PR machine is formidable. Awesome, in a word. It's only January, and they already had their pages set up with links, not simply to Martin Luther King and Valentine's Day, and St. Patrick's Day, but Mother's Day. That link had a telltale cluster of wisteria. And yes, presto! There it was, the next Lucy Lamont novel (which always had wisteria on the cover). Lucy Lamont writes the worst kind of romantic, sexless schlock, but one book or another of hers is always on the bestseller list, and her fans are legion and devoted. This, number eighteen of the Shannonville novels, would be sold with a set of garden tools! Someone's PR brilliance, there.

I made a few calls to my contacts at publishing houses in New York, unsuccessfully trying to interest them in sending their authors out here to San Juan Island. Most of my author events were the same writers who were at Miss Carter's party, people like Frances McTeer and Stanley Lund who produced a Maxwell Dart mystery every year. (Maxwell Dart was very like Stanley, except thirty years younger and better looking.) The only big name author I could reliably get was Tina Frazier, the Green Warrior. Tina was not just an author, she was a Cause, and she was indefatigable in support of that cause. She was a big draw here because the island had a lot of Eco-enthusiasts whom I affectionately dubbed the Granolas (when Miss Carter wasn't around).

Next, I pawed through the stacks of ARCs (advanced reading copies) piled up unceremoniously on my floor where I found a hand-written note on real stationary accompanying a book by a Mary Hill, her memoir of growing up on Vashon Island. Published by Mary herself no doubt, masquerading as a small press. Mary would like to do an event at Carter & Co. I pulled her book out of the pile, and started to read. If I couldn't bring out the big boys, I could at least support the locals.

At eleven I went out to the front desk so Sally could have her break. The front desk was actually a sort of island, there in the center of the store, with computers on either side so two people could be checking out at once. However, it was January, so only one of those computers was on, and it wasn't even in use. Only Statler and Waldorf were in the store. I stood there with nothing more to do than read Mary Hill's book, which had some charm.

When Sally came back, she remarked that Ethan was supposed to be there half an hour ago, and right then, he shows up, whistling. He wore smart shoes and an ironed shirt and pressed pants. He looks like a fashion plate in a town where flannel is king.

'You were s-supposed to be h-here half an h-hour ago,' said Sally.

'Forgive me, Sally. Please. But I just got off the phone. I got some great news!' He snatched from his Staff Pick shelf, *The Body Electric*, and waved it in front of us. 'It's going to be a film! A major picture with a major director and a big star! I can't tell you who yet. I'm sworn to secrecy.'

'Why would you c-care?' asked Sally.

'Win and I went to school together! We're old friends. Have you read it?'

Sally shook her head.

'Tosca, you've read it!' he cried with more enthusiasm than he's evinced, at least in my presence.

'Sorry. No.'

'Really? Really! You call yourself a bookseller, and you don't know this book? Incredible!'

I admit, you'd have to be living in a root cellar in North Dakota not to know about *The Body Electric*. Critics were falling all over themselves looking for superlatives. The book jacket was sort of psychedelic red and black on glossy white with the red letters dripping like blood, and the black ones squirting a little something from a hypodermic. The inside flap featured a picture of Winslow Jefferies, the author. He was good looking in a sort of Harry Potter way, a boyish lock of hair over the forehead, studious eyes behind the glasses, though the mouth looked pursed for pleasure, I thought. Or pain. Hard to tell.

'It's an awesome book! The *New York Times* says Win Jefferies is the Hemingway of his generation,' said Ethan. 'Look at the blurbs! *The Body Electric* is existential truth. "Sex, lice and videotape," *New York Observer.*'

'I d-don't like drugs and b-blood,' said Sally. 'I like Georgette Heyer.'

'Who's she?' asked Ethan.

'She wrote historicals.'

'She's dead?'

'Well, yes. She d-died a long time ago, but she w-wrote wonderful books, f-fifty or s-sixty—'

'Sally, Sally, Sally,' Ethan remonstrated. 'When are you going to learn? The dead don't count. You have to read the living! They're the ones who are shaping the world we live in! They're the ones who are reflecting what and who we are, our times. Who cares about the dead?'

'I do,' Sally replied firmly. 'Just b-because I have to live in the modern world, doesn't m-mean I have to like it.'

'The last I looked Herman Melville was dead,' I remarked to Ethan, 'and he's on your Staff Picks.'

Ethan bestowed upon us a brilliant smile and an artful wink. 'Honestly, who cares about whaling in 1850? I just put that there because Edith said I had to have more than one book. I only read living authors.'

'Frances McTeer is l-living,' says Sally boldly.

'Frances McTeer ...' Ethan frowned. 'Wasn't she at Edith's Christmas party? The one who looks like a fire hydrant in a kilt?'

Sally winced; she and Frances are good friends.

'That's unkind,' I said. (Though it was true.) 'Besides,

The Body Electric is just a narcissist's mirror.'

'If you haven't read it, how do you know?'

'I read some reviews.'

'That's a really narrow-minded way to judge.'

I was not used to being called narrow-minded. I put *The Body Electric* back on his Staff Pick shelf, and said I'd read it later.

'So what's your favorite book, Tosca?'

'I have lots of favorites.'

'No, your favorite book of all time,' Ethan insisted.

'Well, if you must know, *Wuthering Heights*.'

'Really? I'd never have guessed you for a Catherine-and-Heathcliff kind of girl.'

I wanted to ask why not, but my pride wouldn't let me. 'I read it first when I was fourteen, and I still love it.'

'Fourteen? You're still in love with a book you read …' he plainly did some calculations. '… half a lifetime ago? You mean to tell me that you, a bookseller, haven't fallen in love with a book in fifteen years? Another book?'

I cleared my throat, minorly pissed off. '*Great Expectations*.'

'Really? Isn't that the one about the old girl who is jilted on her wedding day, and lives in a moldering heap of wedding finery, never changing her clothes?'

'It's about Pip, but yes, Miss Havisham is a character in the novel.'

Ethan turned to Sally confidentially. 'Can you imagine how bad she must have smelled? Whew!'

I felt a twinge of outraged loyalty to poor Miss Havisham; moreover I'd never once thought how she might have smelled.

Turning back to me, he asked, 'Don't you like anything that's not a hundred years old, Tosca? Really?

Nothing in the last hundred years?'

I took the Ginger Rogers high road with Ethan. 'You asked me my favorite books, not what have I read recently. I'd venture to say I know more than you about the *New York Times* Bestseller list.'

'Maybe, but *The Body Electric* is on that list, and you haven't read it.' He grinned in a good-natured way.

I knew I had been one-upped. 'Our job as a bookstore is to have lots of different kinds of books for lots of different kinds of readers. I'm a professional reader.'

'Aha!' cried Ethan, so animated today I couldn't help but wonder if he'd spiked his Wheaties. 'A professional, but not a passionate reader.'

'They don't have to be different.'

'But they are! You know they are. The professional's always thinking, hmmm, what can I say about this book? How can I sell it? The passionate reader goes for the actual experience, for what the book does to him, how the book makes him feel.'

This was uncomfortably true, but I wasn't about to admit it. At least not to Ethan James. 'As I recall, you told us you were not a passionate reader.'

'No, but I always wanted to be.'

Before I could comment on this unlooked-for admission (for who could imagine ironic Ethan James fessing up to wanting something he didn't already have?) Sally, in a burst of wit, turned to a nearby display and picked up a couple of Lucy Lamonts, the dust jackets uniformly framed in tumbling wisteria.

'I'll read *The Body Electric*,' she said, 'if you r-read Lucy Lamont.'

Ethan looked at the book as though it needed a condom. 'Not on your life. Jesus!'

'Jesus doesn't work here, Ethan,' I said. 'Miss Carter

doesn't like to hear his name unless it's on a book.'

'Lucy Lamont is a pr-prolific writer,' said Sally. 'Seventeen books, and c-counting. I like her n-novels. In Lucy Lamont's Shannonville, th-things come round right. They always do. The g-good are rewarded, there's civility and t-true love. What's wrong with th-that?' Sally took the Lucy Lamont and placed it firmly on her own Staff Picks shelf, right next to Frances McTeer, Georgette Heyer and Hilary Mantel's *Wolf Hall*.

'Oh, Sally!' he cried. 'How you disappoint me.'

'Oh, give it a rest,' I said lightly. 'Lucy Lamont is no worse than some of that trash on your Staff Picks shelf. Pathos in the Hamptons?'

Ethan looked indignant. 'That's not about pathos. It's a modern gender triangle.'

'That isn't modern, Ethan,' I said. 'That's as old as Oscar Wilde and Bosie.'

'It's about ambiguous sexuality and the modern family. There's a young professional woman, whose best friend is a gay guy, and he's hot for her current boyfriend who doesn't know he's gay and she gets pregnant. Spoilers ahead.'

'Believe me, Ethan, Sally and I aren't going to read this book. What happens?'

'Both the men turn out to be concerned fathers and they all live together.'

'Call me a cynic, but that arrangement you describe, not only is that fiction, it's bullshit.'

Just then the jazzy muzak was interrupted with my name coming out of the PA system. Miss Carter's voice. I excused myself. I needed to stop by my office to collect my notes for our first meeting of the new year.

The storeroom was unheated, high-ceilinged and drafty, but the glassed-in office Miss Carter shared with Wendell was toasty, thanks to a space heater. We exchanged the usual New Year's greetings, and I could tell she had something on her mind. Her eyes were unusually bright.

'Popcorn.'

'Popcorn, Miss Carter?'

'Popcorn,' she says, framing the word with moist emphasis. She smiled. 'My new brilliant idea. It came to me, well not in a dream, but when it came to me, I was so excited, I almost called you in Seattle. Still, I thought it would be best to watch your reaction, to tell you in person.'

I managed to knot my features around some expression I hoped would pass for enthusiasm.

'Whenever we have an author event, you should pop up some popcorn, put it in big bowls and circulate it among everyone who comes for the event! We have a microwave right here in the storeroom. It'll be no trouble at all for you to pop up a few bags and hand it round.'

'Well, yes, maybe, but why would I—'

'Entertainment, Tosca! I can't believe you couldn't see that. Didn't think of it yourself! You are Publicity and Events. Every time people smell popcorn, what do they think of? They think of entertainment, of something lively and amusing. It's an inspired marketing idea. Just like Jingle Books.'

'Popcorn won't move titles, Miss Carter,' I protested. 'It will only work on the people who are already here.'

'And what's wrong with that? Imagine! The very aroma wafting through the store, *Ah, entertainment!*'

It was useless to protest that all the popcorn in the world would not plant new butts in those metal folding chairs. So I agreed to pop popcorn, and moved along with the planned events for January and February, including Tina Frazier, the famous author of the *All Things Green* series.

'That was an excellent coup for us,' said Miss Carter. 'Getting Tina Frazier to come here.'

Tina would read at the Arctic Circle to a group of admiring penguins on behalf of her cause, but let it stand as a coup. 'Tina brings in big crowds,' I offered. Twenty people was huge for us.

'Who else do we have?'

'Kind of slow in winter.'

'Then you, Tosca, must do more to draw authors to our store. A bookstore with no authors might as well be selling light bulbs. We want on-site authors. Remember your title, Publicity and Events. And entertainment. Popcorn,' she added with a bright smile.

'Popcorn,' I agreed.

January is the cruelest month. Christmas ho-ho-hos are long since silenced, bills come in, spring is far away. On San Juan Island, the wind came up off the water, and the damp went right through to your bones, no matter how many layers you'd packed on your body. Shelves at the Island Grocery thinned out, and you could park anywhere up and down Spring Street because there was no one here. Some restaurant and cafés closed down altogether. Nonetheless, there was a sense of camaraderie among us year-rounders, locals banded together, self-sufficient, and proud of it. In January and February, temperatures plummeted, and we had snowstorm after snowstorm. No one could move, and life in Friday Harbor shut down. Even Statler and Waldorf stayed home. The weather was so bad that only Ethan and I could get into work because we could walk. (Or in his case, bike. He was fearless on a bike, I'll give him that.) Ethan and I were thrown together a good deal, and oddly, in that miserable cold, Ethan thawed. He made friends with Mr Hyde for one thing. That big fat tabby, whose perspective on the human race could only be called Olympian, actually warmed to Ethan, as he had not to any of the rest of us. When the store was more or less empty, Ethan would turn up the jazzy muzak. There was no reason for two of us to be on the floor (so few customers) so mostly I stayed in my office, worked on Facebook, read emails, made calls, and gave myself a manicure. Once I came out to the counter, and there was Ethan in the empty store, reading *Wuthering Heights*.

He looked up at me, and grinned. 'You're right, Tosca. This is a great fucking book.'

'I thought you had an English degree from Dartmouth.'

He waved that away. 'They taught us a lot of theory and postmodern deconstruction, hermeneutics. Sounds like birth defects, doesn't it? That and post colonialism, the Inbred Id, that sort of shit. I mean, some of the books were great books, but you couldn't just read them, you had to take out your tweezers and pluck at their pubic hairs. I should have majored in music.'

'Are you a musician?'

He scoffed. 'That was a joke. A book like this, though,' he held it up; he'd creased its spine. 'I'm putting it on my Staff Picks. I'll call it *The Body Electric* of its day.'

'*The Body Electric* isn't a love story.'

'You think this is a love story?'

'Isn't it?'

'It's a story about destruction. Just like *The Body Electric*. Just like the Unnamed Narrator and Roger, these two, Catherine and Heathcliff, live at such pitch

73

and intensity, they could only be destructive. They couldn't help themselves. Everyone in their way was going to suffer.'

I'd never thought of it like that, but before I could say anything, the bell over the door rang and Statler came in, his cheeks pink from the cold, his tweedy hat pulled low over his ears.

'I hoped I'd find you alone,' he said to Ethan, ignoring me. 'Game?'

'Go ahead,' I said. 'I'll take care of things here.' I went into my office, and got Mary Hill's memoir, and stood there at the counter, engrossed in her Vashon Island childhood in the fifties till the buzzer at the storeroom door sounded. It was the UPS guy, bundled to the teeth who said he had a shipment from Smithson/Empire, a re-order of *The Body Electric*.

Though our sales in general were woefully down, *The Body Electric* was selling. In February it was still on Ethan's Staff Picks Shelf (though *Moby Dick* and *Siddhartha* had been replaced with *East of Eden* and *Capitalism* by that French economist, neither of which he had read). But for Win Jefferies's novel, he was both a passionate reader and a persuasive advocate. He'd put the novel in customers' hands, and if they demurred (and many did, what with the needle dripping blood on the cover) he'd say, 'Take this—' like it was a communion wafer, '—if you don't like *The Body Electric*, Carter & Co. will buy it back.'

After I overheard one customer succumb to this, I asked him, 'Have you checked out that policy with Miss Carter? I seriously doubt she'll buy it back. We're supposed to be selling books.'

Ethan shrugged. 'All over America, all over the world, people are responding to this novel.'

'Responding how?' I went to the opening paragraph in which the narrator sitting in a pool of his own vomit catalogues the contents. I read it aloud. 'Pretty off-putting if you ask me.'

'I did ask you. Did you read it?

'No.'

'Anyone who doesn't get it, doesn't understand literature.'

'Do you mean they're not cool?' I asked, but he had no sense of humor about *The Body Electric*.

The next time I checked the store's Facebook page, Win Jefferies had friended us! He was following us on Twitter! And, naturally, as this was my domain, we friended him, and we followed him. Miss Carter was ecstatic, and left a card on the lunchroom table with cupcakes from Island Bakery on top for Ethan, who had clearly alerted him to our bookstore. When I asked her if she'd read *The Body Electric*, she equivocated, and I didn't pursue it. Only a certain kind of reader could get past the vomit contents in that opening paragraph, and Miss Carter wasn't that reader.

On a Saturday in early February, I was stapling long strings of hearts to the overhead beams when a woman walked by so fast, the breeze in her wake almost rocked my ladder. I recognized her, Leona Cox, a teller at a local bank. Leona was about fifty, thick-set and no-nonsense. She carried a copy of *The Body Electric* and I couldn't help but wonder if she'd succumbed to Ethan's blandishments because she too, fancied herself cool; after all, she had little butterfly tattoos on both wrists. Leona went right up to Wendell at the checkout desk, and on behalf of her teenage daughter, Jennifer, she slammed the book down, and called it filth.

'And I'd call it a lot worse if I wasn't a lady and this wasn't a public place. I found my 16-year-old daughter reading this in the *bathroom*!'

Wendell, in his studious way, turned the book over in his hands. He adjusted his specs. He asked Leona if she forbade her daughter to read in the bathroom.

'Hell, no!'

'Then what's the problem, Leona?'

'This book, this book —that man, that young man—' she wagged her finger ineffectually, 'where is he? Him!'

'Me?' said Ethan, looking whimsically perplexed.

'He said this was a wonderful novel, a book that everyone was talking about, and reading, a mirror of life, but it's sick and filthy and full of sex and drugs. They end up in jail, in rehab, they screw themselves silly with nurses who are supposed to be caring for them, with girls who are also drugged up and strung out! Then there's a messy suicide!' Leona was breathless. 'Do you know how hard it is to be a parent nowadays? I can't have this book in the house making all that look glamorous. I want my money back.'

Wendell glared at Ethan, but he spoke soothingly to Mrs. Cox. 'Leona, I have a grown daughter and a teenage son, and you are right, it's hard to be a parent. And it is a dreadful book, but I can't give you your money back.'

'He said you would!' Again she pointed a finger at Ethan.

'I'm very sorry, Leona,' said Wendell in his best Atticus Finch fashion, 'but Ethan mis-spoke. It's not our policy to buy books back. We don't do used books, and even if I wanted to,' he lifted it to his nose, 'it smells funny, and the pages don't feel right, they're puffy, like they got dropped in water.'

'I told you Jennifer was reading it in the bathtub. Where she was smoking.'

'Ah.' Wendell handed it back to her. 'I'm sorry, Leona.'

Ethan snatched it from Wendell, tucked it under his arm, and reached into his back pocket. 'Let's see,' he said, flipping through his wallet, 'twenty-four ninety-eight, tax at 8.5 per cent. I'm sorry you didn't like the book. Truly. It is a great novel. As great as *Catcher in the Rye.*'

'Who says?'

'I do. If the store won't buy it back, I will. Here, Leona. Keep the change.' He stuffed a twenty and a ten into her hand. 'I'm willing to stand by my word.' Ethan gave Leona his gleaming smile. 'Is all forgiven?'

'Don't recommend any more books to me.' She shoved the thirty dollars into her pocket.

'I promise. Except,' and he said this without a trace of irony, 'you really should look at *Wuthering Heights.*'

Leona Cox left without taking his advice. Wendell asked me to come down off the ladder and take over the till for a minute. He turned to Ethan and asked him to go to the office Wendell shared with Miss Carter.

The following day, there were two notes pinned on the board beside the tiny staff-only unisex bathroom. The first note said that any customer wishing to return *The Body Electric* would be entitled to a full refund. However, this was not Carter & Co.'s general policy, and employees were asked not to make such promises to our valued customers. Employees were asked to remember that some books were not suitable for certain audiences. However (it concluded) hand-selling was an integral part of the bookseller's art, our calling, and we should never forget our duty to Literature. And the second note? That note reminded employees that Carter & Co. subscribed to the sexual harassment policies endorsed by the Friday Harbor Chamber of Commerce. These were posted on the Chamber's website, and could be downloaded.

'Harassment?' whispered Jessie, as she stopped by my tiny office. 'Does Miss Carter think we'll be sleeping with Wendell?'

We both stifled gales of laughter as Miss Carter walked past on her way out to the floor. She had a sour expression, and though Jessie and I quickly returned to our respective tasks, it really was enough to make you crack up, to think that Miss Carter was so besotted with Ethan James, that basically she'd warn the rest of us off him. As if. Jessie was too broken-hearted over Murph. And me, well, by definition, you can't have a flingette with a co-worker. A co-worker is there in your face. Besides, Ethan wasn't my type. Too surly, too competitive, too much of a loner, too cool and arrogant, and on top of all that, too conventional: the guy who'd trade the Little Ladies the heavy lifting for the gift wrapping. No, thanks.

But the following week, Ethan surprised us all.

He was behind the counter, selling a book to none other than Frances McTeer when Murph strode in, and asked for Jessie. Murph was one of those men, competent when he was completely sober, and bullying after a few drinks. His face was flushed now, but I figured that was anger; it was too early to have been drinking. Ethan ignored him, and he asked again, 'I wanna talk to Jessie.' Ethan continued his transaction with Frances. Finally Murph said, 'Don't toy with me. Do you know who I am?'

'Darth Vader?' said Ethan, giving Frances her change.

'You must be the guy Jessie's dating,' Murph snarled. 'She's dating somebody, or she wouldn't have changed the locks. She changed the locks on me. I can't get into my own house!'

'Jessie's not here,' said Ethan. This was not true. She was in the back on her lunch break.

'I've just listed the place with Island Realty, and put the sign up, and she has to move out.'

'That has nothing to do with me, or with the store.'

'Tosca,' Murph barked, seeing me emerge from the Cookbook section. 'Where is she?'

'Don't ask Tosca. I've already told you, Jessie's not here. You want to buy a book?' said Ethan. 'If not, you should leave. Now. Now would be a good time for you to leave.'

'What! You're throwing me out of the bookstore?' Murph chortled and looked around. Statler and Waldorf had paused in their game, and were watching intently. Even Mr Hyde roused from his late-morning nap. 'It's a public place.'

'Then buy a book or get out.'

'Where's Jessie? Tosca—'

'You need to leave.' Ethan walked out from behind the counter, walked to the door, opened it, and the little bell overhead rang, and cold air rushed in. Murph was spry and scrappy, but Ethan was taller, younger, and outweighed him. 'Whatever business you have with Jessie, you can't do it here.'

And Murph left.

Even though I didn't like Ethan, I thought it only fair that I should acknowledge what he'd done. I told him I thought he was brave. Even impressive.

He shrugged it off. 'I hate bullies, that's all.'

Frances McTeer said, 'I think you must be Scottish.'

'Thank you, Ethan,' said Jessie when she heard what happened. 'A lot of men wouldn't have done that.'

'You were smart to change the locks,' he replied, 'and lucky to be rid of Murph.'

Murph, however, didn't leave the island. At some point during the day, he hit his favorite watering holes and word filtered back to the bookstore that he was drunk and looking for trouble. Jessie agreed to come home with me that night.

Once back at my place, Jessie fell apart, weeping, Kleenex-clutching, and thrashing through all her unhappiness, not just a broken heart (and at last I think she could see that Murph really was a bastard) but a broken life. Could Murph evict her? Could she get a restraining order?

'Look,' I said, 'even if he serves eviction papers on you, it'll take thirty days, or sixty days or ninety days, something like that. It can't happen all at once. Anyway, do you really want to stay there after all this?'

'It's my home,' she protested, 'but even my parents won't help me hold on to it. They say I'd need a lawyer, and what's the point, I don't have a chance. They don't believe in me.' She dabbed her eyes.

'You don't have a great case, Jessie, I'm sorry to say it, but it's true. It is Murph's house. He built it on property he bought, unless you have some kind of agreement with him about ...'

'I didn't need an agreement! We were in love!'

'And now you have to go out, and find a new life and someone new to love.'

'After seven years?'

'After seven years.'

'There's no book for that, Tosca,' she sniffed. 'No self-help, no prescriptions. What can you do? What would

Ginger Rogers do?'

'Ginger Rogers would get her hair cut and a new pair of shoes, and a dress she could not afford. She would move out of Murph's stupid house, taking what was hers and leaving the rest. She would leave the key in the mailbox, or no, she would take the key, and throw it in the harbor. She would go out with different friends every night. She would flirt with so many men, they would fall like leaves at her feet. She would be lively, so lively she would forget she was lonely.'

'Pretend till it was true?'

'*Mais oui!*' I used my French for emphasis.

'That isn't what you did with Vince.'

My French wasn't equal to this, so I just shrugged. I didn't want to talk about heartbreak with Vince.

'And if Murph comes back?'

'Murph isn't coming back, Jessie.'

'But if he did?'

'If he did, I would simply say to him,' I put on my best French accent, '"Murph? Eez that not the name of the petite dog I once had? A disgusting *petit chien* who chewed up women's panties from the laundry basket?"'

'How can you make me laugh when I'm so miserable?'

'Because I am funny, and because I'm right, and because you know I care about you. You want some Chinese? I'll go to the take-out place and get us some.'

'I'm gluten-free these days.'

'I promise I'll eat both fortune cookies.'

Chapter Six

ON THE FEBRUARY night of Tina Frazier's event, I especially wore a bright green sweater in her honor. Tina Frazier, the Green Warrior, was like one of those old saints; the more trouble and woe she endured, the better and more holy she became. She was a Northwest legend, and ordinarily we could have absolutely counted on twenty people for a Tina Frazier reading, maybe even hoping for thirty. But tonight I stood in front of the Masterpiece Theatre set and looked out the window at the swirling snow, drifting all along Spring Street. The worst storm in twenty-five years. Ethan and I were the only ones who lived near enough to the store to walk (or bike) to work. Had it been any other author, I would have called and cancelled, or expected that she would call and cancel, but Tina Frazier was Northwest tough. Alaska tough. She would scoff at cancelling. By seven o'clock, when the event should have started, not one person had come to hear her, and Ethan started taking down the metal chairs.

'Don't do that yet,' I advised. 'She'll come. She's Tina Frazier. And when she gets here and sees that no one else is here, believe me, her tantrum will not be green and eco-friendly.'

He stood beside me at the window. 'Why would anyone in their right fucking mind go out in this?'

'Don't say fucking in the store,' I cautioned him, though there was no one there but us. I sighed. 'Well, I might as well go make the fucking popcorn.'

Ethan and I were nibbling popcorn when the first Islander showed up. Then two. Granolas, people in their thirties, bundled up in Gortex and snow caps with earflaps. Tina Frazier, if she showed, would be preaching to the converted. Two of the three munched popcorn, the third declined because it wasn't organic.

At half past seven, the power went out, and stayed out for ten minutes, and we five lit each other's faces by the light of cell phones. Ten minutes later, even the Granolas were getting restless, and just then Tina Frazier entered, stamping the snow off her boots, informing us that she had walked up from the ferry landing. Stout, tough, fortyish, she eyeballed the three people in a semi-circle, and she turned to me. 'Three? Three people?'

No good in asking what Ginger Rogers would do. I blathered and flailed and blamed the whole thing on the weather. 'Tina, it's the worst storm in twenty-five years! Readers would be here in droves, but there are no snowplows on the island. People can't get out of their homes. No one's moved in *days*.'

'I'm here,' said Tina, taking off her thick gloves, and shaking off the snow from her mukluks. 'I drove up from Seattle, parked my car in Anacortes and walked on the ferry.'

'I know, and I so appreciate it. You are a real trooper, Tina.'

'No, Tosca, I am a real author. And you have wasted my real time. I'm not addressing an audience of three. I could have been home with a cup of sage tea, but I came here to sell books, and look what's here.'

'Who's here,' I corrected her, knee-jerk English major that I am.

'Can I get a ferry out tonight?'

'You're going to disappoint all these dedicated readers?' said Ethan, coming seemingly out of nowhere. 'What kind of activist does that?'

'Who are you?'

Ethan drew Ms Frazier over to the central desk, and the Staff Picks shelf. There was *All Things Organic* on five of the six shelves, and three of her other titles on a couple of Staff Picks as well. 'We've been hand-selling your books like crazy.' He snatched *All Things Organic* off his own shelf and gave it to her, picked up a pen and asked her to sign. 'If it hadn't been for the snow, you'd have had a packed house here tonight. Fifty people. But these few who braved the storm to hear your message, are you really going to walk out on them?'

Oh Ethan, I thought, I take back every mean thing I ever said about you. Every mean thing I ever thought.

Tina Frazier strode in among the Granolas, sat in the Masterpiece wing chair, while she read from her book, and launched into a long description of her progressive views, her predictions, her solutions. She took questions. I glanced at my watch and then at Ethan who sat, feet outstretched, arms crossed over his chest, his gaze fixed on Tina Frazier like she was the Buddha. I glanced outside the window where the snow was swirling. She went on and on. Finally a couple of the Granolas said they had to be going. Look at the snow. I felt vindicated. And, as if to prove to Ms. Frazier what a great place San Juan Island is, the Granolas volunteered to take her to the hotel where we had rented her a room. We sold four copies, including the one Ethan bought.

After they left, I was sweeping up the popcorn. Popcorn adds twenty minutes to my clean up time, and the store mice are the sole beneficiaries of Miss Carter's marketing genius (unless you count Mr Hyde who sometimes catches these mice). Ethan was putting the chairs on the chair cart.

'You were great tonight,' I said to him. 'Honestly.'

'All the girls tell me that.'

We finished, and he pushed the chair cart back to the storeroom, stored it in the corner. We got our jackets and gloves; I turned down the heat, turned off the lights. Ethan strapped on his helmet and took up his bike and we both stepped into the swirling snow. He said goodbye, lifted his bike off the dock and started down the alley. I turned to lock up the storeroom door.

Suddenly I heard a skidding and a tremendous metallic thunk. I called out, but there was no answer, and the alley was poorly lit, no overhead lamps, just the few bulbs burning over back doors, lighting up small pools of snow. I hurried down our steps, slipping once, and falling on my butt, scrambling through the alley. At the end, I saw that the bike had slid into the dumpster; the back wheel still whirred, and Ethan lay sprawled, unmoving and bleeding from his nose and lips. 'Ethan!' I knelt beside him, and turned his face toward me. 'Ethan!' Blood gushed, and stained the snow. He turned to spit out blood, and swore, but at least he was conscious.

'Your teeth,' I said, 'feel your teeth,' but his cycling gloves wouldn't let him. 'Here.' I tore off my own gloves, and brushed the blood away from his mouth. 'Open.' They seemed to be all right. 'Can you stand up?'

'Of course I can fucking stand up.'

But he couldn't. He needed my help, and he was bemoaning the bike as I put his one arm around my shoulder. 'Let's go to my place.'

'No,' he said, amid little blood-and-spit bubbles.

'It's close by,' I protested.

'I'm not leaving my bike.'

So I slid my book bag over the handlebars, and with one hand, I pushed the damn bike. The front wheel was entirely bent and busted, and steering it, even just three blocks was an ordeal. My other arm I put around Ethan James, who dripped blood, bright red drops in the snow, all the way to my apartment.

I managed to get the bike inside my apartment building, but Ethan would not budge till I had locked it. I pointed out that no one was likely to steal it, much less in this condition – the front wheel was twisted – but he insisted. Then I supported him up the stairs, his head thrown back so he would not bleed on the carpet. I opened the door to my apartment, turned on the lights, and Ethan unsnapped his helmet, tossed it on the floor, and collapsed on the couch. I went straight to the bathroom for a damp cloth. The bedroom and the bathroom were both a mess. Oh well.

I came back out, and gently wiped the blood away from his nose and mouth.

'I'm going to look like hell,' he said.

'A black eye, for sure,' I said. 'Maybe two. And that cut is really nasty, but the helmet protected your forehead. You want some aspirin?'

'It won't make any difference. It'll still hurt.'

'Not as badly.'

'Don't you get it? I'm a cyclist. A first rate racing cyclist, a champion cyclist, and I slid into a dumpster? I'll go to work tomorrow and have to tell everyone I ran into a fucking dumpster.'

'Well, the snow, it was—'

'What does that matter?' He pressed the washcloth to his lips and nose. 'You don't have any salve for pride, do you?'

I thought for a minute. 'Wine?'

I went into the kitchen and got down a bottle of the all-purpose red, Chateau Joe, which I stocked up on when I went to Seattle.

'Where's your bathroom?' he asked.

I told him and with his head still tilted back, he wobbled into the bedroom. He was in there a long time, and I turned up the heat, poured two glasses of wine and looked through the cupboards for what I had to offer him. Not exactly Julia Child here. Never mind, who can imagine Ginger Rogers in the kitchen? Still, I knew how to make a mean pizza, and I always kept some Tonnino's dough, mozzarella, and jar of my father's sauce in the fridge.

When he came out, Ethan could only drink the wine in little sips. His lip was slit and a big bruise rose across his nose, and around his eyes.

'Maybe you should go to Island Medical after all. Maybe you need stitches. Maybe you have a broken nose.'

'I've had worse.'

'On your face?'

'No. Not on my face.'

'You might have a scar. It's a pretty bad gash.'

'From a dumpster. Great.' He held the washcloth over the gash, and as if to prove he was fine, he walked around the living room. Ethan seemed over-sized; his sheer height and weight diminished everything else, but then, I remembered there hadn't been a man in my apartment since November when my *petite amour* with the Canadian had ended.

'I see you have a bike on your wall. You cycle?'

'Not seriously. I ride over to Roche Harbor in good weather. Not like you.'

'You mean you don't run into dumpsters.'

'I don't race. I just ride for the fun of it.'

'The race is the fun of it. Like skiing. Why do it, if you're not going to compete?' He stood at the long window staring out at the snow, then picked up one of the jam jars full of sea glass that I keep on the sill. 'I always associate jars of sea glass with old ladies, or little kids. Pretty funky. Who is Emma Calvé?' He pointed to the framed poster on the wall.

'A long ago opera singer.'

'And why do you have all those old posters on the walls in your bedroom?'

'I like Fred Astaire and Ginger Rogers. I like their films, and I like their dancing. Any other snoopy questions?'

'What are you doing over there?'

'Making pizza.'

'Like not frozen?'

'Frozen pizza is an infamy. Are you an anchovy man?'

'I like anything on my pizza except pineapple.'

'Really?' I said. In one night I'd learned two things about Ethan James that made me actually like him. He had saved the day with Tina Frazier, and he wouldn't put pineapple on pizza. This was prejudice I had inherited from my father (though it wasn't enough to make me break up with Vince, who loved Hawaiian pizza). 'I keep the dough in the fridge. I have the sauce from the store.'

'The grocery store?'

'Tonnino's Pizza, my family's place in Capitol Hill. My father's secret sauce.'

'You mean you're going to make the pizza?' he said again. 'From scratch?'

So I told him the story of the pizzeria, of my dad who ran the shop and my mom who ran the business, and all the four daughters who were named after operas, and in turn had pizzas named after each of us. The Tosca was cheese, mushroom, anchovy and olive. My favorites. I told him how we had each worked there since we were fourteen. 'People would come in and breathe deep and roll their eyes and say, that must be the most wonderful smell in the universe! But I hated it. My clothes smelled like pizza. My hair. My hands. So when I went to college, I told my dad and mom, 'I'm done here. I'll never work this counter again. And I'll never eat another pizza as long as I live."

'And did you?'

'Of course not. I've eaten many pizzas, but I've never gone back to work at the pizzeria.'

'You can really whip that dough around!'

'It's in the blood.' I slapped down the dough and whirled it like I'd seen my father and sisters and the cooks do all my life. 'When I make pizza, it's like getting homesick. Do you ever get homesick?'

He gave a short, sharp laugh, then winced. Clearly, it hurt his lip. He took his glass of wine and wandered over to the CD shelves which he perused intently. 'There's a lot of nineties rock bands here. Green Day? Really?'

'Don't be such a snob. I'm sure you also listened to Green Day when you were a kid.'

'There's no jazz.'

'Jazz is an acquired taste I haven't acquired.'

'You're missing out. And all this Edith Piaf. How can you stand her? All that warbling and pain and suffering.'

'I love Edith Piaf,' I declared. '"La Vie en Rose" is—'

'Look at this! Astor! Astor Piazzolla is a god! How do you know him?' he asked, as if Astor Piazzolla were a mutual long lost friend.

'My father, actually.'

'Oh, this one. This one….' words failed him as he took the CD out of the case.

'Opera, tango, my father loves all passionate music. I grew up with Astor, Maria Callas and Dean Martin my whole life.'

'How can you say Dean Martin in the same breath?'

'I like Dean Martin. My dad plays Dean for muzak in the pizzeria. How did you stumble on Astor Piazzolla?'

'No one stumbles on Astor,' he said with more genuine emotion than I had ever heard from him. 'The music of Astor Piazzolla was the best thing I learned at Dartmouth. I had an Argentine roommate, and he played Astor Piazzolla's tangos, and those long, sad passionate pieces. For a whole semester I just drank them in, and every time I listened, I felt as though someone had pinned me to the chair, whispering words of love in one ear, and tragedy and death in the other, and it wasn't as though I had to choose, no, I had to somehow meld them, learn to live with them both. I'd never lived before I heard Astor Piazzolla.' He put one of the CDs on, and skipped ahead to *Tanti Anni Prima*. He said, 'That is the saddest song ever written.'

'When Astor died in '92 my father just sat in the living room, weeping, and playing that over and over. I haven't been able to listen to it since.'

'Your father must be a remarkable man for a guy who slings pizzas all day.'

'Slinging pizzas isn't a bad life.'

'I didn't mean it like that.'

I waited momentarily, poised for him to add something tart and ironic, but he didn't.

Tanti Anni Prima ended, and he went back to the first piece, a fast tango that shattered the mood with its fierce beauty. He lowered himself painfully into one of the rickety wooden chairs at the oak table, and sipped his Chateau Joe. He watched while I flung the oil and sauce and cheese and anchovies on the pie. 'Do you know how to tango?'

'I took a class last spring. I was the best student.'

'Why did you quit?'

'I didn't. The teacher did. She couldn't make a go of it, not on an island like this.' I put the pizza in the oven. 'Did your Argentine roommate teach you how to tango?'

'He tried, but I wasn't very good at it, and I never do anything I'm not very good at.'

'Competition.'

'Yes.'

I made a quick salad with wilted Romaine, flaccid green onions, a splash of capers, and the last of the lupini beans. I got out the plates and flatware, suddenly aware how chipped and mismatched it all was. Oh well, a certain *je ne sais quois* panache can make up for material imperfection. I lit the candles I always kept on the table, but never used.

'That has to be the best aroma in the universe, even if you don't think so. Is this a Tosca pizza?'

'Yes.'

He smiled, though it clearly hurt him to do so. Odd,

I thought, that with his good looks all banged up, and damaged, he was actually more attractive. I brought my wine glass to the table. 'What'll we toast?' I asked. 'My old dad says you shouldn't ever start a meal without a prayer or a toast. You don't look like the praying type.'

'You have one brown eye and one green eye. I never noticed.'

'It's the green sweater.'

'No, you really do.'

'Yes, I really do. What'll we toast?'

'Astor Piazzolla.'

Our glasses clinked.

He savored the Chateau Joe as if it were something special, or at least he closed his eyes and seemed intent on something. 'Astor was a genius. I sometimes wonder if people like that don't do more harm than good. They make the rest of us feel like, well, the rest of us. And for the rest of us, when you strive and work and believe, you get fucked over. It's only in great novels that the brave and lively prevail.'

'You sound like an old fart.'

'I'm a realist. The people who try to be daring and extraordinary, unless they're Astor, or someone like him, they get fucked. One way or another. They lose. Moreover, no one wants them around. Geniuses make everyone uncomfortable, like somehow being around that person, you ought to strive and sweat and achieve.'

'I think they call that inspiration.'

'Bullshit.'

'That's pretty harsh, isn't it?'

'Listen, when you were in college, did you choose the teacher who would kick your butt and insist you live up to a standard? Or did you, and everyone else, flock to the guy who gives out easy A's and tells you all you're frigging geniuses so that everyone has a big grin on their faces, and they'll never have to think.'

'I was just a kid then. I wouldn't do that now,' I replied, though in truth, I wasn't so sure. 'You don't seem the sort of person to live like that.'

'Of course I am. Triumph always belongs to the dull and plain. Why try for anything else? You'll get knocked down and no thanks. That's why I race. It's the one place, cycling, or skiing, even chess, that you can actually work and strive, and feel really good about it. You win, and there's no ambiguity. You lose, and you go back to trying.'

The buzzer went off, I checked the pizza, brought it out and served him a piece while Astor waxed rhapsodic on the stereo. 'Be careful or you'll burn the roof of your mouth with the hot cheese.'

The power surged, went off, struggled for a few minutes, then came back on. Ethan wolfed down his first piece with gusto. 'This is best pizza I've ever eaten, including in Naples.'

And that was the second un-ironic thing he had said in thirty minutes.

'Thank you. I'll tell my father.' I went to re-fill his wine glass, but the bottle was empty. I got another down and opened it. There was a sudden blinking of the lights, and suddenly, everything went black. Astor stopped in mid-arpeggio, though his music seemed to hover, trembling in the darkened room.

'Nothing to worry about. It doesn't usually last.'

'Who's worried? We have the candles, the wine and the pizza.'

In the dim radius of candlelight, I regarded him more closely, looking for attitude, but he seemed to have meant what he said. He smiled in spite of his puffy, swollen lip. He would almost certainly have a scar.

'Another piece of Tosca?'

It took me a moment to realize he was speaking of the pizza. I served it and one for me. The pool of candlelight denting the darkness seemed to enclose us, encircle us. 'Aside from being between things,' I ventured, 'what are you doing up here, working at a bookstore on an island? You don't fit in.'

'I don't mind not fitting in.'

'So what's next?'

'I don't look that far ahead. I don't care.'

'You don't care what you do?'

'I don't care. It's all gas for me, just vapor and gas. Why expend myself? I play video games and watch all four seasons of *Battlestar Galactica* over and over. I'm just an ordinary schmuck. Now, Win. He's not like that. Win's full of fire. He's a damn fine writer, even if he's not the Astor Piazzolla of literature. He's got energy, even if it's not genius. Maybe it doesn't matter if it's not genius. He thinks he's a genius. Anyway, Win goes out and goes after things. You can't mistake him for any old schmuck. When you're with Win, you know you're really alive.'

'And without him you're not really alive? Only gas and vapor?'

'We were like brothers.'

'Complete with sibling rivalry?'

'Oh man, we'd fight and compete, and compete and fight, but when it came to the rest of the world, we had each other's backs. We met at school, boarding school when we were just little. At St. George's, you learned to slay dragons, believe me, it was slay or be slain. Win and I were inseparable. We were like shoes and laces. We counted on no one but each other. When he got into

Dartmouth – and he had genuinely good grades, I didn't – and I thought, oh no, we're splitting up. I told my grandmother I had to get into Dartmouth.' In the flickering light, he tried to smile, but winced with pain. 'So Marjorie bought me in. I don't know that for an absolute fact, just a guess. I got expelled from St. George's once, and she bought me back in there too.'

'I went to Catholic school too.'

'St. George's wasn't Catholic. St. George's was just as Waspy as you could get. They would have been all white if they thought they could get away with it. A few token blacks, Oreos, you know? Black on the outside, white on the inside. A couple of Hispanics, a half dozen Chinese or Japanese, a few Indians from India, and the sons of Middle-Eastern oil magnates. The place was expensive as hell. All the classes were taught by academic fakes who all thought they were brilliant. A few were pederasts, and the rest were pompous asses. And this sorry tribe had basically two lessons to instill in us, the future leaders of the free world.'

'What were those?'

'They taught us to despise everyone who wasn't exactly like us, and that money earned you respect and affection. You could count on money and nothing else.'

'Do you believe that?'

'I used to, I'm sorry to say. But I did. I started to unlearn it in college, the semester Win took off to ski in Switzerland. That's when I had the Argentine roommate. That guy had heart, and he didn't care about all that shit. I thought about taking a semester, and going to Buenos Aires, but then,' he shrugged, 'Win came back and we took up where we left off.'

'And where was that?'

'We were trying to be extraordinary, and we just got

fucked,' he said in a bland way, but the expression in his eyes wasn't mocking (as far as I could tell; his eyes were starting to swell with bruises). 'Do you have any Tylenol? My face hurts like hell.'

I took one of the candles, and went into the bathroom, enjoying the flutter inside me. The snow and the wine and the candlelight, all of that conspired against my better judgment, and I recognized that internal bubbling up of vanity and desire, and I knew what it presaged. I found the Tylenol and checked that I had an extra toothbrush. Brushed my own teeth while I was at it, and combed my hair. Candlelit, in the mirror, I tried out a frankly erotic stare, as though daring any man to be less than dazzled. Then I peed.

I came back out, put the candle on the table, and got him a drink of water, left the faucet on while I was at it so the pipes wouldn't freeze. The power had been off long enough that the place was getting cold. I brought the water to the table. 'You could stay here tonight. Walk to work in the morning. Leave your bike here.'

'Won't your boyfriend mind?'

I was about to say I don't have a boyfriend, but thought better of it. 'I don't need anyone's permission to offer my couch to a friend.'

'The couch.'

'The couch. I do it for anyone who had a broken bike, a black eye, a bloody nose, and a cut lip. I have an extra toothbrush.'

'Thank you, Tosca. I mean it, thank you. You've been really kind. You surprised me.'

I wanted to say he had surprised me too, but I didn't. 'Because I was kind?'

'More than that. You're more than that.'

He rose, and stroked the hair away from my face. I

was afraid to touch his face, but not afraid to look into his eyes. I couldn't kiss him, but he kissed me, or at least his lips brushed mine gently, and he said my name again and again, and I forgot the fiction of the couch, picked up one of the candles and he put his arms around me, and we moved backward in a slow sort of waltz toward the bed, shedding our clothes, breathing each other in as we did. I put the candle on the night-stand, and there, under the watchful gaze of Ginger Rogers swirling to *Let's Face the Music and Dance*, we fell back upon the bed. We rolled over and under one another, and I felt myself moving toward a pitch and intensity I could not remember having felt before. I could not touch his face, but his hands and his words and his body were eloquent. I held him, and his warmth permeated through my very skin, right down to the core.

'I'll be gentle,' I whispered when my hands traversed the length of his smooth torso, and he winced where he was bruised.

'Don't be gentle. Be yourself.'

'You are a wounded man, after all.'

'Yes,' he whispered, 'but not in the way that you think.'

Chapter Seven

FIRST LIGHT WAS late in February this far north, and the windows were frosted over, sheeted, and splayed with ice prisms in silvery patterns. I stirred to waking, and in that wan light turned to look at Ethan. His hair tousled on the pillow, his mouth agape, drooling slightly with big ugly bruises the color of eggplants around his eyes and nose. His looks had taken a beating all right, though the accident hadn't impaired his actions last night. I turned my back to him, gently so as not to wake him. The candle on the night stand had burnt to a stub. I stole out of bed, replacing the covers quickly.

I hotfooted through the blistering cold to the bathroom where I greeted myself in the mirror, not a promising sight. Still, once in the shower, I made the water as hot as I could bear, and stayed there till it got cold. My sweats were hanging on a hook on the back door (souvenir of Friday-to-Roche Harbor Walk for a Cure, 2012) and I flung those on, ruffled my hair dry, pulled it in a ponytail and brushed my teeth. I opened the medicine chest and got out the new toothbrush, put it on the sink for Ethan, and that's when I saw the condom I keep on hand. The proverbial French letter. A woman of the world is always prepared. Well, said my reflection, what does that make you? That certainly wasn't safe sex last night. Maybe sex is never safe, I retorted inwardly. If you want safe, stay celibate, get married, but if you want *l'amour*, then there are always risks. *L'amour, la vie.* I acted on my emotions. I wanted him, and I went to bed with him. And I'm not sorry. So there.

My worldly reflections were cut short by Astor Piazzolla's tango blasting, and the place blazed with light as the power came back on. I sprinted into the living room to turn off the stereo and the lights. The apartment was still freezing, and I got back into bed as soon as I could. 'You want another Tylenol?' I whispered.

'Yes. Thanks. My face really hurts.'

I quickly got him the tablets and some water. He took the Tylenol, and pulled me back into his embrace. His lips were bruised and painful, but his hands were knowing, tender and inciting at the same moment. Spooned against him, I drifted back to uneasy sleep where I dreamed I went to work naked, and that's when I heard my cell phone, which has a particularly obnoxious ring. I flung on a robe, and dashed out to the living room, closing the door gently behind me. I snatched up the phone, and heard Wendell telling me in a voice message that I didn't have to open the store. I didn't even have to come in that day.

'The storm last night was terrible,' his message said, 'but it's warming up out there, it's just rain now, and Sally and I can both get in and work today. I've checked with her. We'll open late, but so what? You and Ethan have held down the fort all this nasty week, so you're both off today. I'm going to call Ethan too.'

Immediately after Wendell signed off, Ethan's phone

rang in his jacket pocket while I looked around the room. Since the heat had come back on, the thick rind of frost had begun to melt, though the windows remained brilliant and opaque. The two empty wine bottles, the cold remains of the pizza, and the miserably wilted salad all seemed especially dreary in the gray morning light. I scraped the dirty plates into the garbage and filled the sink with sudsy dishwater, plunging them in so I wouldn't have to see them. Facing last night's refuse, I felt considerably less worldly, less like a woman in a French film – sexy, defiant, and sophisticated – and more like asking myself prosaic questions, such as What now? Would my relationship with Ethan change? What if it didn't? What did last night mean? Anything? Should it mean something? I advised myself to quit being a dumbshit, and stick to *la vie en rose*. I made the coffee, the grinder's awful noise seeming to reverberate in my teeth. I washed some of the dishes, but that just seemed like the depth of dullness. I took a cup of coffee to the desk, and watched the ice melt on the long narrow windows. Rain replaced the silvery snow, and fell in a straight, gray curtain.

After what seemed like a long while, I heard the toilet flush. I hoped he had seen the new toothbrush and hadn't found the condom. I poured Ethan's coffee, realizing that I had no idea how he liked his coffee. All these months working together and I'd never noticed.

By the time he came out of the bedroom, the coffee was tepid. His face was a mass of black and blue, purple and green, his lip scabbed and puckered. He was completely dressed, shoes even. I went up to him and put my arms around him, my face against his chest, though my cheek pressed into the damp toothbrush that was in his shirt pocket. His body was tense and he did not relax into my embrace. He patted my shoulder.

'Come sit down and have some coffee,' I said. 'Even breakfast.'

'Thanks, no. I have to work in an hour.'

'No, you don't! Neither do I. Wendell called, and he and Sally can get into town today. We're free. Really!' I stepped apart from him, went to his backpack and got his phone, handed it to him. 'Check your messages.'

There were three or four of them, and he rippled through quickly. One was a woman's voice. He came to Wendell who repeated what he'd said to me, including the round of applause for holding down the fort. Ethan turned the phone off. 'I'd better leave anyway.'

'But we have the whole day!'

'I don't.'

I searched his battered face, but his eyes were blank, not glassy, just voids, without affection, without any emotion, without interest for that matter. This was the guy who said my car smelled like old dog.

'What's just happened?' I asked, utterly unlike the woman of the world I longed to be. That woman would have lit up a cig, plucked a bit of tobacco from her tongue, and exhaling a slow blue plume of smoke, said, 'Au revoir, asshole.'

'Nothing just happened.'

'Nothing?'

'Of course, nothing. Come on, Tosca. Don't get all operatic on me.' He nodded to the poster of Emma Calvé on the wall, and laughed, yes, a truly hearty, good-hearted chuckle as he took his jacket off the heater and slid his arms into it. 'Don't do this.'

'You were happy enough to do it last night.'

He zipped up, took his gloves and scarf from the heater. 'You were great.'

'I was great? Was that some kind of fucking audition? A notch for your belt?'

'Look, Tosca, don't put yourself down, but don't make too much of it, OK? You're a sweet kid.'

'I'm thirty.'

'OK, you're a sweet older woman.'

'Are you pandering to me?'

'Oh, stop it.'

'What the hell do you mean?'

'We're consenting adults, right? By the way, I'm clean. I hope you are. I should have brought a condom. The old French letter, huh? Sorry.'

'Are you asking me if I have STDs?'

'I just don't want you to worry.'

'Worry? You're giving me the kiss off!' I was so angry, I was shaking.

'You're being too dramatic.' His lower lip twitched, though whether in humor or in pain, I could not tell. 'Too operatic. This never happened. Agreed? I'll never tell. Anyone who hears about this, it'll have to come from you.'

'What?'

'Remember the store's sexual harassment policy.'

'You think I harassed you?'

He put his gloves on, his scarf around his neck. 'You wouldn't know irony if it bit you in the ass.'

He picked up his helmet, and with that, he was gone, and I hadn't even had the time or the wit to say *au revoir, asshole.*

The ghost of Danny Delvecchio appeared in my apartment, and hovered there. In college I had a study date with Danny one Tuesday night. For econ. One thing led to another, guns turning to butter, so to speak, and we tumbled into bed. We had a good time; it was like being puppies or something, all warm fuzzies and affectionate. On Wednesday morning there in the econ lecture hall, I took one look at Danny and all his friends, their leers and sniggles, and I knew that everyone in a three mile radius had heard I'd gone down with or on him, or whatever we were calling it back in the day. Screwed. A one night stand. A conquest. A name in a little black book. Another brick in the wall. Shortly after that, I met the invincible Vince. Among his other fine qualities, Vince wasn't friends with Danny.

I slumped down on my bed, knowing I should take off my slipper and beat myself. Without youth to excuse me – I was long past college – I'd been dumped after a One Night Stand. A flingette was not a one night stand; it was a modified fling, all fun and no hard feelings. So why I was so undone now? Too stunned to cry. As though someone had punched me in the solar plexus of my heart. How can that be? I didn't love Ethan. I never could. Arrogant East Coast competitive snob. Then why the pain? How could I feel such pain over such a truly *petite amour*? Though it wasn't petite last night, I remembered. I had given more than my body, and I thought Ethan had too. The wine of delusion was certainly sour, and the taste of regret was earthy, bitter, cold, like wild mushrooms. It wasn't Ethan at all, I told myself. I cared nothing for Ethan James. It was pride. Mere pride. *What's mere about pride?* Ginger Rogers's husky voice seemed to inquire.

I marched into the living room, and pulled the candle stubs out, and flung them in the trash. I took Astor off the stereo, blaming him, and the tango in general for the spell he had cast. I turned off the stereo. I washed up all the dishes, took out the trash and the recycle, and by the time I'd got all that done, I figured I could cry. But no. In silence, I swept and mopped the kitchen floor, and still I couldn't cry. I played the *Batman* video game just to truly narcotize my brain, and that didn't work because then I remembered I'd forgotten the goddamn sheets. I stomped into the bedroom and pulled the sheets off the bed. I looked up at the poster above my bed, Ginger in Fred's arms floating beautifully to *Let's Face the Music and Dance*. Only Ginger Rogers could face adversity with that much grace. Not me. The song itself came to me, with its ominous opening line, 'There may be trouble ahead ...'

Chapter Eight

ETHAN'S TWO BLACK eyes, his visible wounds, his sliding his bike on the ice were the talk of Friday Harbor. Everyone – staff, customers, Statler, Waldorf, the baristas at Jumpin Java, Charlotte and all her confections – offered him barrels of sympathy (and free coffee and free truffles). The bike was totaled. But Ethan wouldn't buy a bike from Island Cycles; he insisted they order one, a Scott, though it would take a while to come in. However, Ethan had a second bike, a Scott mountain bike he still rode to work. By the time I arrived for my shift a day later, Ethan was telling his story (sans dumpster) to Frances McTeer, saying simply that he had slid in the snow, and gone down on the road, then steered the bike all the way down to the marina where he lived, bloodied lip, black eyes and a blinding snowstorm notwithstanding. Everyone at Carter & Co. wanted to know where I was in the midst of all this.

'Tosca didn't see it,' said Ethan. 'I left early because of the snow, and Tosca was still cleaning up popcorn.'

Everyone admired his courage, and forgave his foibles. Even Wendell was nice to him. However, everyone agreed he should have gone to Island Medical and got stitches. He would have a scar for sure. Miss Carter, when Nan finally drove her in, was beside herself, worried not only for his good looks, but that dear old Marjorie might blame her. Miss Carter ordered him into her car, and Nan drove him to their very own doctor. Such was Miss Carter's reputation on San Juan Island that she didn't even call beforehand to make an appointment. Miss Carter showed up with Ethan in tow, and he was seen immediately.

Ethan's responses to me, personally, were remote unto robotic. He was civil, but the old wit and lively irritation – the zest, I recognized in retrospect – that had spiced our relationship, that was gone. I struggled to maintain the right attitude, without knowing what the right attitude was. With practice, I got better at being blasé, insouciant, sophisticated (words that reek of Ginger Rogers) though I was none of those things, not really. All an act.

Wendell posted the work schedules every Monday morning, and I was delighted to see that Ethan and I were spared having to be the only two employees on any given day or evening. However, I noticed that Jessie and Ethan were often billeted together. I noticed too in staff meetings, there seemed to be some unacknowledged current between them. Unacknowledged on his part, anyway. Jessie just seemed livelier, no longer bemoaning Murph, but offering up no other info about her love life. I wondered about that because when she lived with Murph, she was always eager to share their intimate details. *The Body Electric* showed up on Jessie's Staff Picks and I wondered about that. Miss Carter seemed unduly snippy with me, snippy and critical, and I wondered about that too.

At work I was a mess and miserable. Outside of work I continued to gnash and fester and take off my own slipper and beat myself. Introspection was for people like Jessie, who actually enjoyed combing through their emotions like looking for fleas on a dog. Not me, thank you. I didn't do introspection, and yet my wounded heart ached, and my wounded ego winced, and my psyche sprouted eggplant-colored bruises like the ones on Ethan's face. I could not shake off the wretched sensation that on that snowy evening, Ethan James had revealed himself to me as the most interesting man I had met in years. Years and years. Since Vince. Now I'd never know if he really was that man, or if he was the bland, sulky, lazy, self-centered dude I'd always assumed him to be. I should have made him sleep on the fucking couch. Dammit. In lieu of introspection, I watched a lot of DVDs including all four classic Fred and Ginger films, a bunch of French films, and I played video games. I went to yoga four times a week instead of twice. I even cleaned my bedroom, and there, at the bottom of the stack of books by my bed, I saw *The Body Electric.*

I read it in one night, staying up very late, and after I read it, I had a hard time sleeping. *The Body Electric* (the title taken from Walt Whitman) was a short, powerful novel, and Win Jefferies had a real writer's gift. The patina of drugged desperation that clings like shackles to the characters comes to hug the reader's mind and heart, leaving you feeling trapped, uncomfortable, which, I was sure, was the author's intent. Certainly after finishing the novel, I felt desperately the need to experience something *not* tainted: a walk in the spring rain, maybe, a spray of sunshine from under a low-lying cloud. At the same time the book did not have that hard-eyed, unflinching lucidity that comes with a novel, by, say, Albert Camus, or George Orwell, where, however gruesome the circumstances, you know the author has stared at the whole, fateful human condition without blinking. But maybe Win Jefferies wasn't going for an Orwellian essence, or Camus's hard clarity Maybe he was doing Holden Caulfield for the twenty-first century. Ethan had compared it to *Catcher in the Rye*. For me, though, Win's Unnamed Narrator lacked the youth or vulnerability that made Holden so sympathetic. Unnamed Narrator and his best friend Roger (for whom Unnamed Narrator feels an attraction, alluded to, but left unresolved) are both slick, wealthy young men who have one drugged and degrading adventure after another. Ostensibly they're looking for meaning, but everything and everyone they touch is maimed or dirtied, or betrayed. They lack all remorse. At the end of the novel, Roger and Unnamed are in adjoining padded rooms in rehab. Roger kills himself and Unnamed feels an existential Nothing. Truly, nothing. *Rien*. The next morning walking to work, I saw an alley cat gnawing on a mouse behind Charlotte's Confections. Just what I needed to see on this rag-end-of-winter day, and after reading an unrelentingly grim novel, and just before my weekly Events and Publicity meeting with Miss Carter. Great.

'I'm very pleased with myself,' Miss Carter announced, as I entered her office, which at least was warm. 'I've got Frances McTeer a slot at the Sunday Book and Author breakfast at the PNBA next weekend.'

'Frances must be thrilled,' I commented. This was a great opportunity for her. The Pacific Northwest Booksellers Association meets twice a year, March and September, and the chance to pitch to two hundred breakfasting booksellers at one whack, well what author wouldn't love it? Especially an author like Frances. These coveted twelve minute slots – like everything else in life – are paid for. The publisher's gift to the author. Frances's publisher wouldn't invest squat in her books; her books didn't make enough money. They sold so poorly, personally I thought it was a fucking miracle anyone went on publishing her at all. 'How did you do it on such short notice? Those slots are set up months in advance.'

'I heard through the grapevine that one of the authors they had slated for the Sunday breakfast had a family emergency and cancelled, so I called JJ, and got the slot for Frances.'

'Did you have to pay for it?'

Miss Carter smiled conspiratorially. 'Between ourselves, I did it because it's what Sylvia Beach would have done for Hem, or Joyce.'

'I'm sure it is, Miss Carter.'

She lowered her glasses over her nose and peered at me. 'What's wrong with you, Tosca?'

'Wrong? Nothing's wrong. I'm fine.'

'The past few weeks, you've been, well, not yourself.'

This was alarming to me because Miss Carter was the least astute, the least observant, the most self-involved person I knew. I gave a wan smile and said again I was fine.

'You're looking peaky. Honestly, Tosca, you haven't looked well for weeks now. You're depressing me. Ordinarily, I'd write it off to Girl Troubles, but that can't go on for weeks. I hope you're not pregnant.'

I certainly wasn't going to discuss my periods with Edith Carter. I grimaced and said maybe I just needed a haircut.

Late that week I had two days off in a row, and I took the ferry over to Seattle, and showed up at my sister Carmen's salon.

I sat in the chair as she shook out the cape.

'Do something,' I said. 'Make me look like someone else.'

Carmen frowned at me in the mirror. 'You've been disappointed in love, haven't you?'

I had to laugh. 'Oh, Carmen, no one but you would talk like that. Disappointed in love! What a crock.'

'Who is he?'

'There is no he.'

'What did he do? What did he say?'

"There is no he. Just make me interesting.'

'Tosca,' said my sister, 'you are an artist! Never let anyone tell you otherwise! And when you walk out of here, you will be as beautiful outside as you are inside.'

'Oh, Carmen,' I demurred, stifling a little sniff. When she called me Tosca, and not Prune, or Prunella, I knew she was serious.

I spent the afternoon there, foiled and crimped and tinted, washed, rinsed, conditioned, dried, moussed, and by the time I walked out, my hair was shorn up around my neck, and fell forward asymmetrically around my face. Moreover it was a pastiche of many colors, few of them my own native dark brown. A long magenta streak ran along the left side. *Trés chic.*

'Call Chris Egan,' Carmen advised. 'Ask him out. Go on. Isn't that what your famous Ginger Rogers would do? Put on a new dress, face the music and dance?'

'I thought you hate it when I talk about Ginger Rogers.'

'Oh that. That was such a long time ago, and I was just in a bad mood. Forget what I said then.'

Carmen waved away a silly quarrel that was deadly serious ten years earlier. I was just back from my semester in France, twenty years old, and in charge of the universe. Carmen had come over to our parents' house with her three kids. They were playing space aliens, screeching through downstairs. My mother was in the upstairs study working on the accounts; my father was at the pizzeria, and Aunt Clara, who usually looked after the house, had taken to her bed to get off her feet. Carmen was in the kitchen making dinner. I was hanging around the kitchen, telling Carmen all the wonderful things I was going to do with my life: I would never live like my parents, tied to ruts, like Dad who would die with only fifty million pizzas (all eaten, gone, pushed through people's bowels) to show for his life's work. I wouldn't live like Mom with all her business acumen having nothing but balanced books for her life's work. I would not live like my sisters, Carmen cutting hair and raising kids, Norma and Aida with similarly boring lives, boring husbands, boring children. Oh no, my life would be fuller! Richer! Deeper! More fully lived, more flamboyant, more daring! I would have lovers and not some dull, balding husband. I would travel! Go to the Lido. Return to Paris. Sip cocktails in fancy places. I would write books that would have people talking and admiring my …

Carmen suddenly reached out and grabbed my wrist. She plonked my hand straight down into the dough where she'd just splashed some olive oil (she was making a pizza. What else?) She rubbed my hand viciously all over the dough.

'That's life, Tosca. That. You feel that?' She gripped my wrist so tightly it hurt. 'That is life. The flour. The oil. The dishes you wash day after day. The fucking laundry that has to be washed, dried, folded and put away, just so it can get dirty again.' She smeared my hand all over the dough and oil. 'The job where you stand on

111

your feet all day and breathe in chemicals and listen to women's woes, and make them feel better about themselves, the fucking bills you cannot pay, the fucking root canals you have to pay for and endure the pain because you don't have dental insurance. The braces for kids. That's life.' I tried to wrest my hand away, but she was too strong for me. 'You hear those kids tearing around the halls? That's life. Mom's upstairs trying to make sense of the accounts Dad can't keep. That's life. Dad's at the store overseeing a bunch of lazy-ass cooks who probably steal from him. My husband's going gray with the cost of gas doubling every year, and my kid is living in middle school hell. That. Is. Life. Whatever you say you want, whatever you say you'll do, this is what it becomes. Rub your hands around in that,' she pressed my hand again, 'and for God's sake get some sense! Grow up.' She released my wrist, threw out the dough, and started over. We didn't speak for weeks.

Shortly after that I slept with Vince, and the rest, as they say, is history.

I called Chris just to say I was in town. He asked me out to dinner at Bellevue's newest chic restaurant.

'You'll like it,' he said, 'it's very French.'

I agreed to meet him, then I remembered I hadn't brought any nice clothes or nice shoes.

'I can't go like this.'

'Never mind,' said Carmen, 'try Chi Chi's. They have a fantastic pair of high-heeled boots on sale, and there's a new retro shop over on Pine. Tell them I sent you. The owner is one of my clients.'

With my new haircut, high-heeled boots and chic black dress with a short skirt, contrasting with an extra-long cashmere scarf, magenta to match the streak in my hair, I felt restored. I could have been Ginger Rogers in

Top Hat. I sailed into the art deco brasserie in Bellevue, and informed the maître d' I was meeting Chris Egan.

'Ah yes, mademoiselle. Mr Egan is not yet here. Will you wait?'

I blanched. Sitting alone in a restaurant is the ultimate test of worldly sophistication. Perhaps it is not so for a man, but for a woman, sitting alone in a restaurant *screams* to the whole place, the whole fucking world: *this woman is alone because she's a failure! She's failed at life, at love!* Worse, I always secretly feared sitting alone in a restaurant presaged some sort of Long Term Alone. A feeling that prickles with foreboding for my future. In my darkest hours, I feared I might end up like Miss Havisham in *Great Expectations,* all alone and weird as owl shit. Nonetheless, mustering my full share of Continental insouciance, I followed the waiter to an empty table, waved away the menu, and ordered a sidecar. I watched the place with a calm, intelligent gaze. Self-consciously calm and intelligent, trying desperately to look calm and intelligent, and not at all self-conscious that I was alone and without a man. What would Ginger Rogers do? Well, she certainly wouldn't feel like that! She wouldn't need a man to make her socially complete. Still, I must say when I saw Chris come through the door, I was so happy to see him, I beamed. Not because his pale Irish face filled me with joy, but because I was no longer publically alone.

Chris and I were midway through the meal when my phone rang. It was Wendell, telling me that Miss Carter had slipped on an ice cube on her kitchen floor. (This was hard to imagine, though I didn't doubt him.) She had broken her hip so seriously that she was airlifted to Harborview Hospital. She was in stable condition, but needed an emergency hip replacement.

'She'll be there quite some time,' said Wendell.

'That's terrible, Wendell. Will she be all right? She's so skinny!'

'They can't even operate right away because she is on blood thinners. The operation, the recovery, everything will take a very long time. She's not young.'

'Oh, poor Miss Carter!'

'The PNBA spring meeting is in Portland Friday morning. Miss Carter wants you go in her stead.'

'She does?' In all the five years I'd worked at Carter & Co., the Pacific Northwest Booksellers' Meeting, only Edith and Wendell ever represented our store. 'Jessie's worked there longer than I have.'

'You're Events and Publicity. You can do the store some good. Set up some events. Get yourself down to Portland. I'll change the hotel reservation to your name. I'll see you in Portland at the show when it opens. Meet me in front of the Smithson/Empire booth.'

'All right, see you then,' I said, sliding my phone in my purse.

'Bad news?' asked Chris.

'Not for me. I'm going to Portland tomorrow on important business.' I clinked my glass to his, and thought, tonight I am out with an attractive man for whom I feel genial affection, and a mild attraction. Isn't that enough? It always was in the past.

Chapter Nine

THE PACIFIC NORTHWEST Booksellers' Association twice-yearly trade shows are a totally gratifying experience for booksellers. All the publishers and distributors set up booths while we move among them, like bees going from flower to flower. We are courted and greeted and applauded, inundated with shop talk, gossip, and gifted with all kinds of swag. I drove down to Portland, leaving in the wee hours, Friday morning, and arrived at the trade show when the doors first opened.

Wendell escorted me all round the hall that day, made sure I met everyone of any importance. He consulted me gravely, as if I were Edith Carter herself, as we made our orders and commitments with various publishers and distributors. Everyone was very concerned about Miss Carter after her accident. Wendell and I were pleased to say that she was doing well, though it would be weeks before she could even return to the island. I was surprised to hear so many people speak so highly of her. They genuinely admired her commitment to bookselling, her high standards, her loyalty to authors whose work she championed. They rattled on about how fortunate I was to work for her. Their respect and affection were genuine, and I regretted having been so flip – and probably shallow – since I'd always thought her notion of Friday Harbor's Sylvia Beach rather comic, even silly.

Luckily, I had little time to feel guilty or shallow; there were tons of people to meet and greet and reconnect with, including lots of Northwest authors like Frances McTeer and Mary Hill, who was delighted that I liked her Vashon Island memoir. Everywhere there was talk of books and sales, and lots of us to bemoan Amazon and Wal-Mart, Kindle and the iPad, Nook (stupid name; why not call it the Nookie and be done with it?) and self-published titles breaking out on the internet, and selling well, by-passing both the indie booksellers *and* the publishers. I got tons of loot, including the latest Lucy Lamont Shannonville novel, the one that would sell with garden implements, and a little packet of seeds tied to it like a high school diploma for a mere $39.95.

'Perfect for Mother's Day,' said the Smithson/Empire rep with a big grin.

I knew most of the publishers' reps who seasonally made the rounds of individual Northwest bookstores. They're on the road so much, they probably live in their cars, but they are mostly all young, a convivial lot. They are always up for a few drinks, a few laughs, and more than a little gossip. That afternoon at a late lunch (paid for by Smithson/Empire, thank you) they bemoaned the video conferencing that was now universal in publishing. Used to be, the publishers would fly them all to some exotic location, and put them up yearly for the sales conference, but now they just sat in their own homes wearing sports coats over their pajamas.

We were at a Mexican place where we could order

pitchers of margaritas. On the strength of all that ésprit and tequila, and feeling rather invincible myself, when I returned to the hotel, I called Vince who I had heard was living in Portland, minus the *Invincible*. Vince now worked for his father's insurance firm. How adventurous could that be? His relationship status on Facebook had recently changed: single.

Vince was delighted to hear my voice, and happy to hear I was in town. We had so much to catch up on. We talked for perhaps fifteen or twenty minutes and then he asked was I free tonight, Saturday night? He'd like to take me to dinner. I certainly was free, and I agreed to be ready at eight. I took a nap, and slept off the Margaritas.

Wendell's phone call woke me just past six. He and Frances would be meeting some other booksellers (a more staid crowd than the publishers' reps) for dinner. I begged off, but told them I'd see them at tomorrow's Book-and-Author breakfast. Then I spent a long, lavish time getting ready to seduce Vince. To make him sorry he'd lost me. I vowed to be Ginger Rogers, the cool, the desirable, while the Fred Astaire character always pined after her, while she remained amused, but aloof. Oh yes! I had a long, hot shower, and shaved with a new razor so that my skin was everywhere smooth and silky, slathered on lotion, cologne in all the right places, did make-up, and skinnied into my smart new retro outfit with the long cashmere scarf. Earrings. Breath mints, toothbrush in the purse. Ready. Everything but the high-heeled boots which I would put on when Vince called from the hotel lobby

I still had half an hour or so till eight, so I rattled through the swag-bags, and stumbled on the ribbon-wrapped Mother's Day package of Lucy Lamont's novel.

I read the press release that endearingly described how Lucy Lamont had begun her career as a garden writer for a small town paper, a column once a week that didn't so much advocate trowels and shears (so said the press release) as bring people together in gardens. Lucy Lamont, and Smithson/Empire were pleased to invite all of us readers to watch Lucy's book trailer on the Smithson/Empire website, where she walked us through her garden, and to commune still further with Lucy at www.shannonville.com.

I cracked open the book. Not surprisingly, all the good people had gardens, and much transpired in these gardens, including most of the novel's dialogue, the characters' intrigues and confessions, their sometimes furtive kisses. The prose was undemanding, and I was deep into Shannonville, probably half-finished when I noticed it was 8.25.

At 8.30 I called Vince's cell. 'Hi, you've almost reached Vince. Leave your name and a number and I'll get back to you as soon as possible. Ciao!'

I left a chirpy message. I didn't want Vince to think that in the last five years I'd turned into a sour, carping, bitter, dried up shrew. 'Can't wait to see you!' I finished off the message and returned to Shannonville.

A Shannonville novel was all I could have read as the time ticked by. I called his cell again. I did not leave a message this time. Nor the next. Nor the time after that. I called down to the hotel desk and asked if anyone had come by and inquired or left a message for Tosca Tonnino, and the answer to that was a resounding no. I was famished. I picked up my Shannonville novel, and took the elevator down to the hotel bar.

'Table for one,' I told the young waiter who seemed to smirk, as though he knew I was a failure at life, at love, and I would always be alone, as though he knew I had been stood up. I might as well have been Miss Havisham herself. I was so hungry and pissed off, I didn't even care.

I followed the waiter to an unobtrusive table near the kitchen door. Ginger Rogers would have never allowed herself to be situated where the kitchen door nearly banged open in her face and she could hear the whoosh of the dishwashers and the clang and natter among the cooks. Ginger Rogers, Katherine Hepburn, any of those wise-cracking *Stage Door* girls, would have withered that waiter with a single stare and demanded a better table, but he told me the kitchen was closing in ten minutes, so I looked at the menu, ordered the biggest steak that they had, salad, baked potato and an entire bottle of red wine: 'Which I would like now, thank you.'

As the waiter delivered the salad, and the wine, cheers went up at the bar as the young lady who acted as DJ for the karaoke, just back from her break, picked up the mike and welcomed us all again. She made especial mention of the Pacific Northwest Booksellers who were in town for the weekend, asking the whole bar to give a big round of applause for reading, and literacy, and books. From across the way came an especially enthusiastic response. Oh God, I thought, a booth full of booksellers and reps, colleagues. I didn't want anyone to see me, much less invite me to join them. I opened my Lucy Lamont novel and dove in.

Yes, Reader, I, Tosca Tonnino ate dinner alone in the hotel bar, my Shannonville novel up against the water glass, like a castle wall in a Frances McTeer novel. I read and ate, and finished the entire bottle of red wine while all sorts of people – some of whom I recognized from the trade show – warbled out *You Are So Beautiful, Can't Help*

Falling In Love, an immortal *We Are the Champions* and a stab at Adele's fading classic. Under these strange circumstances, I have to admit that reading Lucy Lamont was oddly comforting. In her soothing, narrative voice Lucy Lamont assured me somehow that Vince was a mutant. A faithless freak. The crass, the vulgar Vinces of this world who never showed and left no messages, were wretched anomalies because, really, life was like a Shannonville where good women like me did not linger alone in hotel rooms, nor eat alone in hotel bars, while out-of-towners warbled karaoke tearjerkers, and fired up the crowd with their imitations of Freddie Mercury. All that was an aberration. The reader of a Lucy Lamont novel never doubts that good will be rewarded, and all things happily resolved in the garden. I finished the salad, the steak and potatoes, the bottle of an Oregon Cabernet, paid the bill by scribbling my room number on the bill and left the bar with an aplomb that Ginger Rogers herself would have envied.

The next morning, I'm sorry to say, dizzy, dry-mouthed, and groaning, I reached for the phone to silence the wake-up call. I had to be at that Book-and-Author Breakfast. Frances was our local author, and I had to support her. I collected myself (almost literally, as though I were piecing my body back together like the scarecrow in *The Wizard of Oz*). Showered, dressed, and though still shaky in my high-heeled boots, I made my way downstairs to the big banquet room where the Book-and-Author Breakfast was already underway, the president of the PNBA welcoming one and all.

I slid into the seat that Frances and Wendell had saved for me at a table near the front. I poured myself some coffee and orange juice and wished to God I had a big syringe for both. Wendell, who looked very refreshed and spry, his hair slicked down, his bow tie, as usual, askew, asked if I'd had a nice time last night. He introduced me to the people in our immediate vicinity: 'Tosca Tonnino, our Events and Publicity person.'

I nodded and assured everyone I was delighted to meet them.

Frances introduced me to the man sitting next to her, the third author who was to speak that morning, an educator, Dr. SomethingorAnother whose new book was about teaching Johnny to read. He nattered to me about his book, and I stashed him into my mental Rolodex under B for Boring. I blanched to see that across the table from me was one of the singing booksellers from the booth in the hotel bar last night. He mercifully didn't seem to notice me.

'Wish me luck, Tosca,' said Frances. Her graying hair framed a pale face; her freckles stood out prominently. Frances had no eyebrows. She looked less the medieval woman warrior than an elderly wallflower at the AARP prom. I gave her a big thumbs-up, and told her she would get out there and kick ass, just like the Scots.

The president of the PNBA, James Henry Jordan, JJ as he was better known, a genial attractive man of middle years said a few words on behalf of the booksellers' community and the vital link we maintained between blah blah blah. I signaled the waiter we needed another pot of coffee here pronto. And more orange juice too. Someone slammed a breakfast down in front of me. The too-sweet pancake odor floated up. Greasy bacon. I nibbled the orange slice.

JJ went on about what an honor it was for the Pacific Northwest to have Lucy Lamont come from her Charlottesville, Virginia home to address us all. He rattled on about the astonishing success of her eighteen

Shannonville novels (as if everyone in this room didn't know that!). She had created a Shannonville Empire, and since 1998 Lucy Lamont had not set foot in a bookstore to promote her work. She didn't need to. And yet, JJ paused and smiled, Lucy Lamont had graciously consented to join us here at this Book-and-Author Breakfast, and if we checked the number under our placemats, one of those would win the raffle: an entire set of all eighteen Shannonville novels. Moreover, Lucy Lamont and Smithson/Empire were going boldly where few had gone before in marketing, combining the Shannonville garden set in the pre-wrapped gift box with her new book. I scanned the tables looking for Lucy, a sensible-shoe type, no doubt, but then JJ gestured gracefully to his left, and said he was happy to introduce the morning's first speaker, Miss Lucy Lamont.

No straw hat. No garden gloves. No amiable twinkling eye and Shannonville affability. Lucy Lamont was glamorous. Oh, Of A Certain Age, to be sure. Her hair was frosted and perfectly coiffed. Her face had been lifted, even hoisted, but the planes and curves were perfect. Her forehead was so smooth and Botoxed it could have gone on Mt. Rushmore. She was beautiful with long exquisite, manicured hands, heavily laden with flashing rings and an emerald pendant gleaming against her bronze cashmere sweater. The combination highlighted her eye color, accentuated by blue-tinted contact lenses.

'I am delighted to be here!'

She stood at the lectern and addressed us, complimenting us on the beauty of the Pacific Northwest and thanking all of our bookstores for supporting her *oeuvre* (she really used that word) and then adding with a laugh that she suspected that her *oeuvre* actually supported our bookstores. This seemed to me a rather low blow, given the current crisis in bookselling especially for us independents, but she got a laugh and went on. In a voice both breathless and cultivated, her diction crisp, her spiel practiced as the Henry V speech in Shakespeare, Lucy amused us with the story of how she had come to Shannonville through, you might say, the garden gate. Her timing was impeccable: she paused at the very moments she expected a ripple of laughter, and receiving it, moved on. She gratified and ingratiated herself with the audience, flattering us with her confidence, her personal convictions. Whatever perfume Lucy Lamont was wearing, we, all of us booksellers, smelled the musk of success. She invited not simply our compliance as listeners, but our allegiance, as if we were all great, good friends. She got little bursts of spontaneous applause, and waves of warm laughter. She told us how she and Smithson/Empire and her PR firm, headed up by the famous Dawn Philbrick, had differing opinions about which flower seeds to put in with each garden set, how they settled finally on sweet peas because they were practically fail safe. She, Lucy, chose them as a nod of affection to her husband, Ed (to whom she nodded affectionately there on the dais, a well-bred, silver-haired gent) who used to call her Sweet Pea in their courting days. She did the garden thing to death, I thought, though I had to admit she was captivating.

Beside me, I felt Frances squirm. Then I remembered that each author was allotted twelve minutes. That time was precious and finite because the breakfast would end, the exhibit hall would open and all these people would leave, disperse and go back to work. Lucy had gone on longer than twelve minutes. Frances crossed and uncrossed her knees beneath her tartan skirt. She sipped her cold coffee and frowned. She played with her watch, covering and uncovering it with her hand every minute or so. Beneath the tablecloth she clenched and unclenched her fists. I checked my own watch. By my reckoning, Lucy had gone on about twenty minutes. I glanced at JJ who was sitting behind her; he was clearly sweating bricks.

Then, with one last little anecdote and thanking us for our time and support, Lucy seemed to come to a kind of conclusion, at least she got a rather longer round of applause. JJ jumped to his feet, just about vaulted to the lectern to introduce the next author, Frances, but he wasn't fast enough.

'Does anyone have any questions?' asked Lucy.

And of course, someone did. Lucy, her eyes gleaming, her teeth too, answered that question at witty length, in fact, utterly ignoring JJ's noisy throat clearing, and his frantic glancing at his watch. She couldn't see him. She would not have cared if she did see him. Then, she took another question, and in answering this one, launched into a lovely little story about a reader who had emailed her with a request to write a whole book about one of the minor Shannonville characters, and everything she (Lucy) had wonderfully discovered in this charming process. She stood there at the dais and in front of the microphone, like the figurehead on a ship named the Hubris. She sailed forth into that wide sea of time allotted to others. JJ was twitching, just about jumping out of his skin, but there was no way to yank her off stage. It was of course his own poor planning: Lucy should have gone last, but perhaps he couldn't have known the extent of her arrogance. Or her capacity to seduce, to confound and beguile. Her voice washed over us as she intimated without quite saying, implied, insisted as we all concurred, *Screw the educator and Frances McTeer. I sell books by the millions. You love me. You're here to see me. Let me take you and your customers, your readers, your suffering hordes far from the grit and dander of everyday life. Let us all go to Shannonville where true love is rewarded and when people make love, happiness ensues, where the mothers are wise and the fathers are just, where the struggles resolved under the laburnum at the end of the garden walk, and there are no cockroaches, no flies, no faulty drains, no....*

Ours was a grim return to Friday Harbor late Sunday afternoon. Frances, Wendell and I, each in our separate cars took the same ferry. When Wendell and I met on the upper deck, our book bags in hand, and there was no sign of Frances, I said I'd go down and find her.

Frances's car (also a Subaru Outback) was on the second parking deck, on the outside perimeter, and she was sitting inside. I knocked on the passenger side window and she waved me away. I knocked again, and this time she popped the door and I got in, out of the spray and the March rain.

I reached over and put my hand on her shoulder. 'It was just unconscionable what Lucy Lamont did, Frances! Each author was supposed to get twelve minutes, and she ... she ...' Words failed me. Still Frances did not reply. 'You were gracious, Frances. You only talked five minutes so the educator, Dr. Whathisname could have some time too.'

'Three minutes,' she corrected me, her pale blue eyes moist. 'Four, at most.'

I was silent, remembering the general unrest and unease at the breakfast as the time pressed on. When finally Lucy left the lectern, the long applause for her sliced even further into time that belonged to Frances and the educator. As they each spoke, there was a general scuffling of chairs, and whispers of *"Scuse me, please'* as people tiptoed away, including Lucy Lamont, her husband Ed. Wendell and Frances and I stayed till the educator had finished his pitch, and JJ hastened to remind people to put their numbers in the raffle box. JJ came up and outright apologized to Frances who, patently insincere, told him Never Mind.

'Well, don't worry, Frances,' I said, reaching over, patting her hand on the steering wheel. 'We're going to do it up right for your book. We're going to publicize the hell out of it.'

I thought she must be pondering this, but instead she started to cry. 'What kind of Scotswoman am I? To allow Lucy Lamont to make me cry? The Scots are the bravest people on earth.'

Unbidden, *We Are the Champions* played over and over in my head. 'Please, Frances, don't be defeated by this.'

'Oh I am not defeated, Tosca.' She dried her eyes with an ironed hanky. 'It takes courage in the face of adversity to be a writer. People who don't write don't know that. Believe me, Tosca,' she spoke with her chin high, 'I am not defeated by the likes of Lucy Lamont. It's that I had hoped for so much more, and now, it is so much less.'

'If I had my own PR firm, I'd take on your book. All of them. I'd make them great successes.'

'Do you think they are failures?'

Well I'd let myself in for that one, hadn't I? I extolled her books (some of which in fact I'd read) and finally, I coaxed her out of the car, to join me and Wendell on the observation deck. Wendell was waiting for us with a coffee each and the same encouraging message I'd given her: Carter & Co. would expend its very best efforts on behalf of her new book. Frances and Wendell talked books in a desultory fashion and then each found something to read, but I was too restless.

I wandered the vessel, watching, as I always did, the young couples, the families, the oldsters, the backpacking foreigners, the musicians who always seemed to find one another on any sailing. Only this time I did not feel that old warm sense of connection, of all being part of one another's lives for these two hours. On the contrary, I felt cut off, apart. My being alone did not seem dramatic, as though some singular destiny awaited me. My being alone seemed pathetic, with a sour whiff of some larger Miss Havisham-like loss. I couldn't even blame Vince. I knew full well that his reasons for standing me up were every bit as shallow and crass as my reasons for calling him in the first place. I stood at the back of the vessel, the last of a cloudy sunset like a bedraggled purple scarf draping the sky and islands. I could smell the seasonal change in the air, the bright, sharp whiff of salt and spring. The winter was over, as was that snowy winter night, Ethan by candlelight, Astor Piazzolla and his magic, all that was swallowed up by the past as surely as this ferry's wake dissolved in the Sound. Ethan James was behind me.

Chapter Ten

THE BILLS FOR our Portland trek came in April. Wendell called me into his office to ask after the cost of the steak dinner and the bottle of wine at the Portland hotel. He did so in a gentlemanly, oblique way, suggesting that the amount was so high, I must surely have been with someone, and that Carter & Co. could only pay their own employees' expenses. I immediately said I'd pay the bill, that I would give him a check that afternoon.

'Very good,' said Wendell, 'I don't like to bother Miss Carter with these minor matters when she's trying to recover.'

'Any word on when she'll be back?'

'Not yet, but she's getting better by the day. She's quite tough, for all her seeming frailty.'

Frail wasn't a word I'd ascribe to Edith Carter. Skinny, yes.

'She'll be back by Come in Character Day,' said Wendell. 'Have you thought about who you'll be?'

'I have, but I'm not telling.'

That first weekend in May, the opening of boating season (and thus, tourist season) all the Friday Harbor merchants planned special events. One of my first contributions as Publicity and Events was organizing our

Come in Character Day. Staff were required, and customers were encouraged to come in as their favorite characters. We had a sidewalk sale and a raffle for gift certificates. We had a contest as well with many categories so lots of costumes could win. Our loyal customers ate it up, and the tourists thought it was fun too.

Two days later, on my day off, as I was about to leave for yoga, Wendell called me at 9.30 in the morning. 'I need your help today, Tosca. I just got word that neither Jessie nor Ethan can work today. Can you come in and hold the floor? I have to get these invoices ready for the book-keeper before I can do anything else.'

'It's my day off. Where's Sally?'

'It's her day off. She's gone to Seattle. You could really help out today.'

'Why?'

'Why?' asked Wendell, his voice rising with the cosmic implications of the question, 'well because I asked you to, because we're part of a team, because—'

'Why can't they come in? Either of them.'

'They called separately, if that's what you're implying, Tosca.'

'I'm not implying!' I said with too much fervor. 'I am asking.'

'They're sick. Shellfish, I'm afraid.'

'Shellfish,' I repeated as though I was learning a foreign language. 'Shellfish.'

I went to work at the store. I watched Statler and Waldorf at their interminable game. I helped a customer find a sailing book for her nephew. I spent half an hour with Statler's wife, helping her choose the perfect cookbook (after which she no doubt went home and bought from Amazon). All the while I fumed. So it was true: here were Ethan and Jessie carrying on an affair and no one cared in the least, never mind the stupid notice on the bulletin board. *On the other hand,* remarked the louche, observant Ginger Rogers, *Miss Carter has been away for more than a month, and will be away longer yet. Who knows what she might think? Who knows how she might react on her return?* I found this thought comforting, and hoped Miss Carter would come back, have a hissy fit, and fire them both. I didn't mean that. I knew that the hissy fit was mine, and I (metaphorically) took off my slipper and beat myself.

Two days later, Jessie called and told me her father had been diagnosed with a particularly aggressive kind of cancer, and she was taking a week off to fly to Spokane to help her mother who was struggling, and overwhelmed. I felt instantly disloyal for all my negative thoughts, and said I'd drive her to Bellingham airport. Yes, and I would pick her up too when she returned. I insisted. Once we were off island, off the ferry and driving north on Route 5, she cried all the way, and I, the self-help cynic, tried every phrase I knew to comfort her.

Jessie's departure altered scheduling at Carter & Co., such that for my next Author Event, Ethan James was also on the roster. I hadn't had to be alone with him on a shift, save for once when, mercifully, we were very busy. But here we were, 6.30 on a Wednesday, the store mostly emptied out, staring at each other as we got ready for the Stanley Lund reading. Echoes of Tina Frazier night? Not on your fucking life.

I asked Ethan to put out the metal folding chairs. He asked how many. I said eighteen or twenty, Stanley had quite a local following. I asked Ethan to put out the lectern for Stanley and be sure he had a glass of water. Carrying the water, Ethan stopped by my office, the door was open, and asked if I'd read Stanley's book, another Maxwell Dart mystery.

'Of course. I read the books of all the authors who come here.'

'What did you think?'

'I thought it was a very good mystery.'

'I thought it was shit.'

I went to make the popcorn.

When Stan arrived, early – he was a veteran author and very professional – I greeted him as a hostess would greet a guest, said nice things to him about the book (though it was one of Stan's weaker efforts). At a little after seven, I introduced Stan to a good-sized crowd, maybe eighteen people including me and Ethan. He got a round of applause and I locked the front doors so Stan could continue without the overhead bell ringing, and without some harried mother bringing in her brat to have a tantrum while the poor author was trying to hold an audience spellbound. (Yes, I learned that little safeguard from brutal experience.) Then I sat in the front row. Ethan sat down beside me, bubbling, absolutely brewing with bad vibes. So bad that Stan, a salty old gent with good delivery and an easy way with audiences, seemed to lose his way, glancing up now and then, not at the admiring seventeen people munching popcorn, but over at Ethan whose bad juju seemed to snake and coil around the legs of the metal folding chairs.

Stan finished, got a good round of applause, some questions about sailing and Indian artifacts (the topic of this book), sold quite a few copies, but as I was seeing him out, I could tell he was unsettled. I blathered more how wonderful was his book and how I enjoyed hearing him read, on and on. Stan, before taking his leave, remarked it was a pity that not everyone at Carter & Co. shared my enthusiasm.

I bade Stan goodnight, locked the door behind him, lowered one set of lights, and got the broom and dustpan out of my office. I started sweeping up the popcorn where Ethan had cleared the chairs. I said to him, 'If you ever do that again, I'll see to it you're fired.'

'Do what?'

'You were bad-vibing him.'

'Bad-vibing? Why don't you just get on that broom and ride it?'

'You know what I mean.' I wanted to bop him with the broom, but instead I shooed Mr Hyde off the Masterpiece Theatre wing chair. 'He's our author. He's selling books at our store. We have to—'

'So we have to pretend that he can write?'

'His books sell, don't they?'

'What do you care? Do your wages go up when old Stan's books sell? '

'Oh, go to hell.' I turned out the lights, locked my office and went into the storeroom.

Ethan followed me, strapped on his helmet and got his sleek new bike. 'You are such a sellout, you know? You pretend to have a life. You'll never move off this island. You belong here.'

'At least I'm not a damned drug addict, sitting in a padded cell in rehab! Like those characters you admire!'

'You mean Roger? Is that what you mean? That I'm Roger in *The Body Electric*?'

'Take it any way you want.'

'Roger is a tragic figure in a great novel, a novel as great as *Catcher in the Rye*.'

I'd heard enough. 'Roger is an asshole. He's weak, and slavering after the approval of an egotist who is leading him to destruction, the great, the Unnamed Narrator! Another thrilling literary breakthrough!' I flipped the switches and went to the door which I held open for him, while he clipped his pant legs.

'You're jealous,' he scoffed. 'You'd like to write a book and you can't. You haven't got the talent or the discipline, and Win's a great writer.'

'Well then, why doesn't Win just come up here and read from his great novel? You can bad-vibe him!' What had been a light rain this afternoon was now coming down in earnest. We were protected under the metal awning on the loading dock, but the rain pounded on the dumpsters and on the awning overhead. 'Why don't you invite him to San Juan Island, to Carter & Co.? Think how Miss Carter would love that! He's the next Hemingway, isn't he?'

'Win Jefferies is doing stuff, doing work you can't even dream of. He's in Hollywood writing the screenplay for *The Body Electric* which is going to have an A-list star.'

I locked the door. 'You and Win were best friends from childhood. He wrote this book that has the critics calling him a new Hemingway. He's in Hollywood writing a script for the film of his book, and you're on this island. In the alley. Behind the bookstore in the rain. What's wrong with this picture?'

Without another word, he got on his bicycle and rode away, the tires making whooshing sounds through the puddles in the alley.

The truth is, I did once write a book. Or at least I took copious notes and kept journals and wrote constantly what I was certain would become a book, the story of that glorious year that we spent, Vince and I, sailing the open waters of the Puget Sound, a life so glamorous and free that everyone who read my book would envy us, envy our love, our adventure. We were free spirits, in love and invincible.

We explored inlets and islands and abandoned Native villages. Any place we wanted to stay, maybe for a week or so, we'd get lousy jobs, fish gutting, hash slinging, but it was all fodder for my story, and I kept journal after journal. Vince used to laugh at me, gently, and joke that his only competition for my affection was that pen. I was going to call the book *Invincible*. It would be a Northwest classic like *A Curve in Time*. Even our tying up at the Friday Harbor on that golden day in late October was itself, somehow prophetic, or destined, or whatever I thought when I thought like that. We needed a place to spend the winter. Why not here? I got my job at the bookstore so swiftly, it felt like Fate. As they say in *The Gay Divorcee*, 'Chance is the fool's word for Fate.' That night Vince and I drank champagne in the *Invincible* galley and made invincible love.

And then, a couple of months later, one afternoon, opening a carton of books, I inadvertently sliced open my thumb, and Wendell told me to take the rest of the day off so I wouldn't bleed on the books. I walked through Friday Harbor holding my bandaged thumb, all the way down to the marina. There, bobbing by the dock was the *Invincible*, bobbing rhythmically in fact, rocking from side to side with every lusty thrust that Vince was having at a local barmaid. What would Ginger Rogers do? Well, my thumb wasn't the only thing bleeding by the end of the day when the *Invincible* motored off into the sunset. I stood there on the dock at the marina, beside my few possessions, books, clothes, toothbrush, everything in just two trash bags at my feet.

My journals, my would-be book was at the bottom of the marina. I could all but hear the fish reading it, and chuckling among themselves about what a fool I was.

From a payphone I called Jessie, and she came and got me. I stayed with her and Murph that night. My parents gave me the first and last months' rent for the apartment in the Seaman's Union building. My sister Carmen loaned me the down payment for the Subaru, put herself on the title, and drove it over to Friday Harbor the very next day.

As I waited to pick Jessie up at the Bellingham International Airport on her return from Spokane, I resolved to honor our friendship and quit being such a bitch. Men complicate things, but I wouldn't let Ethan James ruin a friendship that had sustained me, sustained both Jessie and me for five years. I wrote him off to experience, which, to be true to my values, I had to savor, no matter whether that experience gave me pleasure or pain.

Jessie looked rather peaked and pale when she got off the Spokane flight. Tired. Things were not well with her dad. She let maybe five miles on Route 5 south go by, a bit of small talk about the store, and then she said, 'I'm making some important changes, Tosca. I'm leaving the island. I'm going to give Wendell my notice and move.'

'But why leave Friday Harbor? You have a job, friends.' I could not bring myself to mention Ethan.

'I struck a deal, an arrangement with Murph.'

'What kind of deal?'

'It was Murph's house. I was a tenant. I loved him, but really? I was just a tenant for seven years, and so I made a deal with him. I'll leave, but I don't have to be out till mid-June. Clinging to that house, or trying to cling to it, to cling to a man who didn't want me, that was stupid. I took the whole thing very hard, but it's over and I understand now that saying goodbye is part of life. Life is probably more about goodbyes.'

'Are you thinking of your dad?'

'My father's dying. My parents are in their sixties, you know? It's shocking really to think of your parents as really old, dying.'

I did a quick calculation on Frank and Donna. They were a lot older than Jessie's parents. 'Does Ethan know you're leaving?'

'Oh, Ethan,' she brushed the name away like a bit of dandelion fluff, literally opened the car window and waved it outside. 'He's too young for me. And even if he weren't, he comes with too much baggage.'

'I thought … you were, well, everyone at the store knows. Except Miss Carter,' I hastened to add.

'And she's not here,' Jessie giggled like a girl who has put one over on the teacher. 'Ethan's a flingette, anyway. Your favorite word. I told you last year when Murph left me, that's not what I'm looking for. Ethan is great in the sack, but who can spend all their time in bed? When we first hooked up, I was really flattered, even a little dazzled, I mean Ethan's very good looking, and not at all like the guys on this island.'

'Such as they are,' I added.

'But he's too complicated for me. I don't like complex men. At least with Murph, everything was clear, up front, you know? Murph was pissed off, or he was happy. He could sulk or smile, that was sort of his range. But Ethan was, is, mercurial, and his moods sometimes shocked me, how fast he could change and how many moods he had. He's like that at the store too. You know, how he'll be Mr Bland, he'll smile, nod, then one of the

136

customers or Statler or Waldorf will set him off, and he's suddenly passionate. Like the way he hand-sells *The Body Electric*, which by the way, was a shitty novel.'

'Why did you put it on your Staff Picks?'

Jessie gave me a look all women understand. 'I couldn't let Ethan think he didn't convert me, could I? I tried to get him to read Dr. Vestri's *Inner Connections*, but he just laughed and flung it aside. I read the book he recommended, didn't I? But when I gave him Dr. Vestri, he just said he'd bike and sweat all his bad juju out. His whole attitude was really pretty contemptuous, you know?'

'I've seen him in action,' I replied.

'And he hated all the music at my house. He had that same kind of ... contempt. Yes, really, contempt. All my indie rock albums, he just snorted at them. One day he presses into my hand – really just like he does at the store with that stupid *The Body Electric* – this CD and he says, play this, and you'll never be the same. Like it has to be a religious experience, or nothing at all.'

'What was the album?'

'Some Argentine guy who plays a, a, bando-some-thing, something like an accordion. It was too, too ...'

'Passionate?' I offered.

'Too complicated.' Jessie seemed uncharacteristically thoughtful; usually she had a ready-made remedy. 'I never got to know him. He never opened up to me. His past, well I hardly know any more about that than I did when we first met. Lots of yachts and summers on the Mediterranean and private schools, and divorced parents, whom he detests, both of them. Dear old Granny Marjorie, who adores him, gave him the only home he's ever known. No long term friends except for Win Jefferies. Lots of skiing and cycling competitions.

He tells like it's all very funny. He'll never face the pain. He didn't want to make Inner Connections. You know what Dr. Vestri says about Inner Connections, don't you?'

I didn't, but I knew I was going to hear all about it. When Jessie had finished her serious rehash of Dr. Vestri's ideas, suggestions and the like, we had gone down the mountain, out into the wide alluvial Skagit Flats. I turned off the freeway, and took the scenic route that skirts along the water. Once there you could see Anacortes in the distance, across the bay, and in spring twilight even the refinery looks beautiful.

'You should take up with Ethan, Tosca.'

'Me? You are a quart low if you think—'

'You two are a lot alike.'

'What makes you say that? I'm nothing like him.'

'You're both, well, deep. Most people aren't deep. I'm not. Murph isn't. I couldn't keep up with Ethan, but you could.'

'I'm done with men who live on sailboats,' I declared. 'He can find someone else to help him grow up.'

'I don't think he needs to grow up,' said Jessie. 'I think he needs to know he can be loved. If you know that, then you know you can love someone back.'

'Dr. Vestri?'

'No. I thought of that myself. By the way, I met a nice guy in Spokane.'

'What? A guy? You were only there a week.'

'I didn't say I slept with him. I didn't, by the way. He's thirty-five, divorced. He has a little daughter who lives with his ex, but he sees her all the time. He's a nurse in the hospital where my dad was.'

'That's part of why you're leaving?'

'Yes. But there are other reasons too. My mom is

138

really happy I'm coming home. She needs the help.'

'I'm sorry about your dad, Jessie.'

'Thank you. I am too. And I don't know if anything will work out with this guy, but he's sweet and uncomplicated, and if I have to be saying goodbye to my dad, I'd like to be saying hello to some new part of my life.'

'I'll miss you, Jessie. I really will.' I bit back tears. 'You've been my best friend.'

'BFFs,' she sniffed too. 'Maybe you'll be leaving Friday Harbor one day. Maybe soon.'

'Why would I leave?'

'Tonnino and Associates? The office in Seattle with the view of the harbor? All those big dreams of yours, contacts and events and high heels on the parquet floor? No one can do that, but you.'

'Are you telling me to Pursue My Dreams? Follow My Heart! Risk All!'

'What would Ginger Rogers do?'

Chapter Eleven

THE NEXT DAY I'm in my office, surveying the Carter & Co. Facebook page when my phone rang, and an oddly accented voice asked if this is Carter & Co. Books, Friday Harbor, Washington.

'Yes.'

'We are looking for the Publicity Manager.'

'That would be me. Tosca Tonnino. Events and Publicity.'

'Excuse me?'

'That's my name, Tosca.'

'Will you hold, please? I have Dawn Philbrick on the phone for you, Miss Tosca.'

'Dawn Philbrick?'

'Philbrick and Peters, New York. Just a moment please.'

Wait! I wanted to say, *as in Philbrick and Peters, New York? Only one of the most prestigious PR firms in the world?* Be still my heart. I took a quick swig of bottled water, reached over, and turned the lock on my office door. It was about eleven our time. Two o'clock in New York.

'This is Dawn Philbrick,' the voice came on the line. Crisp. Efficient. 'Is this Tosca?'

'Tosca Tonnino, Events and Publicity.'

'As in Puccini?' Dawn gave a light laugh, as though we two must share these little jokes all the time, but then she got right down to business. 'We represent Lucy Lamont, and we'd like to set up an author appearance on San Juan Island.'

Lucy Lamont? To come here? I blubbered out, 'What?'

'You seem to be the only bookstore there. Friday Harbor, right? Charming name. I'm sure it's just a lovely place, and Lucy very much wants to come and give a reading at your bookstore ...' Some papers shuffled audibly. 'Carter & Co., Friday Harbor, San Juan Island, Washington State.'

'Yes.'

Behind Dawn's voice, I could hear the far away sirens, horns, the glare and glamour of Fifth Avenue wafting up to her office. I could imagine the Abstract Expressionist art on the walls, Dawn, wearing a blue-tooth, tapping her manicured nails on a glass desk with a pale orchid thriving in the gray urban light. From my smudged window I looked out at the gulls roosting on the dumpsters, and across the alley, Charlotte sat on the stoop behind her Confectionary, smoking a cigarette. What could possibly link my gulls and dumpsters with Dawn Philbrick's canyons of steel and stone?

'Forgive me, Ms. Philbrick—'

'Dawn.'

'Dawn, but are we talking about the Lucy Lamont who sells millions of copies of her Shannonville series, who has calendars and fridge magnets and stationery made in the image of her books, whose latest, number eighteen, comes with a package of designer garden tools, and a seed packet of sweet peas?'

'My idea. I thought it was brilliant. Lucy wanted marigold, but I held out for sweet peas.'

'Lucy Lamont commands huge crowds. We're a small place. A small island, really.'

'You should be flattered. She doesn't ordinarily do bookstores.'

'I heard she hasn't done a bookstore since 1998.'

'That's what I said. You should be flattered. '

'Oh, I am, don't get me wrong, of course, we're flattered.' I blathered on and on, unctuous beyond belief, until Dawn coughed, and I stopped. 'We only have room for about thirty people, Dawn.' And that was stretching it. 'I have to tell you that up front. She can command a much bigger crowd.'

'I appreciate your candor, Tosca. I'm sure Lucy will be able to sell thirty books at your store.'

I have a trilling little laugh while I quickly zapped through my master events calendar. 'We'd be honored. Now, let me see. September? That week just after Labor Day?'

'June,' says Dawn.

'That's in about five weeks. That's awfully soon. Really, too soon. I couldn't begin to publicize it.'

'You'd have more than five weeks. That second Saturday in June. That's the day she wants to do the reading.'

I glanced at my calendar. 'That won't work, I'm afraid, I already have—'

'It will work, Tosca. You will make it work.'

'But I could do it on the 18th or the—'

'Lucy has already put this in her planner. June 12th.'

'Couldn't she—'

'Don't be tedious. You see, here's the thing: Lucy took a leisurely tour of the Northwest last March after the trade show, and she just fell in love with your island. Why, I don't know. There are perfectly marvelous summer homes in the Hamptons, but Lucy was stirred by the scenery up there in Washington and she thinks it will be good for her creatively. She's planning on buying some property there for a summer retreat, and she wants the publisher to pay her expenses out there. Do you understand, now?'

'Hmmm,' I said.

'So if you call Smithson/Empire publicity, and request that Lucy gives a reading at your store on June 12th, then Lucy can agree to it and Smithson/Empire pays the tab for her vacation.'

'So ...' I play with my pencil, pretending that Dawn and I are ironing out a little contractual wrinkle. 'Just so you and I are clear, Dawn. When I call and ask if Lucy Lamont will come here, it will not be a surprise to Smithson/Empire?'

'When you sell as many books as Lucy Lamont, your publisher keeps you happy. If she wants to go to San Juan Island, then they'll send her. If she wanted to go to ...' Dawn sought some place more remote than ours and couldn't come up with anything. 'Call Smithson/ Empire publicity. Ask for Katie. Ask Katie if Lucy will come to your store. I need to answer this other line. You'll let me know when it's all set up, won't you? Good. Thanks. Bye. Oh, and I'm sending you right now Lucy's publicity packet. Everything you'll need. Stay in touch! Ta!'

And behold: it came to pass just as Dawn foretold. I found the number for Smithson/Empire publishers, and from my little office in Friday Harbor, I called into the very belly of the multinational publishing giant. I asked to speak with Katie, Lucy Lamont's publicist. I asked if Lucy Lamont could read here, make an appearance at Carter & Co. on June 12. The answer was yes.

Ask and ye shall receive.

By the time I got off the phone with Katie, I was dry-mouthed and light-headed. This was the sort of coup that Tonnino and Associates would one day pull off. Regularly. But before I opened my door to announce what I had just done I had to make one more phone call. The author I had scheduled on 12 June was Frances McTeer with her new novel of the medieval Scots. Did I feel like a shit? I did. Did I remember what Lucy Lamont had done to Frances at the trade show in March? I did. In my heart I vowed I would make it up to Frances. But she was the only impediment between me and becoming bookselling's Beyoncé. I telephoned Frances, and cancelled her 12 June reading date, citing only a conflict, and not a word of Lucy Lamont. She was very accommodating and agreed to 20 June.

I unlocked my office door and reeled into the bookstore, my shoes scarcely touching the wooden floors as I floated toward the registers. 'Where's Wendell?' I asked.

'Meeting in the back with the Consortium rep,' said Jessie, filing her broken nail.

'You'll never guess what just happened to me.'

She studied me thoughtfully. 'You get laid or something?'

I made my announcement about Lucy Lamont.

Jessie's jaw dropped. 'Way to go, Tosca! That's fantastic! Amazing! What made you think of that? That was brilliant. How did you do it?'

'Well, I just thought, what can it hurt? What can they say but no? So I called Publicity at Smithson/Empire, and talked to Lucy's rep there, and explained to her how much we'd love to have Lucy come to Carter & Co. And they called her, and she agreed.'

'You should go tell Wendell right now. He'll flip!'

So I went and told Wendell the story I'd just told Jessie, which was – which came to be – the story I told everyone: friends, compatriots, competitors in the book-selling biz, Miss Carter, the rest of the staff, the *Island Times*, ShelfAwareness, Galley Cat, Electric Literature, and any book blog that would care or listen. I told my charming David and Goliath story: the plucky PR person from Friday Harbor, Tosca Tonnino, the girl with a dream and some nerve who just thought: *why not?* Why not call and ask if the bestselling author will come to her little island bookstore. The more I told it, the better it sounded. No one from Smithson/Empire disputed my version of events. And Dawn Philbrick? That wasn't part of the story. I never mentioned that conversation to anyone.

Miss Carter had a bouquet of roses delivered to me at the store with a card that said, *Brava, Tosca!* My inbox was flooded with email from people in the book trade, including a note from JJ himself. Their responses were a gratifying gumbo of envy and admiration. Everyone loved the legend: how brave, impetuous Tosca picked up the phone and called the mighty publishing giant and asked publicity if Lucy Midas Lamont would come to our humble store.

Only two people were unimpressed. Ethan declared that the Shannonville novels were shit. This was not the sort of language Wendell liked to hear, especially in the store and he chastised Ethan who did not defend himself. Personally, I think Ethan was jealous, since I had taken his place in Miss Carter's estimation as the coolest employee ever. His Freon treatment of me was tinged with surly which I took to be a sign of triumph. My heart was a good deal less broken than before. This was comforting because it meant he hadn't broken my heart at all. Pride. He'd injured my pride and now I had injured his. So there.

However, there was Frances McTeer. When she heard that I'd bumped her 12 June date for Lucy Lamont, she confronted me directly and with typical Scots bluntness called me a faithless slut. 'What happened to "We'll promote your book, Frances?"'

'We will! Just not on June 12th.'

'To do this to me for Lucy Lamont is just crass, Tosca.'

'It wasn't personal. It was business.' Frances knew as well as I did that her books sell a few thousand copies at best (and only to libraries in hardcover) while Lucy Lamont has *millions* in print. Millions of *each* of the Shannonville series, seventeen volumes and counting.

My coup inspired lots of other bookstores to flood Smithson/Empire with requests for Miss Lamont, all of which were turned down, making me look even better. Finally, on the publisher's and Shannonville websites, there appeared a small statement that Lucy Lamont appreciated all her many fans who were eager to see her at their local bookstores. She had no idea that granting one request would cause such a flurry of interest. She thanked her fans, but declared she must remain at her Charlottesville, Virginia estate working on her next novel, *Christmas in Shannonville*.

On Saturday, 12 June, Friday Harbor would be the center of the Shannonville Universe. From her convalescence in Seattle, Miss Carter went into high gear. She phoned me, perhaps twice a day, planning strategies. We rented the San Juan Island Community Center for that day. We hired extra staff, high school kids to open boxes, set up chairs, generally facilitate. We took out ads in the newspapers from Vancouver, B.C. to Portland, Oregon. We Tweeted and Tumblred, and

Instagrammed and Pinterested. We set up rules: Miss Lamont would sign books bought only at Carter & Co., that had the Carter & Co. logo stamped on the inside cover. The hard work of setting up for such an event fell entirely on me since Miss Carter wasn't there. And just as well, given some of her hare-brained marketing notions. Daringly, Wendell upped our order of Lucy Lamont titles, one hundred copies of the newest Lucy Lamont (the one with the garden tools), twenty-five of number seventeen, and ten of each of the others, and soon, he had to order more. These titles (with our logo stamped inside) danced out the door in the hands of readers. Credit cards and debit cards were swiped again and again, PIN numbers punched in, all of it music to our ears. I, Tosca, I alone had brought this to pass. No one could touch me. I was frigging golden.

Chapter Twelve

IN PREPARATION FOR the Great Day, 12 June, I read a dozen of the Shannonville novels. I did not love them, but I certainly understood their appeal. A Lucy Lamont novel never disappoints. Much like the praline fudge at Charlotte's Confections, you could count on each one for an almost unbearable sweetness. Each Shannonville novel returns readers to a place that never existed. To a time that never was. Batman's Gotham is more realistic than Shannonville. But so powerful is the magnetic pull of longing, the lunar force of nostalgia, you the reader believes that Shannonville is yours. You are not estranged from this pleasant place, nor foreign to it; you *belong* here. These are your people. Like a lovely vacation destination, you will certainly return again, and in the meantime, Lucy Lamont writes you postcards (the novels are short) about all your mutual friends and acquaintances, the best of whom have gardens and whose lives and loves, triumphs and defeats are often hedged about with mossy walks and herbaceous borders.

In light of my Lucy Lamont coup, Sally and Wendell teased me about showing up on Come in Character Day as someone from Shannonville. Sally offered to lend me her garden hat. Ethan, who happened to be nearby when she said this, said that he would contribute a spoon.

'A s-spoon?' asked Sally.

'So Tosca can gag on it.'

I laughed, and brushed off the barb, but Wendell bestowed on Ethan his most disapproving frown. In five months Wendell had never warmed to Ethan, though he treated him with restraint and civility, but that's all. Miss Carter wasn't around to insist on more.

'They say Lucy Lamont is buying a home here,' Ethan remarked.

'Where'd you hear that?'

'Statler told me. His neighbor is a realtor. I guess there's a big rustic estate on the other side of the island that Lucy's interested in.'

'Really,' Sally gasped, 'Lucy Lamont is g-going to live here?'

I felt a little prickle at the scalp. I certainly didn't want anything to tarnish the glow still surrounding my feat.

'Who are you going to be for Come in Character Day, Sally?' I asked, brightly changing the subject.

'Professor McGonagall from Harry Potter. What about you, Ethan?'

'I don't know. I think it's a dumbshit idea.'

'Really, Ethan!' Wendell was emphatic.

'Wendell, are you going to put on a sign that says "Call Me Ishmael"?' I asked.

Wendell chuckled. 'It's certainly easy and clever. And you, Tosca?'

'I'm a classic.'

This year, I'd outdone myself. Carmen and Maddie came over on the early ferry. They walked on so they wouldn't have to park, and I drove down to the landing to meet them, and brought them back to my place where we all had breakfast and got changed. Carmen had brought my costume from a shop in Seattle. For herself she wore a thrift store ball gown, a frothy extravaganza of sea-green tulle and creamy satin splashed with a corsage of camellias from the florist next door to her salon. She piled her dark hair up high. Camille. *La Traviata*.

'Wow, you look more like Ginger Rogers than Camille.' I was astonished really at how beautiful she was. 'I can't remember when I've seen you this dressed up. Your wedding, maybe? You look so young and beautiful.'

'That's the fun of these days. You get to be someone you absolutely are not. Look at Maddie.'

Maddie, a high school sophomore was darling as Pippi Longstocking, her hair in two braids that were worked with wire so they stood out, a spray of freckles across her nose.

'Come here, Prune, Maddie.' Carmen drew us both to the mirror and put an arm around each of us. She smiled happily. 'Look at us. The Tonnino women!'

'I'm not a Tonnino,' said Maddie. 'I don't have a pizza named after me.'

'Well, we'll have to talk to Dad,' I said.

'I don't want a pizza named after me,' Maddie protested. 'Can you imagine my friends once that news hit my social network?'

'Oh my,' Carmen fanned herself with her Camille fan, 'I think you'd get the vapors.'

We cracked up laughing, then Carmen said, 'All right, Tosca, let's put your costume together.'

She exhumed it from the box she'd brought from

Seattle: a mustard-colored, oversized frock coat with wide lapels, oversized pants, a huge hat, with a sign in it that 7/6, right out of the Tenniel illustrations for *Alice in Wonderland*. The Mad Hatter. I rouged up my cheeks, and Carmen painted enormous eyebrows on my forehead.

'Even the one brown eye and the one green eye contributes to the effect,' she declared, stepping back and admiring me. 'Now, tilt your head and look down your nose, just like the Mad Hatter did.'

'Another cup of tea?' I inquired in an arch accent.

We three, arm in arm, walked to Carter & Co., and we didn't take the alley either. The day was perfect for opening day (the weather can be iffy in May) but this Saturday was slathered with sunshine, and the geranium baskets on the lampposts blew about with red and white flowers, and people stopped us just to talk. The guy from the *Island Times* took our picture on his way down to the marina to photograph Opening Day ceremonies.

At the bookstore itself, even Statler and Waldorf got into the mood insofar as they wore straw hats and claimed to be Huck Finn and Tom Sawyer. Wendell did indeed wear a sign that said 'Call Me Ishmael'. Thelma, the book-keeper, helping out on the floor that day, came as The Wife of Bath, with washcloths and sponges pinned all over her clothes and a soap-on-a-rope around her neck. Sally was Professor McGonagall from *Harry Potter*, and Jessie put on a bald wig and a moustache and announced herself as Dr. Phil. Ethan James took off his bike helmet, and shook out his hair which had outgrown from his original stylish cut. His face was powdered, un-naturally pale, and there were black rings around his eyes, his mouth drooping, his lips dark. The scar from the winter was probably permanent. He was the only one who didn't know my sister and niece so I introduced them. I could see that Carmen longed to cut his hair.

'Who are you?' asked Maddie.

'Whatever is the name of that guy, the vampire in the *Twilight* series.'

'Don't you even know who you are?'

Ethan stared at her and unblinkingly replied no, he did not.

'Come back at four and judge for the contest,' Wendell said to Carmen and Maddie. 'You don't live here. You will be unbiased. At four o'clock, all our customers assemble here at the front of the store, for the prizes. We have six categories, including Most Unoriginal.'

Just then, using a cane, walking proudly, and unassisted, Miss Carter herself wobbled into the store with Nan behind her. She got a spontaneous round of applause from one and all, customers and staff. She was clearly touched. She wore a long black skirt, black high-heeled shoes, a white tailored blouse, and a pocket watch on a chain. She sported an old fashioned toque and she carried gloves, and told us she was Alice B. Toklas, and indeed, she was. The resemblance was uncanny, and everyone had a tremendous laugh, and another round of applause. Miss Carter and Nan had to hug everyone. When I put my arms around her, she felt so brittle and frail, I feared she would break.

'I can't stay long, and I'm afraid I can't work the floor at all,' said Miss Carter, 'I can't stand for very long, but I will be coming as often as my strength is equal to it. We have a very big day coming up.' She cast me a long, loving look. She told Carmen and Maddie how wonderful I was at my job, and how fortunate Carter & Co. was to have me. All this fulsome praise made me cringe a little, and I said I had to go to work.

'Oh, Tosca,' said Miss Carter before she wobbled off, 'Please write a note to Miss Lamont, and ask her to join me for lunch at Spinnaker's on the twelfth.'

'Will do,' I promised.

'I notice you weren't included in the lunch invitation,' Carmen remarked quietly.

'Fine with me. Lucy Lamont in person is not my idea of a good time. I've seen her in action at the PNBA. She's arrogant and bullying. All I want is the glory of bringing her here. I have to get to work. You guys go wander down to the harbor and watch the Opening Day ceremonies. Come back and collect me at one for my lunch break.'

At the bookstore we were run off our feet. It was the busiest Come in Character Day that I could remember, and I hoped this was an omen for the upcoming tourist season. God knows after last winter's storms combined with the dismal economic times, we needed a bountiful summer. The sunshiny day grew warm and the store had only fans, no air conditioning. The heavy mustard-colored coat I wore was cumbersome and hot, and I could feel the rouge bead along with perspiration on my face.

The heat was unkind to Ethan's costume too. I passed him in the back room where he was pouring a cup of coffee.

'You look like you're having a nicotine fit,' I said cheerfully.

'I'm a cyclist. I don't smoke.'

'You look terrible.'

'Thank you.'

'But not like a vampire, ready to suck blood. That would take too much effort. You look, well, you look tired, like Roger in *The Body Electric*.' I offered with a dash of vinegar.

'He's a character you don't forget.'

'If you are Roger, then I feel sorry for you.'

'I don't need your pity.'

'And you won't get it.' And in my oversized shoes, I flopped ungracefully away.

Friday Harbor was jumping, and all the restaurants and taverns and cafés were too crowded for my half-hour break, so Carmen brought sandwiches, and my sister and niece and I decided we'd have a picnic down by the marina. We sashayed down Spring Street, stopping to greet all sorts of people on our way. Friday Harbor on that first weekend in May has something of a carnival atmosphere, especially for Carter & Co. When we saw others in costume, we all stopped and talked and laughed. I reminded everyone to come to the store at four o'clock sharp for the judging, that my sister and niece were the judges and they were open to bribes. I was happy to introduce my sister and niece to people who didn't know them, and everyone commented that anyone would know us for sisters. The picnic tables by the marina were all taken, but we found a bench, and ate our sandwiches and drank our Cokes while people wandered by, and the sunlight twinkled on the green water and masts rocked in the wakes of boats coming and going. Lots of people passed us, mostly tourists, including several good-looking men. And one of those good-looking men (though too old for me) turned around, said 'Carmen?' and came back to us. He took off his sunglasses.

Carmen looked up from her ham sandwich, dabbed her lips with her napkin. Beneath the make-up for Camille, she blanched, and her expression ran so many gamuts I could not have counted them. She stood, and dusted off the seat of her ball gown, and she reluctantly offered her hand to a tall man with graying hair, wearing shorts, a logo tee shirt, and a baseball cap with an anchor on it.

'Tom. What a surprise! What are you doing here?'

'I would have known you anywhere, Carmen. Even in …'

'Oh this.' She brushed away the dress and the pale camellias and laughed in a way that must have taxed her larynx. 'It's Come In Character Day at the bookstore. What brings you here? Here!' she added, as if surprised to find herself on the moon.

'We, I come here a lot, well not a lot, summers, though, I, my, our, we keep our boat moored here during the summer.' He waved in the direction of the bigger yachts. *The Gilded Lily*. Are you … do you … what are you doing here?'

'My sister Tosca works at the bookstore, and we came over for Opening Day. And this is my daughter, Maddie.' She pulled Maddie to her feet, positioning the girl in front of her as if Maddie were a chess piece, and Carmen was Statler, facing off against Waldorf.

'Do you live here?'

'Oh no. We're still in Seattle. Oh, sorry, Maddie, Tosca, this is Tom Chase. We went to Garfield High together. Senior class president, weren't you?'

'Something like that.'

'Time flies. Fancy meeting you here. Isn't that what they say? Clichés.'

'I live in Portland now, but I spent years, way too

many years in New York. Sarah!' Tom Chase called and waved at a svelte, attractive woman who had walked on ahead. 'Sarah, come here!' She turned around, boredom draped across her lovely face, and sauntered back. 'Carmen, this is my wife, Sarah.'

'Glad to meet you,' said Carmen, and then we had to do the intros all over again, and explain why we were in those goofy costumes, and how Carmen and Tom knew each other from Garfield High, they had graduated together, blah blah blah.

'Carmen's sister works at the bookstore,' Tom explained to Sarah who nodded sagely. She looked supremely indifferent, or maybe she just had a pole up her butt. 'They have a Come in Character Day, isn't that what you said?' he repeated. 'Carmen is Camille, like the opera, *La Traviata*. Every time I go to the opera, I think of you, of your father, and how he loved opera.' He turned to his wife. 'All the Tonnino girls were named after operas. Carmen was the best. I mean the best opera. Let's see, the others were Aida and Norma, right? I don't remember Tosca.'

'Yes,' said Carmen with an artificial laugh, 'well, here she is. The Mad Hatter.'

Tom was full of questions about the old neighborhood, the old gang, the old days, and in between his questions, he threw in big slabs of info about himself which Carmen had to comment on, or laugh over. It seems he had gone to Yale originally in music, but what was the good of going to Yale for music? He changed to business and now he was a banker. ('But not one of the Bad Guys,' he assured us.) He had remained on the East Coast. For years. Too many years. He never came back to Seattle to live, or even to visit, didn't even keep up with anyone from high school. Then, in 2009, he was transferred to Portland. He loved the islands and every summer, he and his family cruised the Straits in their yacht, *The Gilded Lily*, he said again.

'We should go,' said his wife with a tense little smile. 'Nice to meet all of you.' She touched Tom's arm.

'I have children,' said Tom. 'My daughter stayed in Portland. School. My son too.'

'I have two sons,' said Carmen, 'and one daughter.' She flung her arm around Maddie's shoulders. 'Maddie.'

'Your father made the best pizza in the universe. Really, Sarah,' he beamed, 'the East Coast has nothing on Tonnino's on Capitol Hill. Nothing. Nothing. Really. Are your parents ...'

'Still working,' said Carmen. 'So you see, we Tonninos have not moved very much, nor done very much.'

'Oh I wouldn't say that. It's good to know that some things don't change. Too much does. The older I get, the more I resent change.'

'And your parents?'

'They moved to Arizona right after I went to Yale. My dad always hated the winters here, and he got a job at University of Arizona. I guess that's another reason I never came back. Not even to the Garfield High reunions.'

'You didn't miss much. They're pretty predictable,' said Carmen. 'Swaggering men, tarted up wives.'

Tom gave an insincere laugh, and mentioned half a dozen names, and my sister and Tom blathered, and laughed, and apologized for boring the rest of us. Ha ha ha. Sarah had hold of Tom's arm by now, but he was on a roll and wouldn't budge.

Carmen finally wadded up her sandwich bag, though she had not finished. 'Tosca's on her lunch break. We have to go.'

'So do we,' said Sarah.

'Well,' said Tom, 'seeing the three of you together, just takes me right back to high school.' He peered at Maddie with her sticking-out braids and bright Pippi freckles. 'I'm sure you are the image of your mother.'

Maddie gave him the look of Infinite Disdain that only a teen can muster.

Sarah, with an airy 'Later', pulled at her husband's arm.

Tom still lingered, offering fulsome farewells, everyone agreeing it was so nice to meet one another. He shook Carmen's hand, holding it longer than he needed to. He turned to Maddie, shook her hand, beaming. And finally he turned to me, really for the first time in all this lovely little reunion, blabbing on about my great costume, how unique, blah blah blah as he shook hands. I pulled back, but he suddenly held my hand tightly, gripping it, shaking it up and down, up and down, and then I noticed that Tom Chase had one brown eye and one green eye. He shot a look to Carmen, and then back to me, and then back to Carmen who stood there, chin up, defiant. I snatched my hand back. Sarah actually gripped his arm and they left.

I couldn't quite catch my breath. 'Who the fuck was that?'

'No one. You need to get back to the store. We're going to get some ice cream. Come on, Maddie.'

'Who is he?'

'No one. Maddie, let's go.'

'He's not no one.'

'He's no one, Tosca. Leave it alone for Christ's sake.'

She left me, pulling Pippi Longstocking in her wake. I spent the next three hours dazed, slack-jawed and rather sick to my stomach. I felt as if I'd been hit by a truck. It was hard to breathe. What would Ginger Rogers do? I waited for some sophisticated bit of sass or wisdom, some retort, but Ginger Rogers was absolutely silent.

At four when Carmen and Maddie showed up to do the judging, I pulled Carmen away from the Masterpiece Theatre set where all sorts of readers who had Come in Character were milling. I took her arm, and dragged her back to my tiny office, shut the door, and asked, 'When were you going to tell me?'

She kept her gaze straight ahead. 'Tell you what?'

'Well, I'll ask Mom. Wait. She's not my mother, is she? You're my mother, and that well-heeled asshole out there, the one with one green eye and one brown eye, he's my father? Really? What the fuck, Carmen? What the fuck!'

'Let it go, Tosca.'

'No,' I whispered harshly. 'You owe me an explanation. The whole fucking family owes me—'

'Nothing. You are owed nothing,' Carmen snapped. 'You have a fine family, people who love you, who have always loved you, you had a good home, supportive people who doted on you, adored you, and brought you up right, you had a good education, you are owed nothing. Do you get it? Nothing. Give me the key to your apartment so Maddie and I can change. I want to leave.' She held out her hand and I plopped the key down in her hand with a crack. She turned and left the office.

The crowds cleared out after the contest, but the store would stay open till seven. Wendell and Thelma and Sally and Jessie all got to leave. Ethan and I were to stay. Great, I thought. Fucking great. The Mad Hatter sneakers were hurting my feet, and I felt like blimp, navigating the narrow aisles in my oversized coat and baggy pants. All I wanted was to go home, take off this stupidshit costume, stare in the mirror at my one brown eye and my one green eye and then write a really nasty email to my fucking sister who wasn't even my fucking sister.

Late afternoon light was slanting through the windows, and there was almost no one in the store. I wandered around the store, passed the steamer trunk with Travel. I looked at these titles and my heart started to break and yearn for all the places I was going to go and all the things I was going to be, and do. How I wasn't going to live like the rest of them. Tosca! With a name like that I have to do something grand if not grand opera! All the Tonnino girls were named for operas. Even their bastard brats. Oh God, it was too much to contemplate. I couldn't begin to wrap my mind around the betrayals! My mother – that is Donna Tonnino – involved in such duplicity? Unthinkable. And my dad? My dad. My grandfather? I might have wept, but I suddenly became aware of voices in the aisle behind me, quarreling. Maybe not quarreling. But tense. Raised. One of them was Ethan's.

I took some travel books with me, as though I were re-shelving stock and went back to the last aisle where a customer had backed Ethan into a corner. Really. Into a corner. I didn't recognize the guy, but I figured it was another Leona Cox episode, and that Ethan had overdone it, pressing *The Body Electric* on an unwilling reader. Unlike the Leona moment, when he'd shown some gallantry, and good humor, Ethan gave me a long searing look. The expression on his face, minus the bleeding lip and the bruises, was the same as the night he had been injured: un-ironic, candid pain. Perhaps the proximity of my own injured pain made me butt in between Ethan and this guy.

'Excuse me, I have to put these away. Who are you supposed to be?' I ask Ethan's persecutor.

'What?' He was a fit, tanned, silver-haired man.

'Well it's Come in Character Day. I'm the Mad Hatter. Ethan's a vampire. Who are you? You know, like in the Emily Dickinson poem, "I'm Nobody, who are you? How public like a frog."'

'What?' he said again.

'Let me see if I can guess.' I appraised him up and down. He wore casual clothes laden with logos and a pinkie ring that caught the sunlight coming through our long dusty windows. He was slick, his clothes pressed, and expensive. 'A Tom Wolfe novel. Hmmm. *The Bonfire of the Vanities*?'

'Tosca,' said Ethan, shaking his head. 'This is my father, Barry.'

Oh shit. Beneath my Mad Hatter make up, I blushed so deeply I probably matched the bright rouge on my cheeks. I gulped and chirped, 'Nice to meet you. Are you here for very long?'

'Long enough. Just came to check up on the boy.'

'I'm not a boy.'

'Well, no one's heard from you at all. No phone calls. A few emails, that's it. For months.'

'I didn't have much to say.'

'Well, at least you have a girlfriend.'

'Who told you that?'

'Win. Win says you met some really dramatic girl up here.' He turned to me. 'Are you Ethan's girlfriend? Any man who doesn't have a girlfriend must be gay.'

I laughed in a self-deprecating Mad Hatter manner

while I tried to read the expression on Ethan's face, but it was changing, like the sky and the sea on a stormy day.

'Yes,' said Ethan, 'this is my girlfriend.'

'Yes,' I said, holding out the hand that wasn't clutching books. 'Tosca Tonnino.'

'What kind of name is that?'

'We were all named for operas,' I explained, 'all my sisters and I.' Only now I knew they were not my sisters. They were my aunts. My parents were my … oh shut up, quipped my inner Ginger Rogers, you're in enough trouble here.

Barry grinned. 'How can you call her Tosca in bed?'

'I don't.'

'When are you both off work?'

'We close at seven,' said Ethan.

'I'm taking you both out for dinner,' said Barry. 'No, I won't hear anything else. What's the best restaurant in this burg?'

'The Spinnaker,' said Ethan.

'I'll meet you there at eight.'

'Oh, I don't think so,' I interjected, 'it's Opening Day of the boating season. Every place will be booked solid. You won't be able to get a table.'

'Let me worry about that. I'll see you there. I hope you won't come in those clothes. I don't like to be seen around freaks.' Barry laughed good-naturedly, patted Ethan's shoulder in a comradely fashion, and he was gone.

We looked at each other. We looked like fucking freaks all right.

'Forgive me,' he said. 'It just came out. I don't know why I said you were my girlfriend. I'm sorry.'

'It's all right. I've had a few shocks myself today.'

'You don't have to go. It'll be frigging awful.'

'What're friends for?' I asked, and I meant it. Yesterday I would not have. But today I had felt the full force of parental pain, and I might as well share his as wallow in my own.

'You don't have to do this.'

'On a bookseller's salary, how often do I get to eat at The Spinnaker?'

'How often?' he asked, as though he really wanted to know.

I was about to say that last year my parents had come over and took me to The Spinnaker to celebrate my birthday, but I thought I might cry. 'Let's close up early, and I'll pick you up at the marina at quarter to,' I said. 'Be ready. I don't like to wait.'

Chapter Thirteen

'RESERVATION FOR JAMES, party of three,' said The Spinnaker maître d', giving some complicated hand signals to a waiter. No doubt a big fat tip had changed hands. 'Mr Barry James hasn't arrived yet. Would you care to wait in the bar?'

'Sure,' said Ethan, and he walked away, confident I suppose that I would follow.

That moment of our connection, commiseration, whatever it was in the store, that was over. I knew as much when I picked him at the marina. I wished like hell I hadn't let myself in for this. What an ass I was to have come to his rescue – if you could even call it that. I should have texted and begged off, but no, here I was, stupidly following him into the bar, walking behind him like a servant, and grinding my teeth audibly. I knew my 'date' with Ethan would be all over the island in a matter of hours. Several people, including Frances McTeer, her husband and her neighbors eyed us. All of them except Frances waved. The bar was even more crowded than the restaurant, crammed with lots of well-heeled people in yachting attire, filled with laughter, lively conversation, and the whiff of sunscreen mixed with men's heady cologne. Ethan and I took two stools at the end of bar. Ethan ordered the proverbial something stronger, a single malt Scotch. I ordered a sidecar, a drink so sophisticated that the bartender looked at me blankly.

'Campari and soda, then,' I said.

'You'd better have a Scotch,' Ethan wore his usual pressed shirt and slacks, nice shoes, though he had not quite got all the eye make-up off his face and dark rings remained 'It's going to be a long night, and it will not be pleasant. Don't say I didn't warn you.'

'Do you not get along with your father?' I asked.

'What a stupid question.' Our drinks came and Ethan took a big swig of his. 'You ought to know that my parents are divorced. Have been since I was five or six.'

'Lots of parents are.'

'Please don't patronize me, Tosca. I'm not here to write my memoirs. I'm just giving you some background for a little self-preservation. Yours, not mine.'

'I can take care of myself,' I said.

He shrugged, bolted the rest of the Scotch, ordered another and sat, sulking till it came.

His un-ironic willingness to spare me some awful experience was unexpected, and I regretted my snotty reflex. 'I didn't mean it like that. Please. Go on. Forewarned is forearmed.'

'You are just full of clichés aren't you?'

'All those Shannonville novels. They've eaten away at my brain.'

He smiled before returning to his drink. He faced me squarely, and that too, was unlike him. 'My parents were no good for each other. They should never have married. They fought, and fucked constantly. Their divorce was so toxic, it makes Murph and Jessie's struggle look like a couple of deacons at a church tea.'

165

'Surely your parents aren't still struggling. You were six a long time ago.'

'There's struggle and there's struggle. There was a lot of money, see, so that made it worse. Now, there isn't so much money and that makes it worse yet. My grandmother has money, but she only hands it out with conditions. She's generous, but there are always conditions.'

'Marjorie.'

'Yes. The very one. My dad uses her money to play the stock market, so he doesn't have to have a real job. He remarried once, briefly, and they divorced. Now he has a new beauty on his arm probably every six months. My mother, Karen, has had three husbands, and a bunch of lovers – losers – but rich losers. They get their ashes hauled, and Karen does what she does best which is inflict misery. She's like a tsunami of misery. She cuts a swath that big, that destructive. Karen and Barry are both total narcissists, so not only do I not have any brothers or sisters, but there are no steps or half-brothers. I grew up all alone in that ugly little arena called childhood until I met Win. He was my brother. Even Win was afraid of Karen.'

'Why?'

'I can't explain it. If you ever met her you'd know. Maybe he wasn't afraid of her. He slept with her.'

'Your best friend slept with your mother?'

'I think it was her graduation present to him.'

'That's disgusting.' No more disgusting than passing off one's bastard brat as the child of one's parents. I took a healthy swig of my Campari, and savored its bitterness.

'But Win could always handle my old man. I'll say that for him. I never could. Win could always get him in a good mood. Win's very charming and sociable. I just stayed in his shadow.'

'Well, your dad will be gone tomorrow. It's only this one night.'

'Yes.' He rested his arms on the bar, protectively around his drink. 'But it won't be pretty.'

'Does your dad have any hobbies?'

Ethan looked as if he might guffaw, but he finally settled on a look both withering and pitiful. 'Hobbies? You mean like screwing women and bullying waiters and cheating at golf?'

'We'll have to talk about something with him, and clearly, not the past.'

He laughed. 'You'll think of something. I trust you.' He got the bartender's attention for another Scotch just as Barry joined us at the bar.

In my strappy, high-heeled sandals, low cut dress, and light shawl with beaded fringe draped round my bare shoulders, I followed the maître d' to our table, the James men, single file behind me. It was a very good table, and from the corner of my eye, I could see long-time Islanders who no doubt had reservations, being shuffled to wait in the bar while our waiter (a summer hire, a college kid, no doubt; I didn't recognize him) hovered near Barry's elbow like a barnacle seeking a rock.

Once we were seated, he introduced himself as Our Server, Josh. Barry ordered a bottle of their best, and when Josh said they had many bests, Barry told him to choose a Cabernet. Josh left us menus.

'So how's Lindsay, Dad?' asked Ethan, like a man making the first move in chess.

'Long gone,' laughed Barry. 'My new lady is Ava. Wait'll you see her! Five foot nine. A hundred and ten pounds. Drop dead gorgeous.'

Barry's eyebrows shot up. As he filled us in about his new lady, Ava, his descriptions reminded me of Nan's *Yum yum, don't wrap it up, I'll eat it here.* Ava was a model. The two of them were flying out of Seattle for Hawaii in a couple of days. Ava was staying at the W Hotel in Seattle while Barry drove up to Friday Harbor to spend some quality time with his only son who wouldn't even take the day off. Was that so much to ask? How long had it been since they'd seen one another? Neither, it seems, could remember. At this lull, Barry turned the high beams of geniality on me, easing from me just enough information so that he could feel superior. He was amused that I came from a family of pizza-slingers, and from there he dabbled into the shallows of politics where he made plain just how Republican he was. The waiter returned with a Washington wine. I ordered the most expensive thing on the menu.

Through all this, Ethan's contributions were mostly monosyllabic replies, grunts, or snorts. Drinking did not improve him. He grew more sullen as he drank and dinner progressed. Not surly, not looking for a fight, just low voltage sulks, ongoing, deepening bad vibes like the night that Stan read at the store. Barry, on the other hand, grew more vivacious as the waiter grew more obsequious, and the wine flowed.

'Win says he hasn't heard from you in a long time,' Barry offered.

'Not much to say since the winter,' Ethan replied. 'I cycle. I work at the bookstore. I play chess.'

Barry cast a knowing look at me, as much to say, and you bang this chick. I felt a distinct shift under the table beside me. A knee rubbing my knee. Not the Ethan side. The Barry side.

'Have you seen Win?' Ethan looked up at his father, quizzically, I noticed.

'I sure have! I came through LA, oh, maybe a month or so ago, and we spent a lot of time together. He's great. Just great. He's working on the script of the movie they're making of his book. He's rented a house in Brentwood with hot and cold running chambermaids. That's where I got this great tan. Win's pool.' Barry ran a hand through his silver mane. 'Win's got beautiful girls by the dozens, beautiful babes, actresses, auditioning by the pool.'

Barry smiled, a dazzling smile, eager, hungry for attention, applause. Ethan, whatever else you can say about him, isn't like that. He's competitive, but assessive. A thinker, which is odd because I might not have said that about him before meeting his awful father.

'Did Win bang Ava?'

Barry choked and coughed. I took this opportunity to move my knee. Our server, Josh, brought a very rare steak to Barry, lobster for me, and neon-pink salmon for Ethan.

Ethan toyed with his rice while Barry brandished his steak knife. Ethan took a bite, then he asked again, 'No, really, Barry, did Win get it on with Ava? She's probably closer to his age than yours.'

'Actually, we went to LA for Ava.' Barry collected himself, and assumed his mantle of superiority, which, I recognized, was Ethan's default mode. So that's where he learned it. Very effective.

'So she could bang Win?'

'Will you just stop! Ava's a model, but she'd like to get into acting, and when I heard about the film, I called Win, and told him we were coming out to LA. He put her in touch with a couple of casting people, and he thinks there's a role for her in his film.'

'Ava could be the rehab nurse who fucks the patients while they go through withdrawal. She really gets her rocks off when they go into convulsions.' Ethan turned to me. 'The nurse thinks they're having convulsions because she's such a great fuck.'

At the table beside us, there arose a collective *harrumph*, and I could hear the wife telling the husband that some people have no manners. Luckily, they were tourists, not locals, so I didn't have to care what they thought.

'There's a scene like that, isn't there?' Barry shoved a bite of steak between his lips.

'Ask Tosca. She read it.'

'There is a scene like that.'

Our server, Josh came by to ask if everything was all right. Josh could no doubt feel the air bristle with Barry's money, and he stood like a subaltern awaiting the general's orders.

'Another bottle of wine,' said Barry, 'and none of that Washington crap. French.'

'Tosca likes French,' said Ethan, 'Edith Piaf, stuff like that. She speaks French too.'

'*Mais oui*,' Barry grinned and chewed his steak.

The pressure against my thigh commenced again. Is this geezer competing with his son? What would make him think I'd want to sleep with him? That I'd respond at all? I reached under the tablecloth to push him away, which, I quickly realized was a mistake because this asshole actually thought I was playing with him. With both hands I pulled my shawl around my shoulders. I was suddenly cold.

Barry, clearly energized by what he thought was my participation, sliced up his steak with gusto, and his plate ran with red. 'You and Win are sort of at either end of the chain, aren't you, Ethan? He creates the books and you sell them.'

'Ethan sells a lot of Win's books,' I said, sounding stupid.

'It's a great fucking novel,' said Ethan. 'As great as *Catcher in the Rye.*'

'Maybe Win ought to come up and do a reading at your bookstore.'

'Maybe,' said Ethan without enthusiasm. He ate a few forkfuls of rice to go with his Scotch.

'He'd do it too. Win said he would. He offered. When we were down in LA, we talked about it, and he thought it was a great idea. Think of the fun you guys could have wowing these locals.' Barry gestured around the restaurant.

'I do the Events for Carter & Co.,' I said. 'Win should contact me.'

'This is between friends,' said Barry, not taking his gaze from Ethan. 'Win owes you. Don't forget that.'

There was a short, painful silence while I absorbed the affront. And Ethan? I don't know what Ethan was thinking, but he said, 'I forget nothing. More's the fucking pity.'

The people at the next table waved to Josh, got their bill, and left, dessert uneaten, congealing on the plates. Josh brought Barry a French wine, Châteauneuf-du-Pape, 1992, cradling the bottle in his arms like a newborn. He uncorked the bottle with the panache of a conductor, which, ordinarily, I would admire, but his hammy grandeur just seemed stupid in Friday Harbor. He stood to attention while Barry sniffed the wine, sloshed it around his mouth, savored, and pronounced it fine. Josh poured some for each of us, but Ethan declined, and said he'd stick with Scotch and could he have another.

'All that expensive education,' Barry began, 'all those skiing lessons and tennis camps, and trips to Europe, St. George's from the fourth grade to the twelfth, Dartmouth, all that Ivy League polish and veneer, and here you are, a clerk in a bookstore. That's rich. That's really funny.' To prove it, he gave a dry, rasping laugh. 'Win's the next Hemingway, and Ethan's making minimum wage behind a counter selling books. You guys were like brothers. Inseparable.'

'Shackled at the wrist and ankles,' said Ethan. 'Sometimes literally.'

'Did Ethan tell you the story where they actually got arrested for drunk skiing one year in Vermont?' Barry asked me. 'Drunk skiing!'

'That wasn't the only charge,' Ethan corrected his dad. 'There was disturbing the peace, and creating a nuisance, a few broken windows, as I recall. The bail was reasonable, though.'

Barry was rattling on about various competitions, skiing and cycling that Ethan and Win had engaged in, and how Win always won. 'I guess that's why they call him Win,' said Barry. 'Tennis, chess, girls, he always racked up better scores than you. Winners and losers. That's life.'

'You're wrong. I beat him at cycling. I finished the Eastern States Cup Championship, and he didn't.'

'He had an accident.'

'He faked that.'

'Oh, that's low, Ethan. That's really low. Win was hurt.'

'It wasn't an accident. He skidded out because he knew he couldn't finish. An accident was better than losing to me.'

'You didn't win the championship.'

'But I finished the race.'

The Châteauneuf-du-Pape was probably the best wine that has ever passed my lips, but I nearly coughed it out of my nose when I saw Josh leading Tom and Sarah Chase toward the empty table next to ours. Tom saw me too, and he went white, as though impaled by heartburn.

'I have one thing on Win that he'll never be able to beat,' Ethan said slowly, as if plucking the words like leaves from an invisible tree. 'I heard Hank Jones play with Charlie Haden, and Win never did.'

'Hank Jones?' asked Barry, 'Who's that?'

'A great piano jazz man. One of the greatest. I heard that he and Charlie Haden were playing together in a club, an old club, not a big venue, just a small place in the East Village, a dump, really. Some old jazz friend of Hank's owned it. I told Win, let's go! He said we couldn't, that we were both on probation, and forbidden to leave campus. He said he wouldn't risk it to hear some old piano man and a washed up bass player jam together. I risked it. I went.'

'And you got caught, didn't you? You got expelled as I recall.'

'I did. Marjorie bought me back into St. George's,' said Ethan, focusing on me with some difficulty. 'Who cares? Hank Jones and Charlie Haden together? In person? It was worth it. I was only seventeen, but in all these years since, I've never actually experienced anything that made me feel like the two of them playing *Summertime,* what it made me feel. It was incredible, you know? What they did with that simple song. It left you slain.' His un-ironic earnestness had a weird, an unsettling effect on me, though he was by now seri-ously sloshed. Josh brought him another drink. Ethan turned to me. 'You know what I'm talking about, Tosca?'

'I've never heard of Charlie Haden or Hank Jones. I'm sorry.'

'They're dead now. Both of them.'

'I'm sorry.'

'Like Astor Piazzolla.'

'I'm sorry,' I said again, all the while surreptitiously glancing at Tom Chase. Tom Chase's gaze kept flicker-ing in my direction too. He gave me a weak smile, and a wave. I wanted to give him the finger.

Barry laughed. 'You should have seen them, Tosca.'

'Who?' I asked, realizing that the conversation had gone on without my paying attention. I'd clearly missed some cue, or switch, or shift in the wind; the father/son struggle had intensified, and I was the only barrier between them.

'These two were a bad influence on one another. Always competing to be the best. Ethan and Win were in a race to the finish for a while there. Looked like one or both would be checking out.'

'But then we got religion. Kind of like, Gimme that Old Time Religion.' Ethan threw his head back, eyes closed, palms out. 'Lord, lemme outta here! Lord, before I do something really fucking dumb, before I really fuck things up again.' He took another swig of Scotch, laughed in his old ironic way, and turned his bleary attention to me. 'Forgive me, Father, for I have sinned. Isn't that what the Catholics say?' He looked to his father. 'I forgot to tell you, Barry, Tosca's Catholic, not nice Waspy Episco-Aliens like us. A mackerel snapper. No, wait, that's what they call the Irish. What do they call the wops? Well, at least she's not Jewish, huh, Barry?

You couldn't tolerate a Jew, could you?'

I finished my lobster, and Josh, ever at the ready, took my plate. 'Could I have a fresh glass of water, please?'

'Dessert menus, Josh,' ordered Barry, his paw stroking my thigh again, clearly delighted with himself.

'Tosca has a plastic Virgin Mary on her dresser,' Ethan went on drunkenly, 'and poster of Ginger Rogers on the wall above her bed, and some old opera singer in the front room, and a butterfly tattoo on her butt.'

This was true and I coloured, and wondered how, in the darkness, he could have …

'I'd like to see that,' said Barry with a wink and a grin.

'Religion,' Ethan returned to his topic, 'just a closer walk with thee, Win, down the cold white halls. Win and I made a holy ghost out of marshmallows and ate it. Wholly. We smoked a lot of incense and drank some wine and communed again and again with cocaine, who forgave us for everything we'd ever done. Ever. Gimme that old time religion.'

'You never got religion,' Barry snorted, his lecherous moment dissolved, his hand withdrawn from my thigh, and pointing at his son. 'You got rehab, and after rehab, Win wrote a novel, and you relapsed, and went back on drugs. You broke her heart, you ungrateful shit.'

'Karen doesn't have a heart.'

'Not Karen. Fuck Karen. My mother. Marjorie! You broke your grandmother's heart, you brute. You stupid, asinine brute.' Barry's eyes were glowing and beneath his tan, he had flushed pink, the color of Ethan's salmon, as he said to me, 'It was Marjorie's idea that Ethan needed to come to this island, to be away from all temptation, though I can see,' he added with a leer, 'some temptations you just have to give in to.'

'Yep, that was the deal, Tosca.' Ethan grinned; he was now seriously drunk. 'I have to spend a year in Washington working for Marjorie's old college room-mate. A year on this glorious, goddamned, godforsaken Ere-last-I-saw-Elba island, a year holding down a job, like any ordinary schmuck. It's a condition, but she passed it off as a bet. My grandmother made me a bet I couldn't do it.' Ethan watched, interested, as Josh brought me my water and poured the last of the Châteauneuf-du-Pape into Barry's glass before taking the bottle from the table. 'She's afraid I'm just a loser. There's winners and losers. There's Win and Ethan.'

'She's paying your salary,' snapped Barry. 'Did you know that, you loser? Marjorie is paying your minimum wage salary so Edith Carter will keep you on.'

'That's not true.' Ethan focused on his father with difficulty.

'Ask her.'

'Oh,' Ethan flapped his hand at mythical flies. 'What do I care?'

'And the boat,' Barry went on, his hot breath close to my face, 'the boat he lives on, that belongs to Karen's husband's brother, or his cousin, or one of his fucking relatives. Ethan lives there rent-free. Ethan's never held onto a job longer than a year, and that's why—'

'Give it a rest, Barry,' Ethan shrugged. 'No one gives a shit.'

Probably long before this, Ginger Rogers would have stood up and left these two to stew in their own toxic juices. But leave Ethan to be destroyed by Barry? I couldn't do it. Reader, I could not do it. It was like watching a fellow creature caught in a trap and chewing off his own foot. No matter what I thought of him, I could not abandon him. I touched his arm. 'I think we should leave,

Ethan. You know how it is, Barry, us working schmucks have to get up early. Come on, Ethan, let's go home.'

But Ethan stared at my hand on his arm. Then he brought his face to me, his eyes glazing, squinting, as if I were in the far distance. He lowered his voice and offered confidentially, 'Tosca has a pizza named after her, Barry. Did you know that? Anchovy and olive and mushroom. I'll bet old Ava doesn't have a pizza named after her, does she? She might be leggy and gorgeous and half your age, she might have bubble boobs, and give a great blow job, but no pizza.'

'We should leave, Ethan,' I said, with a glance to Tom and Sarah Chase who, like everyone else in our vicinity, were following this tableau with a mix of horror and delight.

'A pizza and an opera,' said Barry as his hand made a long slow caress against my thigh while the expression on his face never changed. 'That tells you something, doesn't it?'

'She isn't my girlfriend, though,' Ethan drunkenly waved away the possibility. 'She's just some girl I banged one night. A one night stand. No strings. Not one. I feel nothing. Nothing.'

I rose, and tossed the glass of ice water all over Ethan, and in the same motion and moment, I reached out, and threw the last of the wine in Barry's tanned face. *'Au revoir,* assholes!'

The restaurant hushed into appalled silence, outraged at my act, and Barry's shrieking obscenities after me, and Ethan's long, jagged, raucous laughter as he mopped his face, smearing what was left of his eye make-up. Josh cursed me outright. So much for his tip.

I walked out, pushing past Tom Chase. Ginger Rogers could have done it no better.

Chapter Fourteen

GOSSIP THIS RICH on an island was like the Exxon Valdez oil spill; it washed up in conversations everywhere. Word of my hissy fit at The Spinnaker traveled with the tides. When I went into work the next day, I could hardly say in my own defense that Barry was feeling me up, that Ethan had told the world he'd banged me in a one night stand, that the man who had fathered and then abandoned me was sitting there looking sheepish beside his bitch wife. I couldn't even tell Jessie the truth of it. No, I said nothing, preferring to keep my pride intact at the expense of my reputation. Let them eat cake.

After Come in Character Day, Ethan lapsed into the total prick I always knew him to be, visiting his churlishness on me and everyone else. He was gruff with the unoffending Sally, snappish with Jessie, and downright caustic with Wendell. Miss Carter blamed me for Ethan's bad behavior. Then, even she suffered at his sarcasm. Everyone froze in their tracks at that. However, she was not Edith Carter for nothing, and she bore the remark with regal hauteur. But the *coup de grâce*? She overhead him being short and sharp with a customer. She called him into her office, and though we don't know what was said, he left the store immediately. Wendell outright accused me of having brought all this on. I told him to bugger off. All in all, not the best working conditions.

Moreover, Lucy Lamont declined to have lunch with Miss Carter, and did not deign to address her directly. Dawn Philbrick's office (not Dawn personally, but her assistant) called me and said Lucy had her own plans for lunch on 12 June. However, I was informed that Lucy would want a parking space reserved for her that day, right beside the venue. I said I would accommodate. Then I had to go tell Miss Carter that lunch with Lucy was off. Miss Carter seemed not to take offense. She had another great idea: tickets for this event. Free with buying the book, otherwise ten bucks a pop. If it were free, the Community Center might not be able to hold all the readers coming for the rare public appearance of Lucy Lamont. This way, we made money no matter what. This was her first marketing idea I actually admired.

A few days after Come in Character Day, my name blared out on the in-store intercom. Wendell asking me to come to the front desk. As I emerged from my office, Wendell pointed to Tom Chase. 'This gentlemen would like a few words with you.'

'Oh, just some book suggestions,' Tom said quickly. 'I respect your opinion.'

We stared into each other's one green eye and one brown eye, looking to see if we resembled each other. No wonder I was taller than the rest of the Tonninos. The mouth? No. I always thought I had my father's, that is, Frank's mouth. Carmen's mouth. I had not shot off my angry email to her. I had done nothing with or about my new, nasty and unwanted knowledge, though my anger at Carmen and all the rest of them bubbled and boiled and smouldered and roiled in my guts. After I'd returned from the fiasco at The Spinnaker, I found a voice mail from Carmen: *I know you're terribly upset. I don't blame you. Please say nothing of this day to Mom and Dad. I will talk to you, explain everything privately. I love you, Tosca.* Mom and Dad, I wanted to say. Are you fucking kidding me? I would have lashed out, believe me, but the thought of what this would do to Frank and Donna (I kept forcing myself to call them Frank and Donna, not Mom and Dad, or Granny and Gramps) stopped me and made me cry. Worse, and more confusing yet, that ghastly evening with Ethan and Barry had underscored for me what a fine, an enviable childhood and youth I'd had among people who adored me. Parents, grandparents, did it really matter? They'd already given me everything a daughter could want. Except the truth of my identity.

But as I looked at Tom Chase, here in the bookstore, did I want his identity? Did I want anything at all from Daddy Fucking Dearest? 'What do you want from me?'

'I need a book.'

'What kind of book?'

'Uh … a gift.'

'For whom?' I could feel Wendell's beady eyes behind me.

'For my daughter.'

'How old is she?'

'Uh … college.'

'What kind of book?'

'I don't know.'

'What does she like?'

Tom was puzzled. 'I was hoping you could …'

'She's your daughter.'

'Travel?'

I marched him over the steamer trunk. In fact I marched him all around the store, responding to his questions about books, and books alone. Asking no questions of my own. I wanted nothing from this dickhead. When all was said and done, I was trembling, and Tom Chase had bought two hundred and fifty dollars' worth of books, including *Galley Cooking*, especially for boats and RVs.

'It's good to see you again, Tosca,' he said when I had rung up his purchases. 'I'd like to see you again this summer. Maybe we could have lunch some afternoon. Talk. You know?'

'I don't know. I don't want to. Don't come back. Don't ever come back.'

Wendell was nearby, and when Tom Chase left, he started to give me a tongue lashing about how we treat customers. I did not stick around for Wendell's shit. I left him with a split infinitive hanging from his lips, and returned to my office to cry. But no one heard me.

They say that people who believe that Nature reflects or responds to their moods succumb to the Pathetic Fallacy. It may be pathetic and it may be a fallacy, but nonetheless, since Rain first rhymed with Pain, people have believed that Nature secretly sympathizes with their sorrows or joys. Just as that Saturday, Opening Day, had been gloriously sunny, a harbinger of a fine summer to come, right after that, rain set in. Spring rain, unrelenting, unforgiving, utterly disheartening. If I didn't have to go to work, I didn't go anywhere. I missed yoga, a friend's birthday party, and an important Tourist Board meeting. I heard absolutely nothing from Carmen, never mind her promise to explain everything, and I didn't trust myself to call. I cracked pistachios till my lips stung, and asked myself over and over, *what would Ginger Rogers do*, but there was no answer, no reply, no assurance that any of her sexy, defiant confidence would do me any good at all. On any front. Personal or professional. And my own lovely confidence, hallmark of the Tosca Tonnino we all know and love? Shattered.

Thursday was my day off, but Wednesday night Miss Carter sent an email to the staff, asking us all to come in at 9.30 before the store opened. I dreaded this, fearing I would be publicly chastised, or made to suffer my actions in The Spinnaker. (Josh had come into the store the day before, and I had to wait on him. He had some choice words for me. Nothing vulgar, but no mistaking his attitude.) That fear subsided when I came into the storeroom and there on the long table were two bottles of expensive champagne and seven Waterford crystal glasses, each one of which Nan was hand-polishing with a dishtowel. Miss Carter, wearing a peach-colored suit that lent a glow to her face, sat smiling like the Cheshire Cat. Clearly, all was forgiven. But what was the occasion? A mini-farewell for Jessie? She still had a couple of weeks to go. Jessie looked over at me: *WTF?* Wendell looked perplexed. Sally looked expectant, but not hopeful.

And Ethan? He sprawled his great frame across two metal folding chairs. His clothes were rumpled, as if they had been plucked from a pile, and his usually clean shaven jaw was stubbled. He looked bored shitless.

Leaning fashionably upon her cane, Miss Carter stood, once we were all assembled. She signaled Nan, who handed us each a champagne flute. We stood too. Even Ethan hauled to his feet. Miss Carter began.

'When I named Carter & Co. in honor of Sylvia Beach's legendary Paris bookshop, Shakespeare & Company, I always meant to do more than merely sell books. I wanted to serve Literature.' She lingered over the word as if it were confectionery. 'And now, I am going to see my dream come true. In Sylvia Beach's great tradition, Carter & Co. finds itself at the heart, the veritable beating heart of American letters, the crossroads of American literature. Thank you, Tosca and Ethan!' She raised her glass and sipped, as did we all. 'Tosca's energy, and verve and insight brought Lucy Lamont to this island. We are the only bookstore where Lucy Lamont has appeared since 1998! So Tosca,' Miss Carter raised her glass to me again, 'whatever it was you said to her, you were very persuasive. Carter & Co. – and literature – thank you.'

Everyone had to have another sip on my behalf. I smiled wanly. *Oh, brother....*

'Tosca must have inspired Ethan! Because now I have the honor to inform you all that Ethan has prevailed on his dear friend, Win Jefferies – the next Hemingway! – to come to Carter & Co. to read! Ethan already got Win to friend us on Facebook, to follow us on Twitter, but an author like Win Jefferies, well, he might do the big Seattle bookstores, he might do Barnes and Noble or even Costco!' Her voice went up into a little shriek. 'And now he's coming to Friday Harbor. Making a special trip, a special reading, a special occasion just for Carter & Co., and his dear friend, Ethan. I give you Ethan James!'

There was a moment's silence. Ethan accepted the accolade with a shrug.

'And best of all! Oh yes, I have saved the best for last! We are going to have a double feature! The two bestselling authors in America will be here at Carter & Co. on the same day, June 12th! At last!' Edith declared, holding her glass aloft in triumph. 'Carter & Co. will make literary history! We will see two of America's greatest authors in one day, in one place. Not New York, but here in the Northwest. Here on our little island, two of America's finest will come together. It's as though Walt Whitman and Emily Dickinson, contemporaries who never met, will stand upon the same podium, as though Henry James and Mark Twain gave a reading together, Balzac and Dickens!' she rattled on and over the undercurrent of our collective disbelief, or wonder.

Wendell knew what she wanted to hear, and he knew that she could not say it herself, so he did. 'You are the Sylvia Beach of Friday Harbor. The Sylvia Beach of the West.'

We all toasted her, and she smiled at Wendell as though they were the proud parents of a masterpiece. I excused myself and went to the employee bathroom where I barfed up my Cheerios.

When I returned to the storeroom Nan had finished off the champagne, and opened a box of donuts and muffins. Everyone was talking logistics for the great event. I cleared my throat, and then I said to everyone present, 'This is not a good idea. Lucy Lamont will never take a back seat to anyone. *Anyone.*'

'Oh,' said Miss Carter, still dewy and glowing. 'I'm sure that's not so.'

'It is so. Trust me.'

'It's an opportunity for Literature,' Miss Carter contended sweetly.

'It is fucking fiasco in the making.'

'Tosca!' said Sally. 'R-really.'

Wendell scowled at me, and moved slightly closer to

Miss Carter to protect her. 'You go too far.'

'You know I'm right, Wendell, you saw Lucy Lamont that day in Portland. Back me up here.'

Wendell glanced from me to Miss Carter whose expression remained dreamy, no matter what I'd said. He offered: 'Lucy Lamont can be difficult, there's no doubt of that. But I'm sure she'll see it as an opportunity.'

'An opportunity to what? To share the stage with a kid who writes about drugs and sex and padded cells, and pokes through the contents of his own vomit?'

'Really, Tosca!' Miss Carter, suddenly alert, rebuked me, *The Body Electric* is the most talked about novel in America. It's chic.' She cackled in her old lady way, delighted with the word.

'*The Body Electric* is the dark side of the American dream,' said Ethan, speaking for the first time that morning. 'They're the perfect pairing. Win Jefferies writes about the dark underbelly of Lucy Lamont's America.'

'There. The dark underbelly.' Miss Carter looked pleased. 'You see? Walt Whitman and Emily Dickinson. Oh, look at the time! We have to open the doors. Ethan, would you tell Win again how much we appreciate this?'

'I will,' he replied. Straight-faced too.

'It will be so … so …' Miss Carter sought the word, as if seeking a monarch butterfly with her gauzy net. 'It will be so cool.'

What would Ginger Rogers do? Put on her tap shoes and dance till she dropped? Buy a new ball gown? Fly down to Rio? I went home, took my bike off the wall, put on a backpack and rode like hell through the rain ten miles to Roche Harbor. Once there, I walked the windy beaches, feeling less like Ginger Rogers and more like Tess of the d'Ubervilles. I knew I had been screwed, but I wasn't sure how it had happened.

Chapter Fifteen

THE FOLLOWING DAY, I opened the store, mercifully with only Sally for company. When I saw Nan helping Miss Carter up the front steps, I held the door for her. I walked Miss Carter back to her office, saw her comfortably seated, and proceeded to apologize for my little outburst the day before.

'Of course, Tosca.' She waved away any bad feelings between us.

Having mollified her, I dove right in. 'I apologize, but I still have to say if you have these two authors here on the same day, the same stage, the PNBA, the whole American bookselling community is going to think you've lost your mind.'

'That's what they said of Sylvia when she published *Ulysses*.'

I tried to explain the concept of marketing to mutually exclusive sets of readers. I used analogies, like the Hatfields and McCoys, tree-huggers and capitalists, like putting Tina Frazier on the same bill the same day with George Bush. Never, never the twain shall meet. But Miss Carter was convinced this was genius. She reminded me of the successes of 'Jingle Book Jingle Book'. The popcorn. She flailed about again in literary history, Balzac and Dickens, Henry James and Mark Twain. Her eyes were bright with anticipation. Then she said she had work to do.

I retreated to my office, and closed the door, put my head on my desk. I felt sick. I had lain awake all night, preferring insomnia to dreams of Lucy Lamont, her careful coiffure, her flashing rings, her arrogant smile bearing down on me like a huge, over-inflated balloon at the end of a short tether.

Though I wasn't scheduled to work the next day, I came in at six thirty and telephoned the East Coast. It took me twenty minutes to get past Dawn Philbrick's assistant who kept telling me Dawn was in a meeting, or on another line, or away from her desk, and would I like her voice mail.

'Lucy Lamont!' I finally shrieked. 'Do you hear me? Lucy Lamont is going to have a heart attack and die next month unless I talk to Dawn Philbrick right now.'

Dawn came on the line two minutes later. I could still picture the Abstract Expressionist art on her walls, the pale orchids, but I knew that her red nails and stiletto heels were about to be ground into my eyes. I started easy, blaming Sylvia Beach, and Miss Carter's wish to be a Literary Legend.

'I don't have time for this shit. What is it?'

So I explained briefly about the double feature and Win Jefferies sharing the podium, or at least the day with Lucy Lamont, swearing throughout that I had nothing to do with this complete snafu.

'Win Jefferies? Mr Sex and Cocaine, the guy with his vomit in the first paragraph and the nurse who gets off on patients' convulsions?'

'Yes.'

'Are you out of your fucking mind?'

'I didn't do this. It was—'

'It doesn't matter. It can't happen. End of story.'

'That's why I'm calling you, Dawn. You talk to Lucy and get her to cancel.'

There was moment of silence. Somewhere beyond Dawn's windows, in the New York canyons of steel a siren blared. And here, beyond my windows, somewhere in the alley by the dumpsters, two cats were getting it on.

Dawn spoke in an even voice. 'Lucy has made her plans, Tosca, as you very well goddamned know, and Lucy will carry through. You will get this twerp, Win, to change his plans. Lucy is coming there on the 12th with a certain set of expectations. Great Expectations. Do I make myself clear?'

'Yes,' I said beating myself with my own slipper for having called this hard-hearted bitch.

'And just for the record, let me give you a little advice. If someone said to me, "Dawn, would you rather live through Hurricane Katrina in the New Orleans' Ninth Ward with no supplies and no flashlight and standing on the roof waving to a helicopter while raw sewage laps at your ankles, or Lucy Lamont in a rage?" I'd say, "Katrina, New Orleans, Ninth Ward, here I come!" That's the last bit of wisdom I'm giving you. Take care of this.' She slammed down the phone.

Not only did she hang up, but my efforts to call back were met with 'Not here' and a refusal to take a message. Then my number was blocked.

Next I tried Smithson/Empire and asked to speak to Win's publicist there, Zach Harrington. I explained to him the situation, in slightly different terms, leaving out Sylvia Beach. He just said it wasn't his responsibility. Win had set this up on his own, not through

189

Smithson/Empire. All Zach knew was ... and I listened to some computer keys natter ... that there was an order for fifty cartons of books to be delivered to Carter & Co., Friday Harbor, Washington in a week.

'Awesome!' he said. 'You musta done something right. Fifty cartons!'

'You don't understand. He's sharing the stage with Lucy Lamont.'

'Shannonville Lucy?'

'The very one.'

'Pardon me, lady, but you are out of your fucking mind. Win Jefferies is the real thing, a real writer. Lucy Lamont is a power-hungry, man-eating Godzilla who passes herself off as a cream puff. Everyone around here knows that. She's driven four publicists here to quit, or she has had them fired, just since I've been here.'

'How long is that?'

'Eighteen months. And the last one, Katie, you know why she got the axe?'

'Why?' I asked, dry-mouthed.

'For sending on a bad review! Right. Kill the messenger time. They forgot to tell Katie that any review sent to Lucy Lamont had to be glowing or doctored. Or both. Hey, Katie's probably in lockup with the Unnamed Narrator.' He gave a horsey, mirthless, youthful laugh.

'What's the new publicist's name?'

'Tiffany.'

'I suppose they told her no bad reviews.'

'Tiffany is scared shitless every time the phone rings, thinking it be might Lucy.'

'Give me Win's number. I'll talk to him myself. '

'I have to go. Email me your request.'

I did, and received for my pains, the 'Out of the Office Reply.' The one that doesn't even have a Re: in the subject line. The one that means you've been blocked forever.

I called Tiffany who had a New York accent and a reedy voice. Tiffany did not think she could undo what Lucy Lamont had set in motion: let no man put asunder what Lucy Lamont hath wrought.

'Don't you see what I'm telling you? Let me talk to your boss.'

'All those requests have to be in writing. Email me.'

She hung up. I emailed. The result was the same as with Zach.

It was nine o'clock by the time I'd finished. I checked the work schedule. What would Ginger Rogers do? Well, probably not what I was about to do. I felt pretty fucking sure of that.

I walked down to the marina. One of those glorious spring mornings, the air, tender, refreshed, washed anew. The hanging baskets on the lampposts blooming with the promise of summer. The hillsides coming down to the harbor were alight with green, the evergreens dark, straight sentinels, the deciduous trees a still-tender green. Sunlight splashed along the blue-green water and the white matchstick masts in the harbor. The slurp of water lapping at hulls, the gentle clang of halyards sounded as, amid all this cloying beauty, I walked the docks, fruitlessly looking for the fucking *French Letter*. I saw a middle-aged duffer smoking on the deck of *Mom's Revenge* and asked him for the *French Letter*. He chuckled, and then winked at me, and told me where I could find it.

As I came closer I could hear a heavy metal band, Rage Against the Machine maybe, shaking the *French*

Letter's timbers. I stood on the dock and called out Ethan's name over the thrashing guitars. More than once. 'I know you're in there, Ethan. I need to talk to you.'

The music turned off, and he came out, half-shaved, and half-clad, wearing shorts, barefoot. 'What do you want?'

'Call this off, Ethan.'

'Too late.' He started to go back inside.

'It's not too late. Look, you've had one on me. You showed me up good. Now the joke's over.'

'It's not a joke.'

'I'm sorry I called you an asshole.'

'You did? I've forgotten.'

'I'm sorry I threw ice water on you, and wine on your dad. He was feeling me up. Honestly, he was massaging my thigh.'

'Typical.'

'I'm sorry I was snotty to you when you first came here.'

'Were you?'

'I'm sorry, OK?' I opened my arms wide. 'Big blanket apology.'

'I don't need a blanket.'

'Please call it off.'

'Look, Win called me. Win wants to come.'

'Fine. Not on June 12th.'

'It's Win's schedule, not mine.'

'I'm sorry about that night last February.'

'This isn't about you. It hasn't got anything to do with you. It's me and Win. Understand? Don't take it personally.' He regarded me with equanimity you might have given a rutabaga in the produce aisle.

Ginger Rogers would have called him out, accused

him of being the big, wounded, nasty baby that he was, asked him what the world had done to him to make him so spiteful and careless, and cruel. I, however, tuned up the violin and appealed to some last shred of decency.

'Do you have any idea what it will do to Miss Carter once the shit hits the fan? She is an old lady.'

'You saw how happy she is. It'll be good for business, sell a lot of books. You know that's true. Edith is a tough old bird. She'll be grateful.'

'I have seen Lucy Lamont in action. She will eviscerate your friend.'

'You mean, like disembowel?'

'Exactly.'

Ethan shrugged. 'Win can take care of himself.' He went back into the *French Letter* and turned on Rage Against the Machine.

I drove out to False Bay to Miss Carter's house. Nan was surprised to see me. I said I'd like to see Miss Carter and I was led to the sunroom to wait. I strolled around, inspecting the orchids and tropicals for about twenty minutes before Nan came back, and said I should go to Edith's study which was on the second floor, first door on the right.

Clearly, the twenty minutes had been taken up with hastily applying make-up and getting dressed, and I confess I admired the old girl's respect for pride and propriety. She wore an outfit, casual for her, a neat cotton sweater and silk pants. Her eyeliner was applied crookedly.

'Now, Tosca, what was so urgent that it couldn't wait till I came into the shop?'

'Miss Carter, it pains me to say this, but this whole

thing, Lucy Lamont and Win Jefferies, has been a dreadful error, and it should not happen.'

'Oh please Tosca, not more jargon about mutually exclusive readership.'

'No, although that's entirely true, what I said.'

'That remains to be seen.'

'This is happening for the wrong reasons. Ethan set this whole wretched thing up because he's mad at me.'

'I heard you threw water on him and wine on his father at The Spinnaker. That was very unwise. Everyone is talking about it. You represent Carter & Co., even when you're not working. Word even got back to Marjorie. Marjorie called me and asked if you were Ethan's girlfriend.'

'No. No, I'm not. It's nothing like that. It was all his father's fault.'

'Marjorie said—'

'Look, Miss Carter, I don't care about Marjorie. Please. I'm here to talk about Lucy Lamont and Win Jefferies. Ethan only did this to get back at me. To make me look bad.'

'You look like the most brilliant Events person in the Northwest! Maybe in the whole country! First you get Lucy Lamont, and then Win Jefferies joins her! Ethan has done you and the store a tremendous favor, Tosca.' She paused briefly. 'Are you worried that I'd give Ethan your job?'

This had never occurred to me. But I said, 'I'm sure Win Jefferies isn't looking forward to joining Lucy either. I can just imagine what he thinks of the Shannonville novels. They're drivel, of course, but—'

'We never describe our authors' works as drivel. I can't believe you said that. You're the Events Person!'

'Here's the problem, Miss Carter. I really don't think

you can have both Lucy Lamont and Win Jefferies. You have to choose.'

'Why?'

'If Lucy Lamont has to share the stage with *anyone*, she'll cancel. She won't come.'

'Not come? What do you mean?'

'She has a towering ego. She's a power-hungry, man-eating Godzilla. As soon as I tell her Win Jefferies is coming, she will cancel. You will lose Lucy. If you asked Lucy Lamont to share the stage with Shakespeare, she'd refuse to come.'

'Now, Tosca,' Miss Carter's voice oozed between her thin lips, 'if Lucy Lamont does not show up on June 12th, everyone will be so disappointed. I will be so disappointed. It will disappoint people who believe in Carter & Co. It will be bad for our reputation. We will look like fools, having promised something you cannot deliver. It will be very bad for you. Very bad.'

That cheery thought hung like crepe in the air while Nan brought in a tray with two cups and a china coffee pot. Miss Carter poured. 'One lump or two?'

'Two.' This bitter pill needed sweetening. I started to cry, yes, just like a little bitch, a whimpering dog. I didn't even need to take off my slipper and beat myself. I wasn't being coy, or ironic. I was crying. From afar Ginger Rogers frowned at me, wondering how I could be so disgusting as to abase myself. I wept away. Miss Carter looked alarmed and passed me a tissue. Asked what was the matter.

'I lied to you,' I sobbed, 'Ethan and I had an affair.'

'I thought that was Ethan and Jessie. Jessie's too old for him. Good thing Jessie's leaving. He's only twenty-eight.'

I snuffled, annoyed. Sexual harassment, my ass. 'It

was Ethan and me first, and he wanted it to go on.'

'I do not approve, you know. Sexual liaisons between employees are against company policy.'

'I know! That's why I said no. I told him it just couldn't be.'

'I thought you said you actually had an affair.' Her eyes were a little brighter and her sharp little teeth showed in her smile.

'Yes. Well, sort of yes. I went to bed with him, but then, he wanted the affair to continue, to go on and on, and I said no. No sex. That's what I told him. Company policy. Your very policy. I was very emphatic, and he got all hurt and angry. That's why he's doing this to me.'

'He's not doing anything to you. What do you mean?'

'Setting these up on the same day to ruin the whole Lucy Lamont thing. Ethan's just doing it to get back at me. It'll look like I screwed up.'

'You were quite right not to continue to sleep with him. This is a business. We must all be professional, even if he is very attractive. These Dartmouth men, you know. Have another tissue. Quit crying.' I dried my eyes. I quit crying. I was wasting more than my tears here, more than my time. My breath, my very soul.

'Never mind all this personal stuff. As long as you're not sleeping with him now. Are you?'

'No.'

'Good. Then Lucy is your responsibility. Win is Ethan's. Just do your job.' She did not smile.

I did not ask myself what Ginger Rogers would do. I asked myself: how desperate are you, Tosca? Desperate enough to take the operatic step of informing her that in going through with this fiasco, she is sabotaging

196

her dear old Bryn Mawr roommate? That she is cruelly undoing everything Marjorie had hoped for when she sent her grandson to this island to deliver him from evil. Not metaphorical evil. The real thing. Could Edith even begin to fathom Marjorie's desperation? The circumstances under which a woman would pay her grandson's salary for a year up here in the northwest corner of the northwest corner? On a *bet* that he couldn't keep a retail job? Couldn't keep himself off drugs and out of trouble? Couldn't stay away from the very companion who had brought him so low? In bringing Win Jefferies – with his swagger, his success, and no doubt his suitcase full of glam drugs – Miss Carter was setting Ethan James up for a fall. Ethan was weak, and perhaps one day that could change. Win was venal, and that would not change. *The Body Electric* proved that much. There was no redemption in that book. Nor even friendship. Only high times for Roger and the Unnamed Narrator, then crash and burn. Unnamed crashed. Roger burned. Roger died. Unnamed lived on, and felt nothing. Nothing. Win cared nothing for the destruction he might wreak. Nothing. I rose, thanked her for the coffee, said I would do my job, she needn't worry about me.

Like the Titanic plying toward the iceberg, Carter & Co. paddled its way toward 12 June. I alone thought it was going to be a disaster. Everyone else – each for their own reasons – thought it was going to be funny, or fine or legendary or some other stupidshit thing.

Smithson/Empire sent us big displays, one for the Shannonville series (complete with embossed lavender wisteria) and one for Win Jeffries's book, in black and red, a black needle gushing out a little spurt of red blood. They were too big for the window, and so we cleared away the Masterpiece Theatre set, put the wing chairs and the chess table in the storeroom to the shrill outcry from Statler and Waldorf. Ethan soothed them. He promised it would only be for ten days, and then everything would go back the way it was.

'Right, Tosca?' he said to me as I was arranging Shannonville novels.

'Shut up, and fuck off,' I snapped at the very moment that Wendell was passing by. Wendell asked me to come to his office.

'Change your attitude, young lady.'

'Don't young lady me! I'm not your daughter! I work here. I'm a professional! This is going to be—'

'We're going to sell lots of books and that's the only thing that matters.'

'Really?' I demanded of Wendell. 'You really think so? Do your wages go up when we sell a lot of books?'

'That's crass, Tosca. Don't be so petty.'

Petty? Petty doesn't begin to describe what I felt. Try palsied with anxiety. Every night I suffered shuddering insomnia, and every morning, I woke pale and panicked. How could I possibly tell Lucy Lamont of the change in plans? How could I tell her that she will be on a double bill with a young debut novelist whose book had the critics fawning, while her own work inevitably had the critics barfing. How would I tell that to a woman who would not suffer so much as a bad review? How could I? Reader, I did not do it. I never informed Lucy Lamont that there was to be double billing. I felt certain Dawn would not do so. (Remember Hurricane Katrina.) Nor would dear little Tiffany. The responsibility was not theirs, after all. The responsibility was mine. At least, if Lucy showed up, I wouldn't lose my job, though I knew full well I might lose something else. Something more important. My self-respect, perhaps? That I might well lose some deeply held conviction that I was a woman who could meet the world with confidence and courage, with panache! That woman blurred in the bathroom mirror, increasingly lost to me. I was a weenie after all.

One Saturday I was volunteering at the Walk for a Cure Community Garage Sale that Sally had helped to organize. I was sitting at a card table, taking cash and making change, and I looked up and saw Frances McTeer clutching some old books. She handed them to me. I added up the prices. 'That'll be $10.50, Frances.'

'I thought I knew you better, Tosca. I thought you were a person of some loyalty, some dedication. Some sense of honor.'

Only Frances McTeer would be talking about honor at a garage sale.

'Ten fifty,' I said.

'First, you give Lucy Lamont a slot that should have been mine. You bump my book for Lucy Lamont. Lucy Lamont! That spineless, sugar-fried, mincing poseur passing for a writer! With all her little garden intrigues. Will Cecily and Arthur kiss in the gazebo? Oh dear! They aren't even characters! They're fridge magnets on a page!'

Her husband murmured, *'Frances, dear ...'* but she shook him off. She was one fierce Scotswoman, and the British ought to be glad she didn't live three hundred years ago.

'And you double-bill her with a writer whose opening paragraph recounts everything that's in the pile of his vomit! How could you?'

'I didn't. Honest.'

'If you were going to do two authors on June 12th, Tosca, why not Lucy Lamont and *me*? Why bring in Win Jefferies?'

'This wasn't my idea, Frances, I swear. I wish I'd never heard of either one.'

And that, Ginger Rogers snapped, *is the first true thing you have said in weeks.*

Chapter Sixteen

My BIRTHDAY OFTEN coincides with Memorial Day weekend, and my family was always fond of saying, 'Look, Tosca gets a national holiday to celebrate!' This year my mother, that is, Donna, called to see if I could come home.

'Your dad and I could come over to Friday Harbor, and take you out to dinner, but the long trip wears him out these days, and we don't much like restaurant food. Neither does Aunt Clara.'

'So if I come home, what'll we do?'

'What we always do! We'll have a nice dinner with a lot of the family.'

'Like who?'

'Like the family!'

'Will Carmen be there?'

'What's the matter with you and Carmen? Did you two eat the same bad fish or something? Dad says she's been weird.'

Trust my dad, I mean, Frank, to catch every little quiver, and Donna to notice nothing.

'Hey,' she cried, 'you can invite Chris to your birthday!'

I said, 'Oh Mom!' before I remembered how pissed

off I was, and determined not to call her Mom, 'Chris is not the man for me.'

'OK. He's a man, though, isn't he?'

'Is that enough? Is all you want is that I should have A Man? Don't you care what kind of man?'

'What's with you, Tosca? You got PMS? You coming or not?'

I went. I worked a half shift on Sunday and took the afternoon ferry and arrived at the East Valley street house at dusk, surprised to find the kitchen door locked, though the lights were blaring. Aunt Clara was in the kitchen. She had been crying. She sat there at the table with a knotted hanky in one hand and a rosary in the other.

She looked up from her hanky. 'So, at last you come. Thank God.'

'What?'

'We've been waiting for you. Carmen says we can't go till you get here.'

'Go where?' The place was quiet. No Maria Callas. No Astor Piazzolla. No NPR on the radio. No theme from *Hawaii Five-0* in the other room. Carmen sailed into the kitchen, her arms full of folded dishtowels.

I said, 'What the hell is wrong here?'

Aunt Clara had her mouth open to reprimand me, but Carmen butted in, 'Dad's had an incident.'

'He's at death's door,' said Clara, and she started to bawl.

'Aunt Clara, stop! He is not at death's door, and you do no one any good by saying so!' Carmen sounded just like Mom, or Norma, all knuckles-and-know-how. 'You are making things worse. Tosca, Dad has had what they call a TIA, a mini stroke. He is at the hospital.'

I collapsed into a kitchen chair. 'When did this

happen? Where?'

'It happened at the store. This afternoon.'

'Why didn't anyone call me? Isn't that what cell phones are for?'

'Would a phone call have made the ferry move faster? You were already on your way. There was no point. Besides, we had to get him to the hospital. One of the cooks came running down to the salon, and told me Dad fell over, and his speech was suddenly slurred. I called 911, and Mom.'

'And?'

'They're keeping him overnight at University Hospital. They'll probably release him tomorrow. Probably.'

'How bad is he?'

'I don't know. Mom, everyone is there, with him. I said I would come back here and wait for you. I'll take you.'

'And me,' said Aunt Clara. 'I am going too.'

'No, you're not,' said Carmen. 'You will slow us down. I need to talk with Tosca.'

'Everyone treats me like dirt here. Everyone thinks I'm just an old woman, poor, widowed, what do I know? Oh, who cares about Clara? She's in the way.'

Carmen waited for her to finish her lament, pointless to interrupt. 'Really, Aunt Clara, it wouldn't be good for your health. You know hospitals are nasty places. We'll look after Dad. You need to look after yourself, Aunt Clara. Everyone will need something to eat when they come back. No one can cook like you. Why don't you make us some dinner?'

Now she sounded like Dad, soothing and knowing just the right emotional note to touch. Then Carmen turned to me, and for the first time I saw the years in her face; when she was an old woman, she would look like Frank. Whatever else we are to one another, she and I are the female images of Frank Tonnino. 'Go pee,' she said, 'and let's get going. I'll explain everything on the way.'

Once in the car, though, she was silent. I was bleak with anxiety about my dad, that is, Frank, but I was still oddly reminded of the night I'd first met Ethan, driving him home from the Christmas party, that air of false enforced intimacy between strangers that had settled upon us, enforced because we were alone in the car, false, because we hardly knew each other, my sister or my mother or whoever the hell she was. Thirty years of falsehood.

'Do you need a coffee?' she said at last. 'You wanna stop?'

'No. I need the truth. You need to tell me the truth. At long fucking last.'

'I haven't got a lot of time, and I'm not going to make a lot of excuses. What I did, what we did, lots of people do. They don't talk about it. We didn't talk about it, but it's a lot more common than you think.'

'I thought you weren't going to make excuses.'

Carmen cleared her throat. She didn't speak right away. 'In high school, Tom Chase and I were like Romeo and Juliet. West Side Story, tragic lovers. Forbidden to see each other. Yes, I know your generation thinks all that is quaint, and who can tell you what to do, and all that, but it was a different day, Tosca. We met in band sophomore year. Tom had just moved here from Washington DC, and by senior year, he was so popular and smart, he was senior class president. And talented! He came to Garfield High for the music program there. Oh you should have heard him play the soprano sax.'

'Great,' I scoffed, pissed off that I, too, had played soprano sax. Just like Daddy.

'His parents had moved to Seattle because Tom's father got a job at UW, professor of international relations, or something. He had been a diplomat, hob-nobbed all over the world, something high up in the foreign service. Tom's mother, I don't remember what she did, some sort of artsy philanthropic thing with the symphony, a snob. They were both detestable snobs. One night, after Tom and I had been dating about a year – and we were serious, truly in love – they forbid him to see me. They said they'd checked out my family, that they'd actually gone to the pizzeria. Did Tom know we were shopkeepers? They told him all I wanted was to get knocked up, and hold onto him for life, to get out of the pizzeria, out of the house. The house! Our house was bigger and nicer than theirs any day! They lived over in Wallingford and we lived on Capitol Hill! Tom told his father he'd never give me up, and his father said, "We'll see about that." So Mr Chase, that bastard, he comes into Tonnino's one day, and asks for Dad. He told Dad they had forbidden their son to go out with me, and Dad had better keep his daughter away from their son. That their son was going to Yale, and would not be sticking around to marry a wop. You can imagine Dad's response to something like that.'

I could, and it wasn't pretty.

'Dad hit the roof, and I paid the price. Tom and I were forbidden to see each other by both sets of parents. So we met when and where and however we could. We'd say we were going out with others – all our friends were on our side, of course, we were teenagers – and we'd be together for as long as we could. Romeo and Juliet. And whenever we got caught, which we did, Dad would rail and wring his hands and splutter and yell, holler at me, how could I go out with a boy who despised me, and Mom would just call me a stupid Bimbette. They both kept beating me with the same old slipper, how I was the youngest Tonnino, I was the one who had the chance to make something of herself! Aida and Norma had got married, Aida knocked up, and Norma knocked up by that awful first husband of hers. Why couldn't I see that I should make something of myself? But all I wanted was Tom, and I told them so: I could not live without Tom. Mom and Dad could not understand how I could love a boy who would never respect me. I told them he did respect me, only his family didn't, and what did I care? "Oh, you'll care," they said. "His parents will make your life a flaming misery and there will come the day he will hate you. He will learn from them how to hate you."'

She drew a deep, indignant breath. 'Now I understand how right they were. Now, as a mother, it would break my heart to see Maddie crazy about some boy whose family had nothing but contempt for her.'

'We're not talking about your daughter, Maddie. We're talking about your daughter, *moi*.'

Carmen waited for the light to turn green before she went on. I could hear her gulp, but I had no mercy, and I did not speak or ease her tension.

'Someone saw us and word got back to my father. Caught again. Mom was stoic, furious but stoic. Dad was in a rage. I became like the princess in the tower. And like any princess, I escaped whenever I could, and I ran to Tom, and he was always waiting for me with his arms open.' She stifled tears. 'Now, I think, if they had just let us be, we might have outgrown one another. If his parents hadn't come to the pizzeria that day and told Dad, if—'

'I don't want if, Carmen. I want to know when and how.'

'Yes. Of course you do. Tom and I were crazy with love for each other, with longing, and for me, the more I was forbidden to be with him, the more nothing mattered but being with him. My grades were shit because all I could think about was Tom. His grades fell too, but his father was a Yale alum, and nothing was going to keep Tom Chase from New Haven. He was accepted early. We kept making all these plans that somehow we could be together – short, naturally, of my going to Yale,' she added with an acerbic tang. 'By September, he was in Yale, and I knew I was pregnant.'

'Just like his parents feared,' I offered unsympathetically.

'We had been sleeping together since January. Well, sleeping together suggests you had the whole night to roll around in a bed. We didn't. We had the backseat of his Chevy. It was all fast and furtive and fraught with emotion. Love, blind, wild, soul-searing passion.'

'Like opera. Or tango.' There was a time I'd loved Vince like that, and the pain he inflicted was commensurate with that love.

'I hope you never love anyone like that. It will kill you, unless you're very young, and then ...'

'I'm thirty.'

'So, you're already too old. Lucky you.'

'We're almost to the hospital.'

'When I realized I was pregnant, what was about to happen to my life, Tom was writing me passionate letters that he sent to my girlfriend's house. His letters were all about Yale, and how wonderful it was. I sobered up fast. I can tell you that. I knew no matter what, he was not coming back from New Haven to marry me, and I could imagine the look on his rotten mother's face when she found out that I actually was knocked up. His father!' Carmen took her hand off the wheel to wipe her nose. 'No more lovesick girl, Juliet to his Romeo, forget that. I was knocked up, alone, no money, no man and no options. Abortion was out of the question. It might have been legal in all fifty states, but I assure you, in the kingdom of Tonnino, it was out of the question, even if I'd had the money, which I didn't. My friends said they'd chip in money for an abortion, but I couldn't do it. Too Catholic. And my parents?' She drew a long breath. 'I had to tell them. It was the most painful hour of my life. I knew they'd wail and weep and accuse me of every stupidity and ingratitude they could think of – and they did – but finally they helped me. I knew they would. Except I could not bear the thought of giving the baby away to strangers. I still loved Tom and I could not bear to think of my child, our child, being raised by people who wouldn't know us, or who we were. I couldn't bear the thought of never seeing the baby again.'

'Me.'

'You.'

We went a few blocks in silence till University Hospital loomed in the distance.

'I dropped out of community college, and told everyone I had been accepted by the airlines, Pan Am, to be a flight attendant. I would travel the world! What a fucking joke. To travel the world. I said I was going to New York for training. I went back to Jersey and lived with Aunt Clara.'

'Oh God, even Aunt Clara knows?'

'You can imagine what those six months were like.'

I could, but I didn't want to offer her any sympathy. 'And Mom? I mean Nana, or Donna or whoever she is.

She went along with this … this … charade?'

'Mom never blinked. In a couple of months, every time she so much as went to the grocery store, or the pizzeria, or even the backyard to hang out the clothes, she stuffed a pillow under her dress. When she went to church, she'd say, "'Oh God, that Frank is a rascal, look what's he's put me through at my age!'"

In spite of myself, I laughed. We both did. 'Mom putting on an act like that!'

'She was great. And hey, she did the accounts at home, so who was to know the difference? Three weeks before you were due, she told everyone she had to go visit her poor sister Clara. Clara was sick.'

'Clara who has never had more than a head cold.'

'Yes. Mom just shrugged when people said, "oh Donna, you're too far along to travel." She said her own mother had made the Atlantic crossing in steerage when she was eight months pregnant with Clara, so shut up. She came back with this beautiful baby daughter, and they named you Tosca. For an opera. Like all their other daughters.'

'And you? What did you do?'

'I stayed in Jersey for another couple of months, then I came home. I told everyone I found out I had claustro-phobia and couldn't be a stewardess after all. I picked up my life, went back to community college, gradu-ated, went to beauty school, met Mike, married him, and became who I am, mother to Maddie and Sean and Tyler.'

'And me.'

'No. You were always my sister. I got used to it. The truth is, it didn't even bother me, really. I was too young to be a parent. I was happy to be your sister. To dote on you. The whole family doted on you. You were the best thing that ever happened to Mom and Dad. You kept them young. Dad would come home from the pizzeria between the lunch and dinner rush just to spend time with you. He would wake you up, even if you were asleep so he could play with you. He used to do his magic trick, and pull a pepperoni out of your ear and make you laugh and laugh.'

'I remember,' I said, glum at the thought of all that happiness.

'Even Clara, she sold the Jersey place and moved out here with Mom and Dad because she doted on you, couldn't stand being apart from you.'

'Aunt Clara doted on me? She's always telling me everything that's wrong with me.'

'Oh, she's like that with everyone. But when you were a baby, a little girl, she was crazy for you. Little bows on your shoes and ironing all those frilly dresses. If you want to know the truth, I have a suspicion – only that – that the reason this solution came so easily to Clara and Mom is that they might have done it before.'

'Clara and Mom? You think Mom is Clara's daughter! You think Aunt Clara is really our grandmother! Your grandmother.'

'They're sixteen or seventeen years apart. But I'm just guessing. Don't you dare say anything to Mom or Aunt Clara. If you're going to be spilling beans around here, make sure they're your own and not someone else's.' Carmen drove around the University Hospital parking lot till she found a place. She turned off the car. It was full dark now, sunset a mere stain across the sky.

'And Tom?' I asked. 'Did you ever tell Tom?'

Carmen pulled the key out and the inside light came on, illuminating us. 'I did. Aunt Clara had no idea how crafty a girl in love could be. Remember, I had years of experience lying to my parents, so it was easy to think of a lie that would do for Aunt Clara. She never had any children.'

'As far as we know.'

'I took the train up to New Haven. Tom said he'd meet me at the station. When I got off the train he wasn't there.'

'He didn't show?'

'He was late. I waited on a bench. When he walked through the waiting room doors, I stood up. He took one look at me. It was obvious by then. His face fell and I knew in that instant that Mom was right. There *would* come the day he'd hate me. That day had come. I was living it. Oh, he put his arms around me, kissed me, but ...' Carmen closed her eyes, and waited a while, and I could see tears eke out. I dug in my purse and found a napkin from Jumpin Java and handed it to her. 'Tom and I went into the station coffee shop, and had a cup of coffee and a sandwich. He said if he'd known he would have paid for an abortion. I said to him, you really don't know the first thing about me, do you? And then I realized he was just like his parents, an expedient snob who might charm the socks off a world of diplomats, but inside he was just as hollow and empty as they were. I took the next train back to Jersey. He returned to Yale and I never saw him or heard from him again until that Saturday in Friday Harbor.'

'You told him he was a father and he never saw you again?'

'What does it matter what he did or said or didn't do or say? My parents knew he would despise me, and he did. I grew up fast after that, but at least I didn't have to grow up fast and try to be someone's mother. I couldn't have done it. You owe everything to Mom and Dad.'

'So do you.'

'They saved my reputation at the time. Thirty years ago. Who gives a shit now?'

'Tom came by the bookstore a couple of days after… He said he wanted a present for his daughter.'

'And?'

'He bought some books and I was snotty to him.'

'Good.'

'Does Mike know?'

'Sure. Of course. He's my husband. I told him before we got married. But you, you'd better think long and hard before you start inflicting misery and blame on people who don't deserve it. I'm not speaking of myself. For myself, I don't care. I don't even care if you tell Maddie and the boys. I got over it a long time ago. I am who I am. What are you going to do?'

'I don't know,' I said honestly. 'But don't you want me to forgive you? Don't you want to apologize?'

'Why would I apologize?' She looked at me like I'd just asked for pineapple pizza. 'Pull up your big girl panties, Tosca! You didn't go to strangers. You aren't a grown up adoptee, gnawing your knuckles and wondering who the hell you are, wondering why your people gave you away. You know who you are. You're a Tonnino. Only you have one brown eye and one green eye. Now let's get in there. Mom needs us.'

There in the ER waiting room, Aida, Norma, their husbands, and Mike and some of the older kids including Charlie and his wife were all clustered together around Mom, who was dry-eyed. But when she saw me and Carmen, she stood, walked to us, put one arm around each of us, wept and called us her babies, her youngest daughters. And we are, I thought to myself, holding her, holding Carmen. What does it matter if

212

these people are my sisters or my aunts, my nephews and nieces or cousins? We're here because we're all Tonninos and we care about my dad. Frank. I am lucky to have these people. Lucky I didn't get adopted. Lucky they had the foresight and ability to put together a little ruse to save face for Carmen and save family for me, and if everyone knew it for thirty years, clearly no one cared. And then, Reader, I confess, I started to cry, not just a little sniffle, no, a full-fest crying jag, and everyone put their arms around me, telling me my dad would be fine, everything would be fine, it was my birthday, after all.

Chapter Seventeen

O<small>N THE FERRY</small> home, while it wasn't exactly Pathetic Fallacy, Nature reflecting emotions – still, the timing was remarkable. I was feeling buoyed and warm and loved and happy, and behold, I saw my first ferry wedding! I'd heard how sometimes people who couldn't afford a big wedding venue got all their friends on the ferry and had two hours, start to finish, to accomplish the whole thing, clean up and get back in their cars. This was a young couple, really young, looked to be not much more than teenagers, and all their friends were young. The bride, Cassie, put her dress on in the bathroom with help from a couple of girlfriends. Cody (the groom) and the rest of their friends hustled around, claiming a bunch of tables down the center of the top observation deck. Two people brought the cake up. Others, not just their friends, but people like me, people who didn't even know them, but wished them well, we all got out the paper plates and plastic silverware, paper cups and jugs of punch, helped to put the celebration together.

A guitarist and an accordionist readied their instruments, and at a signal from a bridesmaid, they started to play. The bride emerged from the bathroom to meet the groom. Cody's hair was tied back in a ponytail, and he was wearing a suit and sandals. Cassie walked toward him on the arm of another young man. Not her father. No one's parents were there, that much was clear. That young man too wore a suit and sandals and he walked her up to meet Cody and the minister, who also wore a suit and sandals. While there were only about ten of their actual friends there, Cassie and Cody had a huge wedding, everyone on the ferry happily in attendance. When the minister said 'Dearly Beloved,' we all got out our hankies. We were part of this memorable occasion, and suddenly, not strangers at all. Everyone cheered and applauded when they said 'I do,' and Cody kissed the bride. Everyone got a piece of wedding cake (they had enough wedding cake for the whole ferry) and cup of punch. Everyone pitched in for the cleanup. Everyone was happy. Cassie and Cody were having a camping honeymoon at San Juan County Campground, a small, intimate campground with a view of the water, and often the whales. Everyone wished Cassie and Cody the best, good luck, much love and happiness, (and they were so young, you just knew they needed every bit of luck they could hold on to) and everyone left that ferry feeling like a million bucks, like we'd all just participated in True Love.

The hospital kept Dad longer than overnight, and sent him home with a couple of new prescriptions and strict instructions to work less, to reduce his stress level, to get more exercise, lose twenty pounds, lay off the pizza, get some rest. The usual remedies for overweight older people who work too hard and take things too much to heart. Dad made light of it. A lot of fuss for nothing. No big deal. A little dizziness, that's all.

My very next day off from the store, I went home again just to be sure he was all right, a flying visit, overnight. Dad told me he was fine. Don't make a fuss. Don't come back to Seattle till the Fourth of July. He said that knowing full well no one in retail in a tourist town gets the Fourth of July off. On the return sailing that weekend, I had another unique ferry experience, equally weird as Cassie and Cody's wedding, but not nearly so pleasant. Quite the contrary.

I was slumped in a seat by the windows, with a book in my lap, watching the gulls and nibbling from a bag of Cheetos, when I looked up, and saw someone familiar reading a book. This is a common occurrence when you've lived on an island. You really do know everyone – even if you don't. I wiped the yellow stuff off my hands, and strolled over, peering at this guy. I couldn't place the face. He was too slick and handsome to be from San Juan Island. I mean, a guy that good-looking, you'd remember. The Harry Potter spectacles, the tousled hair, the voluptuous mouth with its little twist of cruelty. I sat down across from him. 'You're Win Jefferies, aren't you?'

He gave me a grin with his blindingly white teeth, while he also gave me the once-over, that swift, apprais-ing glance. Men are so transparent. He was tanned and fit, and had salon-streaked hair, like Ethan had when he first moved here.

'What are you reading?' I craned my neck to see the title. It was literally in a plain brown wrapper.

'An advance reading copy. I'm reviewing a new book for the *New York Times*.'

'Is it any good?'

'Brilliant.'

'When is the movie of your book coming out?'

'Don't know. We're still in pre-production.'

'Do you have another book about to be published?'

'I'm a professional writer. That's what I do.'

'I'm a professional reader. I'm with Carter & Co. Books. I'm Tosca. Tosca Tonnino.'

He had heard of me. I could see it in his expression, which he quickly mastered and returned to the ironic smile that was clearly his default. 'Ethan's mentioned you.'

'Did he say I was a great lay?'

'He did, actually.'

'Ethan was only mediocre.'

'Yeah well, that's Ethan for you. I'm a lot better.'

'Let me just cut to the chase here.'

'You wanna hook up?'

'Dude, you seriously overestimate your appeal.'

'You don't know that for sure.'

I rewarded his arrogance with a sour little smile. 'It's the competition, isn't it? One of you always has to win.'

'Usually me.'

'Yes, I know. Win. That's your name. But if someone always has to win, then someone else has to lose.'

'Winners and losers. That's life.'

'That's what Barry said.'

He chuckled. 'I talked to Barry after you threw wine all over him, and water all over Ethan. He said you were pretty amazing, that he'd never met such a hot-tempered bitch.'

'Barry was feeling me up.'

'Ethan wasn't?'

'He and Barry were drunk as skunks.'

'Excess runs in the family. Competition.'

I wanted to shrivel his balls with one well-placed verbal squeeze, but I'm not that clever. So I said, 'If it's competition you want, then pick on someone your own size. The next Hemingway. The one after you. Or maybe the one before you. Lucy Lamont is not your competition. She's not cool. She's not worth the effort it will take for you to make her look bad.'

'I don't care what she looks like. I'm coming up to give a reading. I mean – my best friend works in a bookstore. I'm an author. Why not?' His big bright teeth gleamed at me.

'Was this Barry's idea? So Ethan will fail?'

'You think Ethan's a loser?'

'I don't think anything about him. I don't care anything about him. But I have to wonder why you'd come up here.'

'Vacation. Time away from the Hollywood rat-race, you know?'

His cell phone rang, and he answered it, chatting in an animated fashion. The galley slipped from his lap, and the plain brown paper fell away. Only it wasn't an advanced reading copy of anything. It was a paperback book. Wisteria framed the title. Lucy Lamont. I felt a cold hand clutch my heart, a spasm of fear, probably something like Frank felt when he fell over with his mini-stroke. I couldn't move.

Win ended his call, put the phone away. Then he opened his briefcase and tucked the Lucy Lamont novel in there with two others. He ran his hand over the glossy wisteria, embossed on the cover. 'Don't you think this is a kind of pornography? I mean really, like porno with powdered sugar. It's sex, but it has to be all rummied up with whipped cream, as in whipped-cream-your-jeans. It's so smothered in sweetness that it's obscene. The organist's orgasm while she feels those big pipes rumble up her butt? The stirring Dennis feels while walking among the swelling rosebuds? Getting some in the gazebo? These characters use chintz slip-covers for condoms.'

'It's not what you'd write or read, but some people like it. There's room for all sorts of readers in this world.'

'You read my book?'

'Of course. I'm Events and Publicity. I read all the authors who come here.'

'So what did you think?'

'Lucy's stuff is no worse than the drug-and-fuck-fest you wrote.'

Fleeting shock rattled his handsome features, then he scoffed. 'My work is clean. My book is brave about facing ugliness.'

'The dark underbelly?'

'Yeah, exactly. Lucy's writing takes simple human impulses and makes bon bons out of them. Then they eat each other up.'

'Hers is pretty disgusting, but so is yours.'

He smiled, pleased.

'I don't mean disgusting like that,' I said cooly. 'Your work isn't that different from Lucy Lamont's. *The Body Electric* is really only a Shannonville novel stood on its head. There are no surprises in either. In a Shannonville novel all emotions are tidy and lead to happiness. In *The Body Electric* all emotions are ugly and lead to despair. Lucy Lamont's characters have unions but no sex, and your characters have orgiastic, polyglot sex, but no one creates any unions.'

'Orgiastic and polyglot! Wow! What a vocabulary, Tosca!'

Now he's pissed me off. 'You – the author, you – killed off Roger because he'd served his narrative purpose, and you didn't know what else to do with him.

219

And his death didn't even matter. Not to anyone. Roger followed the Unnamed Narrator into oblivion, but what else could he do? I saw his suicide coming from page ten. Ethan James isn't Roger. He won't kill himself to get out of your way, but I feel sorry for him. He actually admires you, and look what you did to him. What you're doing.'

'It's a novel. Not a memoir. I can't stand literal people. What happened to irony?'

'It died. Stung to death by gnats.' It was, without doubt, one of my best Ginger Rogers performances ever. I gave him a shrug and walked away, though it was a wholly pyrrhic gesture. Nothing was going to change. Like in the old poem, mine was not to reason why, mine was but to do or die.

I stayed at the front of the vessel for the rest of the run. I threw the last of the golden Cheetos into air as gulls swooped and squawked, and dove and scavenged. Usually I prefer the back, with its frothy wake. But not this time. I knew what was behind me, but I could not begin to guess what lay ahead

Chapter Eighteen

JUNE 12TH WAS a high, fine, breezy day; cloudless, and sunny. The geranium baskets swayed gently from lampposts; the water in the harbor twinkled and winked in the sunshine, boats bobbed in the marina, the great ferries plied the Sound, disgorging at the Friday Harbor dock what looked to be record numbers of walk-ons, people eager, chatting, high-fiving one another, and clearly in fine communal fettle.

All along Spring Street and beyond, bunting billowed from shop fronts. In honor of this day Charlotte had concocted a special Shannonville Truffle, chocolate with lavender flavor and lavender color once you bit into it. I know this because she brought over a whole box, just for me. I asked if she were going to do a nice blood-red cocaine-flavored one for Win Jefferies's book. Charlotte just laughed, but she had in fact concocted an Electric Truffle, and I heard through the retail grapevine that she gave a whole box of those to Ethan, and a box of each to Edith Carter. Oh yes, we were awash in commercial kindness and fellow-feeling on 12 June. Everyone just thought this was the best day Friday Harbor had enjoyed since the Pig War ended in 1872.

By ten o'clock the line for a latte and a muffin at

Jumpin Java was around the block. Every eatery and donut place was jumping. Strawberry Fields Forever, Lavendaria, every art gallery, pottery place and tee shirt shop had sidewalk displays. You couldn't park in Friday Harbor for love or money, and by eleven, I noticed that some enterprising high school students were cruising the roads and picking up fares, literally, using their parents' cars as taxis, to take people who had to park far away to the Community Center. People milled in front of the center, eating ice cream, fanning themselves with the leaflets that enterprising businesses were handing out, chatting to one another till the doors would open at one. The event would start at two.

Unlike every other shop in Friday Harbor, Carter & Co. Books was closed for the day, all our resources concentrated on the Community Center. I was the general overseer, having dealt already with the nuts-and-bolts: hiring high school kids to hoist book cartons and open them, renting extra computers and cash machines, arranging for 400 chairs in a community center designed to hold maybe 250. (Lying to the fire department about the numbers, that too was my responsibility.) In the Community Center foyer, Wendell and Sally and Jessie (her last day here) set up the cash registers, and had the high school kids lining up cartons of Shannonville novels and cartons of *The Body Electric* to sell. There were also high school kids instructed to stamp the Carter & Co. logo on the inside cover of each book bought. The foyer was dominated by two big easels with pictures of each author, Lucy's captioned: *Smithson/Empire Proudly Presents the Bestselling Lucy Lamont, author of the* Shannonville *novels.* For Win's: *Smithson/Empire proudly presents the Critically Acclaimed Bestselling Win Jefferies, author of* The Body Electric. A hastily added sticker, *Soon to be a Major Motion Picture*, was slapped along one side.

I kept thinking of Gabriel Garcia Márquez's *One Hundred Years of Solitude* and the character who is standing, facing the firing squad, and remembering the ice before the volley sounds. I awaited only the arrival of the soldiers, the rifle, the blindfold, which naturally, brave as I am, I would refuse. Or maybe not. Anyway, I was resigned to my fate, and to my responsibilities which were simple: Lucy Lamont.

My attempts to set up cell phone contact, to be able to text or email, to have some sort of frigging plan where/when we'd meet beforehand, all of that had come to naught. Lucy was elusive and uncooperative. She responded to nothing. I was on my own. So be it, I told myself with the stoicism of the condemned as I carried a big RESERVED sign on a sawhorse to the Community Center parking lot. I set it up in the parking place nearest the door, just as I'd promised. Lucy's own parking place. I waited there for her.

Leona Cox's daughter, Jennifer, came out and said Wendell wanted me inside, wanted my approval.

'Really?' I said. 'He didn't ask for my approval weeks ago.' The back door was locked, so we walked round to the front.

'I borrowed someone else's copy to finish *The Body Electric*,' said young Miss Cox confidentially. 'Don't tell my mom.'

'I promise.'

'I thought it a was really cool book. Like everyone says. Awesome.' Her voice betrayed misgivings.

'But?'

Jennifer Cox made a face. 'All those needles, and the people just freaking the fuck out? I mean,' she shivered, 'who'd want to live like that?'

'The Unnamed Narrator wants to live like that. Feeling nothing. Ever.' As we came to the front, I was shocked to see the huge crowds milling before the Community Center doors. Jennifer showed me a side door and we scooted into the foyer.

'Where's Wendell?' I asked Sally.

She pointed me through the double doors and into the auditorium where 400 chairs, neat as church pews, were set up to face a dais. On the dais, there were five chairs for Miss Carter, Ethan, Win and Lucy Lamont, and me. The lectern was in front, and beside it there was a small table with bottled water, and a vase with a bouquet of miniature roses. I made sure that the steps up to the dais were in place, and a rail for Miss Carter, that the light worked on the lectern.

'Testing, testing,' I said into the mike. Only my own voice came back to me.

'Who is doing the sound?' I asked one of the kids. He didn't know, and I sent him to find out.

'What do you think, Tosca?' asked Wendell. 'Is everything all right?'

'No, Wendell, everything is not all right. I've already told you that.'

'I mean here.'

'I mean here too.'

He ignored all that, and asked if we should open early. He was flushed and the hair swept over his pate gleamed with moisture. 'There's quite the crowd out there already.'

'We said the doors would open at one.'

'But have you seen them? They may be blocking traffic.'

'Let 'em wait. Not our problem.'

'It's coming on noon. I don't see why we can't open early.'

'Because they'll all be picnicking in here, Wendell, and the city will charge us overtime for the clean-up. I am a veteran of the popcorn wars. Trust me on this.'

'What about blocking traffic? The city won't care for that either.'

'All right, open at quarter to.' I conferred with the sound guy who had righted the problem, and went back out to the foyer to be certain there were plenty of pens at the signing tables.

'So, Tosca,' said Jessie, clearly worried. 'What would Ginger Rogers do?'

'Ginger Rogers would have never got herself into such mess.'

Jessie gave me a hug. 'Just stay true to your Inner Connections. You'll be fine.'

My cell phone rang, and I answered, hoping it was Lucy Lamont telling me where to meet her, but no, it was Edith Carter calling from The Spinnaker, and saying what a lovely lunch she was having with Ethan, Win, Barry and the lovely Ava.

'Yes, more champagne,' Miss Carter said to a waiter invisible to me, then after a trilling laugh, she returned to the phone. 'What time should we be at the Community Center, Tosca? Well?'

'Be here by one,' I said and hung up. Barry and Ava too. Now the madness is complete.

I went back outside to the parking lot to wait for Lucy in her reserved parking place. But when I got there, I saw that the sawhorse had been moved, the RESERVED sign tossed in the bushes, and the spot had been taken by a Toyota with California plates. I swore inwardly. What to do now? The parking lot was completely full. I walked out front; the crowds had grown to hordes. They were blocking traffic. You could see at a glance these were two groups of mutually exclusive readers. Sorry, Miss Carter, but it isn't rocket science. The Shannonville readers were dressed for a garden party, pastel pantsuits, crisp blouses, silk scarves. Their smiling, paunchy husbands wore golf shirts that had been ironed. Their ages ranged from youngish matrons (that is, women who were matrons even at a young age) to grandmotherly sorts, and a good many well-preserved Old Girls, dyed hair, painted nails, face powder clumping in the heat. *The Body Electric* crowd was more eclectic, some slick Abercrombie and Fitch types, but mostly jeans, tank tops, sandals, with a lot of tattoos and pierced eyebrows for distraction. There were some ponytailed graybeards and their skinny women as well, middle-aged hipsters. But mostly, Win Jefferies's admirers looked to me to be a fairly youthful crowd who were here to be entertained. Like a rock concert or something. They were boisterous, high-fiving each other. *The Body Electric* fans condescended to the Shannonville readers, who returned their gazes with barely concealed indignation. Astonishingly – given that Lucy had seventeen novels and Win had one – it looked to me that *The Body Electric* partisans at least equaled the number of Shannonville ladies and their husbands. It was past noon.

I caught a glimpse of a stone-faced Frances McTeer among the throng, and ducked out quickly before she could see me. I returned to the parking lot where I placed the sawhorse behind the offending Toyota so Lucy would know that I meant well. I paced. I checked my phone: ten minutes till the doors opened. I could feel my hair going white, my ovaries drying up, my arteries hardening, my skin puckering. My mouth was parched and my palms were wet. I sat on the sawhorse, sweated, and awaited the firing squad. I saw a red Cadillac SUV with tinted windows pull through the lot. The window rolled down. 'I told them to save me a goddamned parking place! There's nothing here, Ed. Let's go.' She rolled up the window.

I jumped up and ran after the SUV, waving my arms, calling out, 'Miss Lamont! Miss Lamont!' Ed must have seen me in the rear view mirror. He slowed and stopped. The passenger door opened, and out stepped Lucy Lamont, all coiffed and Botoxed, crushed silk pantsuit, high heels. An amethyst solitaire set about with diamonds flashed as she held the door open, bent and spoke to Ed. 'You go park, Ed. I'll meet you back here. Don't get lost. You're such a klutz sometimes.'

'Miss Lamont!' I cried out, bounding up. 'I reserved your spot, but someone took it!'

She was about to chastise me, but swiftly, she took in the front of the Community Center where the crowds were filing in. Her face smoothed out, and a smile arranged itself across her features, cool as a doily on a porcelain toilet tank.

'Why, Edith. How good to see you again. Look at all these people! This is quite the turnout you've arranged for me.' She held out both of her bejeweled hands to me. 'This is a wonderful reception, Edith, and you're looking so well.'

Of course Lucy Lamont expected to be greeted by Edith Carter herself. I didn't disillusion her. Disillusion enough lay ahead. Worse. An epic disaster about to be conveyed to the whole world via viral Twitter and Tumblr, and Facebook and Instagram, by Google, and YouTube, and Salon, that whole vast, un-moored ether known as the blogosphere, all of which provided links to the catastrophe. Just about everybody here would take pictures and video with their cell phones, and spray them across the universe.

I quickly took Lucy's arm, escorted her back to the parking lot and through that side door. I was hoping I could ease her through the foyer quickly, but our progress was impeded by a number of her fans coming up, exuding enthusiasm which Lucy returned with practiced charm. She was gracious to pose for selfies with them, smiling, even exchanging bits of Shannonville gossip ('Now, if I told you what happened to Margaret, you wouldn't read the next book, would you?') walking with them amiably until, beyond her admirers, she saw the huge poster for Win Jefferies' book beside the poster for Shannonville.

And then – Lucy Lamont was no dummy, after all – she figured out that she had been misinformed, misled, probably outright lied to. She went gray beneath her makeup. Momentary confusion rattled her forehead as though she were trying very hard to frown, but the Botox wouldn't let her. Her jaw clanked into place like the visor on the Man in the Iron Mask. She looked around wildly, for Ed no doubt, but there was no one but me. I remembered what Dawn Philbrick said about Lucy in a rage, about Hurricane Katrina, and New Orleans. Collagen seemed to drip from the corners of her lips and her blue-tinted eyes got hugely black. She was about to erupt. I took her hand and pulled her out of the foyer, quickly through the Community Center and into a narrow, small hall that opened on to the parking lot.

There, Gentle Reader, I more or less flung myself on her mercy, braying apologies, swearing I had nothing to do with it, nothing, nothing at all, blaming Ethan, blaming Win, blaming Sylvia Beach, Hemingway and James Joyce, Charles Dickens and Balzac. I was reduced to a puddle, blathering and blabbering and blaming the weather because it was so sunny and so many people turned out.

Her pupils were seething pools of rage. 'You will regret this, Edith. I promise you.'

'I already do, Lucy. I regret it terribly.' I begged her to look on the bright side, on her many fans, her slavish admirers, her devoted readers who had all come here to see her today. 'Don't disappoint your readers, Lucy. You never have before.'

'Shut up. Let's get this over with.'

Just then the side door opened and in from the parking lot came Miss Carter, flanked by two young handsome men, Ethan and Win. I could smell a faint spray of champagne on the three of them. Clearly, they had come from a lively lunch, jolly and pleased with themselves. Win was radiant, his eyes unnaturally brilliant, Ethan's too, though he looked pale and miserable. Right behind them came a leggy, gorgeous blonde; Ava stood up very straight so her boobs would not fall off. Barry followed her in, and on seeing me, his lip twisted. Their eyes too were unnaturally bright.

'Lucy Lamont!' Miss Carter cried, stepping forward to hug Lucy, or trying to. Lucy remained stiff, unmoving, unmoved. 'What an absolute pleasure to meet you at last! And what an honor to welcome you to San Juan Island. This,' she gestured to her left, clueless as a cabbage, 'is Ethan James, and of course you know the brilliant young novelist, Win Jefferies? Or you know his work. Everyone knows his work. The Hemingway of the twenty-first century.'

Lucy responded with arctic disdain, though she did not actually reply. Miss Carter rattled on, delighted, thinking herself at this moment the epicenter of the literary world, waving gaily, posing for the photographer from the *Island Times* weekly, who had found us there in the otherwise empty hall. She linked arms with Win and Lucy, and smiled for posterity. She would live to regret this picture. On Facebook and Twitter, *#literarycatastrophe*, it would be fucking immortal.

After the photo, Win turned to Lucy, and in a deep, fake, buttery accent, declared, 'Miss Lamont, you write the sweetest little books I know. Yes, indeedy, Miss Lamont, why that last little number ... now what was its name?' Win tapped his fashionably-stubbled chin. 'Oh, yes, Little Margaret's Seaside Fuck. Or was that the one before? No, no, surely that was cream on the bun. Or is that brown lips that pucker become every fucker?' Ethan laughed. Barry guffawed. Ava laughed so hard, you could hear her breast implants slosh. 'Chapter Two. Isn't that called *How to Lick It and Stick it*? Bottoms up! Yoo hoo!'

Win actually unzipped his fly, then zipped it up again, so quickly you almost didn't know he'd done it. Shock radiated out cosmically, and I swear I felt tectonic plates collide beneath my feet. Lucy Lamont froze motionless. Miss Carter hushed Win as though he were an errant toddler.

Win ignored Edith. 'The pederast on a pedestal. Oh yeah, bro! Sodomized in Shannonville! Orgasm from an organ pipe! Cool!'

Against this gross mockery, Lucy Lamont had no resources. Despite her arrogance, her tough audacity, she stood there like a hapless mouse, pinioned to the wicker while the cat chewed off her head. Blood in the gazebo.

Laughing, arm in arm, Win and Ethan moved away, through the doors and into the main hall where they were swallowed up in a pool of eager well-wishers, a couple of hundred fans with cell phones eager to take Win's picture. I could hear them calling out, and saw their cell phones aloft, waving, *Hey, Win! Hey, over here, Win!* Barry and Ava followed.

That left me with Lucy and Miss Carter, the former rooted, trembling visibly. Miss Carter had gone green, and her mouth dropped open, her jaw slack, as if she'd suffered a stroke. Tough shit, Edith, I thought to myself, you brought it on yourself. My responsibility was to Lucy Lamont.

I took Lucy's arm, clutching her silk jacket and propelled her up toward the dais at the front. Her readers applauded. Some even stood. But Lucy seemed scarcely aware. I sat her down in one of the chairs behind the podium. I turned on the mike which shrieked, and though it was only one thirty, I asked people to take their places so we could begin. *Yes,* I thought, *begin and end, and get it fucking over with.* I started speaking even as people flailed their way to their chairs. Ethan and Win took their places on the dais behind me. As I spoke, from the corner of my eye, I saw Edith Carter, frail, puzzled, pale, and alone, making her way toward the dais, tapping with her cane. The white-wine glow of lunch had vanished. She plopped down in her metal folding chair like a load of laundry, all rumpled and heaped

I introduced Lucy Lamont at fulsome length, '... who needs no introduction to her vast legions of readers, who has created ...' My gaze went over the crowd. Nearly every one of the four hundred seats was taken. I saw Nan, her brow creased with alarm. I waxed eloquent on behalf of the pleasures of a Shannonville novel, the gift of Lucy Lamont to her readers, blah blah blah. The room quickly quieted, voices lowered, chairs quit creaking, coughing and feet shuffling hushed, and only then I said into the microphone, my voice echoing, 'Please welcome Lucy Lamont to Friday Harbor.'

Lucy Lamont's extraordinary powers of marketing, timing, and delivery did not fail her this day. She wasn't the altogether commanding woman I'd seen in Portland in March, but after the applause diminished, she began by thanking her fans for their loyalty to the characters peopling her eighteen novels. She began her talk – much the same as she had given in Portland, about how she had entered Shannonville through, as it were, the garden path – and earned smiles from her many readers. Her remarks were punctuated with affectionate applause.

Behind her on the dais, Win and Ethan smirked and made faces, shifted their weight uneasily in the folding chairs; they twitched and whispered. Lucy could not see them, but I could. And so could the audience. I debated going over there and smacking them both, like you would a dog, like Buster and the slipper, but it was too late for any such theatrics.

Lucy moved seamlessly forward. Delivering this oft-repeated address seemed to soothe her; she stood taller, gained confidence, and I began to think perhaps all would be well. Perhaps Lucy would save the day. She talked and talked, twenty minutes, sailing through the time allotted to her. They each had half an hour. She went on, smiling, well beyond that, forty minutes, forty-five. As she had in Portland, she swam out into that broad delta of time that belonged to someone else. Time that belonged to Win Jefferies.

Lucy did not stop, not so much as to take a breath, or insert a comma, either utterly unaware or absolutely uncaring that a restless undercurrent of audible scorn began to snake around the room. She went on and on, the same refrains that had made Shannonville a household word, that had brought her millions in merch, in fridge magnets, and stationery, and calendars, just as she had in Portland, her voice intimating, if not quite saying *Screw this kid and his filthy first novel. You love me. You're here to see me. You believe in Shannonville where there are no drugs, and where all the mothers are wise, and all the fathers are just, and there is no buyer's remorse, and sex always means romance, not vulgar hook-ups, but long, loving unions, and no one talks dirty.... Canker-less roses. Ever-purple wisteria. Love requited. Goodness rewarded. Unions that prospered. No flies. No rats. No cockroaches....* She absolved her audience of nostalgia, assuring them that in her world, their world, all was well.

'Aw, put a sock in it,' someone cried out from deep in the crowd.

On stage, Win and Ethan laughed through their noses. The audience tittered.

'We want Win!' came a voice from the back.

Others picked up the chant. 'We want Win! Give us *The Body Electric!*'

Lucy kept on talking, her voice smooth, emollient, unimpaired, as though she were a recording. She never acknowledged these hecklers, but a few Shannonville ladies turned in their chairs, saying hush and shame on these young people, and accusing their mothers of teaching them no manners.

'Aw, leave my mother out of it,' cried a girl's voice.

'We want Win! Give us *The Body Electric*!'

Lucy's readers made indignant harumphing sounds on her behalf. They looked to Lucy for guidance, but she kept on. Oblivious. Absolutely oblivious, smiling, and still talking about the pleasures of Shannonville.

Win's readers set up a sort of low chant, '*Body! Electric! Body! Elec-tric*!' The chant grew louder, and the floor started to rumble with their pounding feet.

I looked over to Win and Ethan. Win was cracking up. Ethan too. Ethan James had gone – spiritually, mentally, spatially – somewhere so very funny no one but Win Jefferies could follow him. Beside me on the dais, Edith Carter went rigid. She could see what she'd unleashed, what she'd agreed to. She saw what a damned fool she was. She gave me a hard, narrow-eyed, pinch-lipped look. She actually wagged her finger at me.

'Sorry, Edith,' I said, 'this isn't my fault, and you damn well know it.'

Shouting matches had broken out in the audience, the Old Girls holding their own against the insults, while Lucy, her lips still flapping, her eyes gone blank, as if they'd rolled up into her head, just raised her volume up a notch each time someone called out, 'Shannonville sucks!' Or worse. I was looking madly round the hall for Ed, though I could hardly remember what he looked like. Why didn't he come up and rescue Lucy?

A young man yelled out, 'Shut the fuck up, Lucy!' Behind him, a white-haired lady stood up and used her handbag to thwack him, again and again. Down he went. People all around laid hands on the old lady, and then her cohorts and their husbands jumped into the melee. The bodies electric were out of their chairs, not about to take this sitting down. Mayhem erupted. Metal folding chairs were falling right and left, banging noisily against one another. Voices, shouts escalated, curses, a few shrieks and screams. Cell phones snapped pictures and videos that would be all over YouTube by nightfall, Twittered and Tumblred and Facebooked around the world in an instant.

I jumped out of my seat, and dashed over to Lucy Lamont, took her arm. She shook me off, clutched the lectern, and kept talking. I pulled at her, but she wouldn't let go, her voice rising to a scream.

'Lucy,' I said, speaking low and right up against the pink shell of her ear, 'there are more adoring fans. They're waiting at the bookstore for you. They can't wait to see you. They want to ask about the garden tools....' Talking all the time, sweetly, softly, even as the chaos around us heightened, and First Amendment rights were being practiced with furled fists and slashing handbags, and people shoving and kicking, I pried Lucy from the lectern, took her arm firmly, and led her swiftly out the side door, and down the street, still talking.

If she faltered, I asked a question, enough to send her off again, nattering with that same gaiety, as though an audience lay at her feet. I sure as hell didn't walk along Spring Street; I took the alley to the loading dock, and pulled her up the stairs. I opened the back, the storeroom door at Carter & Co. and ushered her in, shuffling her toward my office. The place was empty, only the silent books, and the slowly approaching, pitiful mew of Mr Hyde.

Chapter Nineteen

I DRAGGED A Masterpiece Theatre wing chair from the storeroom into my tiny office, wedged it between my desk and the Electrolux and told her to sit down. Leaving her there with a book cartoon for a footstool, I pawed through the office fridge till I found a Coke which I offered to her. She waved it away.

'Perrier, please.'

'Sure, Lucy.'

I got some tap water from the bathroom and gave it to her in a rinsed out glass. She drank it one gulp and then released the glass, not dropped, not spilled, just released. It rolled to the wooden floor where Mr Hyde toyed with it. When the glass stopped rolling, Mr Hyde jumped in her lap. Trembling, teeth chattering despite the June heat, Lucy scratched his ears, and crooned kitty talk at him for ten minutes. Then she started to weep. Mr Hyde jumped down and wandered away. Her hands over her face, Lucy cried her eyes out, heaving sobs. Heartbreaking, genuine emotion. Nothing coiffed or Botoxed or falsified. I looked for a box of tissues, but could only find a roll of toilet paper. I knelt by the wing chair, patted her hand, and gave her a wad of T.P. She blew her nose and snuffled gently, hiccoughed another burst of tears. I let her cry. Sometimes you just need to cry.

I turned on my computer and sat there staring at its placid, unchanging face, the Carter & Co. logo. I knew what I had to do. And I knew that once I started, I would not stop, nor should I. Everything was clear to me. My eyes misted up. In five years I had settled – not as in settled down—but settled for, compromised. I had lived with pre-printed wallpaper when I might have had a life splashed with color. As a reader I had relinquished passion for prim professionalism. As a woman, I had allowed a string of flingettes to satisfy my heart and define my self-regard. I had believed myself wonderfully erotically independent, instead of merely alone and without genuine connection. Genuine connection *is* messy, just like Carmen's splashing my hand down into that raw pizza dough that day. Deep, abiding connections are difficult, demanding, and yes, sometimes painful, like listening to Astor Piazzolla instead of Beyoncé. I started to cry while I hit *delete delete delete.* Everything personal and professional in my computer. *Delete delete delete.* I sent all my email contacts and addresses to my home computer, and then deleted them.

Finally I mopped my face with my palms, smearing mascara everywhere. I was suddenly famished. 'You want some popcorn, Lucy?'

She sniffed, mopped her eyes, smearing her mascara. A false eyelash hung off. She nodded.

'I'll be right back.' I popped a whole big bowlful and brought it to my office.

I put the bowl in her lap. Lucy ate in a haphazard fashion, bits of popcorn dribbling down her silken blouse. The smell wafted around us, and I chortled out a bitter laugh.

'Ah, entertainment,' I said, shoveling another handful into my mouth. And then, I started to cry, to weep in earnest. 'How did this happen? Do you think it was Vince?'

'Who's Vince?' She seemed genuinely interested.

'My old boyfriend. The one who left me stranded here, motored his little sailboat off into the sunset with that slut aboard, and left me at the dock at the marina with my heart broken and my stuff in garbage bags around my feet. Did Vince really break my heart so badly I never tried to love again? I can't believe that. He never did deserve me.'

'He never did, Edith.'

'He left me here, but I got this good job, and this nice apartment, and I love to read and every summer it seemed like the place was crawling with attractive men who had boats and bikes. Like Ethan,' I sniffed, and wiped my eyes, and took another handful of popcorn. 'He really got to me, that weak-kneed weenie bastard.'

'No bastards in Shannonville. Everyone gets married before the baby comes.'

'You're right. I can't blame him. I can't even blame Vince. I let this happen. I've become so dim, so dull, so complacent, I didn't even know how much I was compromising. And I can't just blow the whole thing off.'

'There are no blow jobs in Shannonville.'

'It's my own fucking fault. I've been living in a tourist town, never seeing that I was a tourist in my own life! Like I was visiting my own fucking life!'

'No fucking either. We make love. True love. To have sex is gross. Like going to the toilet. To make love ...' Lucy chewed reflectively. 'To make love is a lifelong act, not a mere night's dalliance.'

I stared at her, astonished. 'Lucy, that is awesome!'

238

Her eyes softened, and her expression went misty. 'I remember Ed, that time in Myrtle Beach. We weren't married yet, but oh Edith, I knew then I would never be complete without him, that whatever might lie ahead, any success I had would be meaningless without him, and any failure, any adversity, I could face it with him by my side.'

'True love.'

'Yes. I waited a long time.'

'Was he the only man you ever loved, Lucy?'

'Oh no. God, no. But Ed was the only man who never said to me, in one way or another, You Are Too Much for Me.'

'Too much?' I paused, popcorn midway to my mouth.

'Yes, you know, Too Much. Too smart, too lively, too ambitious, too eager, too beautiful. What have you. You see, even when I didn't know what I wanted, I knew I wanted *something*. Something more than my mother had, a stifled life, all quite lovely, but well, to me it was like being smothered with a sachet pillow. I went to college, joined a sorority, all that, but the fraternity boys, they were no different from my dear reverend father. They wanted me, they wanted women in general, and certainly they wanted their wives to stand behind them, and look lovely and prim and remain, well, motionless. I didn't think I could do that. I was, well, Too Much.' She nibbled thoughtfully on a piece of popcorn. 'I thought I was going to have to move to New York just to meet someone who was like me. Then I met Ed. And Ed, he …' Mascara lay in two, great half-moons beneath her eyes; her colored contacts gleamed with happiness, and she peeled off the fake lash.

'He what?' I said, fighting off the awful notion that I was about to learn something of lifelong value from none other than Lucy Lamont.

'He didn't stand in the way of what I wanted, no matter how long it took me to find it.'

'How long did it take?'

'I don't remember. A long time. It always takes a long time. But Ed never said, Be Less, or Stand Behind Me, or Don't Move While I March Forward. In my books, the truly unworthy men say that. Don't tell me you didn't notice, Edith!'

'Oh, I noticed,' I lied without a qualm.

'Ed is such a dear man.' Her brow furrowed with difficulty. 'Where is Ed, Edith?'

Right. Ed. I asked her to tell me Ed's cell number and dialed it.

He stammered with anxiety. 'Thank God! I didn't get to the Center till late. I had to park a mile away, and by the time I got there, all hell had broken loose. I've been looking everywhere for her. Is she all right?'

'Yes, she's here with me at the bookstore.'

'Thank you, Edith, thank you so much for looking after her.'

'You're welcome,' I said, not bothering to correct him. 'Drive down the alley behind the bookstore and we'll meet you there at the loading dock.'

'It might take me a while. I have to walk all the way back to the car.'

'Flag down some high school kid and get a ride from him. I'll be here. I'm not going anywhere,' which, I reflected was patently untrue. One last professional act.

Dear Miss Carter

No.

240

Dear Edith,

It will come as no surprise that I am resigning as your Events and PR person. I am resigning from the bookstore altogether. I do not expect any references from you, and so I guess I have squandered the last five years. So be it. I have given you years of service and you have given me nothing but shit.

Not true. I was going to be professional, so I left it at years of service, then added:

You have created a lovely bookstore here for this community, but for what it's worth, you have no gift for marketing. I want it fully understood that I am not resigning because of what happened today, though I certainly warned you. This event, egregious as it is, has finally cleared my vision. In quitting this job, I'm hoping to find my way.

Hit print.

I found a box to carry my personal things out of the office, family photos, my old-fashioned Rolodex, a few knick-knacks and little jars of sea glass, some hand-written notes from authors who had enjoyed reading here. In my top desk drawer where I had taped the picture of Ginger Rogers, I peeled it off, but the tape had gone all yellow and brittle. The picture tore, and I just left it. I took the store keys and my letter of resignation and put them on the front desk.

Returning to my office, I found Lucy standing, erect, her resolve everywhere apparent; this was the woman so steely she made the Statue of Liberty look like a cream puff. 'I want Ed.'

'Follow me. Ed's coming.' We went to the back door and stepped out on the loading dock.

'You will be sorry for what happened there, Edith. Someone will pay.'

'I don't doubt it.'

'Not just you. Others.'

'I can't wait.'

'You're very cool in the midst of all this.'

'I always ask myself: what would Ginger Rogers do?'

Lucy puzzled. 'As in Fred and Ginger?'

'Yes. Glamorous, sure of herself, talented, not afraid to work, and not afraid to say what she wanted. That's how I've tried to live.'

She pondered this. 'I, too, have tried to live like that.'

'Well, you succeeded, Lucy. I admire you. Me, I've fucked up. Big time.'

The red Cadillac SUV lumbered down the alley, and stopped by the loading dock. Ed got out, raced up the stairs and took Lucy in his arms. She burst into tears and he led her away with barely a nod to me.

I locked the storeroom door, and then, as I had for many years, I walked down the alley toward the old Seaman's Union building. When I got home I would call Carmen and tell her that I needed the whole tribe of them, as many as could be spared to help me move. Tomorrow. Bring pickup trucks. I would call Mom and ask if I could have my old room back for a while, even if it meant I shared the bathroom with Aunt Clara. I would call my dad and ask if I could work part-time at the pizzeria, never mind my youthful vow never to smell like pizza again. I had to have some kind of job while, with my trusty, antique Rolodex, and my list of contacts, I would start up Tonnino Associates, operating not from downtown Seattle with the view of the harbor, but from my old bedroom with the same view of East Valley Street, and the copper beech that I had looked at since the day I was born, or if not the day I was born, at least the day I came home from New Jersey.

I was in the midst of packing when Jessie called me, late, about ten thirty or so. She was on the ferry. She told me to check out YouTube. The whole disaster was all over YouTube and Facebook and Twitter, and anywhere else you cared to look. 'It was awful, Tosca. Injuries everywhere, blood even, and some of those old people were staggering around. Some of them fell down and couldn't get back up without help. I was afraid Win's fans would start a mosh pit with the old folks. I don't know how many people went to Island Medical, but at least no one died, though I heard one guy had a heart attack. Someone called the sheriff, but by the time they got there, most of the fights were over, and they were just calling paramedics for the people left on the ground. Frances McTeer got a black eye when she waded in to break up a fight.'

'Holy shit. I'll bet she gave as good as she got. What about Miss Carter?'

'The paramedics offered to help Miss Carter, but she wouldn't move. Nan tried to get her out of there, but she just sat there glued to the chair, and she wouldn't even talk. Oh, Tosca, you know why?'

'Why?'

'She'd peed her pants and she would not move out of that chair. She was too humiliated.'

I winced on her behalf. No wonder they hadn't all come running back to the store.

'She just sat there with Wendell and Nan on either side, protecting her, till the paramedics found a blanket, and they draped her in it, and escorted her out. Poor Miss Carter. She's so proud.' Jessie gulped. 'Wendell and Nan had to walk her all the way back to her car wrapped in that blanket. I stayed with Ethan to try to save the books.'

'Save the books?'

'Win's fans were like, gaga, like at a rock concert. Once they'd spilled out into the foyer, they just started grabbing books out of the cartons, and circling around Win who just stood there, like some kind of rock star, signing looted copies of his book.'

'I'm sure he and Ethan were having a great time.'

'Ethan was the one who finally stopped the looting! He got a couple of those high school boys to help him push the fans away, and to pack up the books that hadn't been looted. He made Win and his fans move outside, really, he and the high school boys pushed them through the doors, and then Ethan sent me to get the van, and bring it to the back. He and I and the high school kids loaded the cartons in the van, and when I finally got back to the store, I found Wendell reading your note.'

'And?'

'Just as well you quit. He was going to fire you.'

'BFD.'

'The store is staying closed tomorrow anyway. The Community Center called when I was at the store, and told Wendell they expect Carter & Co. to pay for all the damages. And, you won't believe this, but just before I left, Lucy Lamont's lawyer called! Yes, from the East Coast! Imagine how late it was there! He said Lucy was suing everyone involved.'

'For what?'

'I don't know. Wendell just told the guy to put it in

writing. Wendell's really worried.'

'Tell him to forget it. They have no grounds. There was no contract. She asked to come here. She set it up herself.'

'Lucy Lamont? She did?'

Out with it. I knew I had to tell the bitter truth. 'Yes, I just never mentioned that part. Her publicist called me and told me she wanted to come to San Juan Island because she was looking for a vacation home. You tell Wendell that.'

'Then all that stuff about you calling Smithson/ Empire and asking for her, that was a lie?'

'Yes.' I bit down on the word. 'Yes.'

'Oh Tosca....' The disappointment in Jessie's voice cut me to the quick. 'You should call Wendell.'

'All that is behind me,' I said, willing myself to picture the wake of the ferry, the island diminishing in the distance of my life. I adopted a tone of totally false bravado. 'It's on to bigger and better things.'

'Yes,' she said, though I knew from her voice she didn't believe it. I knew I had truly fallen in Jessie's estimation.

'What about Ethan and Win?' I asked to change the subject.

'Win and all his fans finally left in a big crowd. They all went down to the ferry together, like a big party, having a great time, the walk-ons, the drive-ons. They bought a bunch of beer and had a kind of block party at the ferry landing.'

'Are you on the same ferry?'

'No. That was much earlier. They're long gone. I just heard about it.'

'Ethan too?'

'No, that was the weird part. Ethan just kind of

vanished once the books were packed up.'

'Oh, don't kid yourself, he was out there with the rest of them.'

'He wasn't. His dad, Barry, isn't that his name? What a jerk! He came back up to the store and banged on the door and demanded to know where Ethan was, and Wendell and I, we didn't know. Barry said Win wanted his stuff off the *French Letter*, and he, the dad, had gone down to the marina to get Win's stuff, but the *French Letter* was gone. Just gone. The *French Letter* had sailed away.'

'Ethan can't sail.'

'The boat's gone,' Jessie insisted.

'He must have figured out how to turn on the motor. Anyone can turn on the motor and steer.'

'Tosca, Ethan said to tell you he was sorry. Just before I drove away with the books, he asked me to give you the message.'

'Sorry for?' I flopped on the bed, staring at the poster of Ginger Rogers.

'He didn't say. Just that he was sorry and that he couldn't face you again until he could earn your trust.'

'That will be fucking never. Never.'

'Aren't you even worried a little bit, knowing he can't sail, and he's out there somewhere on the Sound?'

I thought about it for a moment. I could picture the *French Letter* out there in the Puget Sound, alone, a speck against the mountains, a mote upon the tide. 'Frankly my dear, I don't give a damn.'

Chapter Twenty

SEATTLE IS A city awash in coffee. Of the gizillion coffee places, my favorite for meeting clients is the large, airy Starbucks at University Village, once a sleepy neighborhood shopping center, now an upscale mecca for ultra-chic corporations passing themselves off as designer boutiques. As an independent publicist for authors, you'd think Tonnino and Associates would meet with clients in bookstores with their lovely, literary ambience, the smell of fresh print, perfume to writers, especially since there's so many great Seattle bookstores with smart little coffee shops, three near Capitol Hill alone. But I don't hang out in those places. My old pals and colleagues in the bookselling biz are, at best, cool. Not like chic cool. The other kind, frosty. They blame me for the disaster. It's unfair, but there's nothing I can say in my defense. God knows I took the credit last March when Dawn Philbrick and I had our secret conversation. And if I can't defend myself, what's the alternative? To laugh at the Shannonville Massacre? Ha ha ha? That's the YouTube title that went up on Salon, the Shannonville Massacre. They played it for funny. I mean, no one died. And really? For all these *readers* to riot over a couple of books? That's pretty funny, isn't it? Readers are supposed to be curled up alone, reading, not beating the shit out of one another. Funny? No. I can't laugh at it. I can't do anything really, except feel my heart tighten in my chest, and my face flush whenever the Shannonville Massacre comes up. However obliquely.

Everyone in bookselling knows Carter & Co. was sold in September to a couple from Chicago who got rid of the Masterpiece Theatre set, but kept the name. They kept Wendell and Sally too, though Wendell's no longer manager. He had to accept the demotion; he's too old to do anything else, and too young to retire. Jessie emailed me in October to say that she'd heard Miss Carter sold her False Bay home, that she and Nan were moving to a posh golfing gated community in Bellevue, and they would do winters in Palm Springs. This was so unlike Miss Carter. She wanted to serve Literature in the Northwest. Now she'll spend the rest of her life putting a little white ball in the company of pastel-clad ladies, and leathering her skin beside turquoise desert pools. The thought makes me sad. People who respected Miss Carter think it's a tragedy. And, as I had learned at the PNBA meeting in March, many people respected her.

I arrived early at Starbucks to meet my client. The place was tastefully tarted up for the holidays. Lots of ho ho ho. I got misty for Jingle Books, but I bought my double latte, and in strolling to a table, I saw someone reading Lucy Lamont's *Christmas in Shannonville* (holly instead of wisteria on the cover), and two people had the trade paperback of *The Body Electric*. There's been no word at all of the film.

I situate myself with my laptop so I can see the door. I'm meeting my client Mary Hill (*A Charming Memoir of a Vashon Island Childhood*). Mary Hill may have written a book, and published it herself, but that doesn't make her an author. She's unprofessional, always late, scattered, over-fond of her own voice. She's critical of the press releases I write for her book, but unable to add to, or say quite why she doesn't like them. I got her a gig on a podcast, and a speaking engagement with the Puget Sound Preservation Society to promote her book; both times she dithered, and went off on tangents. In short, Mary Hill drives me bonkers, but she's a client, and I need her more than she needs me.

She was not my first client. My first client was Frances McTeer. I worked for Frances for free. I owed her that much, and she agreed to tout my services to others if she was pleased with my performance. Frances's Scottish novel got some notice it would not otherwise have had, readings at Third Place Books and University Bookstore, a slot on The Conversation, KUOW's artsy chat show, as well as a Seattle Library panel on fiction and history, hosted by none other than the famous librarian, Nancy Pearl. I did right by Frances, and she was pleased, though I know she never quite forgave me. She endorsed me to my second client, a pseudo-spiritual writer. Compared to fiction about medieval Scotland, he was easy PR. There's always a hunger for pseudo-spiritual bullshit, as Jessie has proved. I did a nice multi-media platform campaign for him, resulting in a dozen podcasts, radio interviews, lots of hits on his blog, and enough buzz so that his small, independent publisher actually paid his transportation (though not lodging or meals; he stayed with admiring friends) for a West Coast tour. Quite a success. I had two other authors I worked hard for, but without that great of a payoff. And here I was waiting for Mary Hill. I was on my second double latte. I texted her twice confirming that this was the day and time of our meeting. I watched the clock. If she didn't get here soon…. I debated just leaving, but if I failed my client, I'd look like a flake, even though she was the flake. My phone rang, and it was Mary Hill with a thousand apologies! I listened to all the many, many difficulties that came between her and getting over to the mainland from Vashon! All the reasons she's not just late this time, but a complete no show! I listen, but I don't give a shit.

Finally, she says, 'Listen, Tosca, we don't really have to meet, do we?'

'I thought that's what you wanted. That's what you said. Face-to-face contact was important to you.'

'Yes, but I have Face Time on my iPad. Let's do that when you get back to the office. Or we can Skype. Whatever works for you, Tosca,' she added, expecting applause for her thoughtfulness.

'None of this works for me, Mary.' I did not say why. I did not say that anyone on Skype would see in the background of my 'office,' my unmade bed, wallpaper that's older than I am, a lamp with a torn shade, a bunch of library books on the floor, a bureau with sweatshirts hanging out of the drawer, and a plaque I got in high school for Most Improved in Marching Band, 1999. There are no parquetted floors, no stiletto clip of high heels, no view of the harbor.

'Why don't I call you tonight, Tosca?' said Mary cheerfully, 'and let's get something done then.'

'I'm busy tonight. In fact, I'm late.' *Because of you* went unsaid.

I packed up my laptop, and left Starbucks. It's a long, cold, wintery walk out to the nether reaches of the parking lot which is full of Christmas shoppers driving BMWs, Mercedes, Audis, Porsches. At last I came to the Subaru. The heater had stopped working. Chafing my hands against the cold, swearing under my frosty breath, I drove up to Capitol Hill, to the pizzeria. I parked in the back beside the delivery van which the guys were loading up. Five o'clock on a Friday night in mid-December. Business was booming.

'You're late,' the driver told me, as he started the delivery van. 'And Greg is really pissed.'

I went through the back door, and into the tiny restroom where I changed from Tonnino Associates (high heels, sleek pants, silk scarf) and into my counter-clothes: jeans, denim shirt, *Tonnino's* embroidered on the pocket flap, socks and comfortable shoes for standing up hours on end. We wore special aprons, white so they could be bleached within an inch of their lives, and I tied that on and went out to the counter where Greg was taking an order. Greg, whom I had massively inconvenienced by being very late, gave me a filthy look. What could he say? Firstly, there was the customer right there, so he couldn't even growl at me. Secondly, I was the boss's daughter, and Tonnino's new manager. I apologized, but not at length. I knew Greg didn't care why I was late, just like I didn't care why Mary was late. Greg handed me the pen mid-order, took off his apron, and left without another word.

I smiled at the customer, and then, in the great tradition of English majors since the dawn of time, I said, 'Extra cheese with that?'

Yes, Reader, contrary to my youthful vow, I now work at Tonnino's Pizza. Manager, part-time, afternoons and evenings so that my dad doesn't have to work full-time anymore. The rest of my working day I labor away at my new independent PR firm, Tonnino and Associates.

There are no Associates. There's only me, up early every morning, cup of coffee in hand (I keep a coffee pot in my room). I'm on the computer, creating buzz and image, creating campaigns, working on behalf of my few authors, and hustling up new ones. I pursue any contacts I can think of, sometimes outright cold-calling small, independent publishers for PR work. I was certainly on Facebook now, never mind my old disdain. I texted, Tweeted and Tumblred, and was even using Instagram, I browsed the blogs, the web, the Cloud, the Google alerts looking for … what? I did not always know. Work? Authors? Books? Buzz? Something.

I thought if I had a coffee pot in my room, I could avoid the family. Futile. By 7.30 one of them, Mom or Dad or Aunt Clara, would bring me a fresh cup of coffee, a bowl of Cheerios and some toast. I would hear Mom or Dad's heavy tread upon the stairs. Aunt Clara was more than a heavy tread.

'Oh God,' Aunt Clara would call from the landing, 'these stairs are killing my knees! I should move to a retirement home. At least they'd have an elevator. If I had assisted living, I wouldn't be bringing breakfast upstairs to you, Tosca!'

So now I go downstairs and have breakfast with the old folks. Ditto lunch. My mother and Aunt Clara are insistent on a big lunch, because I work late. I have put on five pounds. Okay, seven pounds. In the afternoons, I shower, get dressed and go to work, manager at Tonnino's, so Dad can come home and rest.

In the late afternoon, Carmen sometimes ambles down from the salon, and if the pizzeria's quiet, we have a coffee together. Carmen is on a mission, joining my other sisters, my mother and Aunt Clara. In the six months I've lived at home, they have been seeking the

Next Nice Young Man non-stop.

Carmen was unusually chirpy one afternoon. 'One of my clients keeps telling me about her son. He's thirty-two. He's single. Never married. He works for Starbucks in marketing. He might be a good PR contact for you, Tosca. I have his number. You want to—'

'No, Carmen, I don't. There'll be no Nice Young Man at Christmas this year. I can't stand the thought.'

'It's too bad about Chris Egan getting a girlfriend.' Carmen shook her head and sipped her coffee.

'Not too bad for him.'

'I heard he met this girl through online dating. That's so dangerous. They could be anybody. Tell you anything.'

'Hey Carmen! That's what I'll do! Sign up for online dating! Fill out my profile! Let's see,' I fluttered my eyelashes, 'I like to go to picnics and take walks in the rain. Beaches at sunset. Woodsy walks at dawn. I want someone with a good sense of humor so we can laugh and laugh and laugh. I'm sure I'll meet Mr Right, and I won't care about his bald spot. I'm looking for inner beauty. He and I will go on TV and beam at one another, really gush how happy we are forever. Thank you, algo-rithms, thank you!'

'No need to be snotty. I'm thinking of your well-being. All you do is work, PR, the pizzeria, PR, the pizzeria. You don't have any love life. You ought to get laid now and then anyway.'

'I'm learning to bond with the spin cycle.' Sotto voce, I told her what that meant, and that hushed her on the subject of men. For a while.

Our old instinctive sisterly closeness had returned, and that was gratifying to me, to us both. If anything, all those revelations last June brought us closer. After my initial shock, my sympathies were all with the youthful Carmen who had loved Tom Chase like Catherine had loved Heathcliff, only to find that Tom was just a pale, ordinary mortal. How like Carmen to have a love affair of such pitch and intensity. Like Dad, well, like Frank, she was deeply emotional, and brave or foolish enough to show it.

I was not brave or foolish, but I was not very smart or resilient either. If I were, I wouldn't keep thinking about Ethan James, would I? I never mentioned him to Carmen, not to anyone, but that didn't keep me from thinking about him. He rankled with me. I'd go out with my old high school friends to local bars, or out with college friends to upscale restaurants, and in the crowds, I'd see a tall guy at the bar, or hear someone's ironic laughter, and I think, *Ethan*. I was relieved when it was not. Sometimes when several of us went cycling around Green Lake, or played frisbee in Volunteer Park, I'd see some man in the distance with Ethan's easy walk. I actually tapped one guy on the shoulder, then he turned around. Oops. And why? Why did I still think about Ethan James? So I could tell him what I really thought? Speaking of schmucks. Was it because I felt the imperative – too strong a word – the need for some kind of closure, or understanding? To ask: why did you fuck me over like that, Ethan? Bring Win and destroy everything? Why did he dump me unceremoniously after a night that had seemed to me…. No. None of the above. I needed a big emotional enema. I needed to beat myself severely with my own slipper. Or maybe I just needed to go to bed with an old college beau for the fun of it. I did this. It wasn't that much fun. It wasn't any better than the spin cycle.

As my frustrations, my restlessness mounted, I tried

to applaud myself for pursuing the career I always wanted. Brava, Tosca! But the work I had dreamed of doing was not that compelling or rewarding. And this too left me frustrated, restless. The glamour I'd once so vividly imagined? It's all as fragile as soap bubbles, as fleeting and meaningless. PR takes place in the ether, the blogosphere, the Cloud, the world of mobile apps. It's virtual. It has no substance. As I once so blithely told my father, creating buzz does not have anchovies. Moreover, I kept thinking of that day long ago when Carmen had slammed my hand down in the dough, telling me *That's life, Tosca. Roll your hand around in that!* I had to admit – only to myself, rest assured – that at least when you finished rolling your hand around in dough, you had something in your hand. OK, so it was only a pizza. When you created buzz, what did you have? Nothing you could touch or feel, or point to. Buzz was but a surface ripple on a shallow pond. Buzz would blow away like the fluff on a dandelion stem. And then? Then everyone raced off to hold and clutch and covet the next bit of buzz and the next new thing. How long could you keep that up? I don't mean physically. I mean how long could you go on giving a shit?

The truth is this: I have spent the last six months unsettled, unsatisfied in every way. I once believed that my life would be a proud ship sailing on a vast sea of possibility, that I would make waves, but instead I found myself in a tepid bathtub, adrift with a rubber ducky.

Chapter Twenty-One

LATE ONE MONDAY afternoon, circa four, the lull before the families-with-kids rush, I was mopping down the counter, and this guy came in. He was young, but he looked tired, grim actually. He ordered a small pizza, cheese, that's all, nothing to drink. Water was fine. I knew him, but could not place him. As I handed him over the plates and flatware and a handful of napkins, I mental-Roladexed through my island acquaintances, and still no name came to me. He took everything back to a table and sat so he could see the door. He slumped. A girl came in, and his face lit up. He jumped up and hugged her, not just a little polite hug, but a hug where you could see he was taking in the scent of her hair, and absorbing the warmth of her being, as much as her body. They sat down across from one other, hands locked, talking brightly, and when I called their number, they came up together. The newlyweds!

'Cassie and Cody, right?' I cried. 'Hey, I was at your wedding on the ferry! That was such a cool wedding. How's it going? I'm so happy to see you! What else would you like on this pizza?'

'We can't really afford—'

'Hey, it's my gift! A wedding gift. And what do

you want to drink? Cokes? Sure. Here.' I poured them two Cokes, and called back to the cooks, 'Hey, make a Supremo for my friends here, a wedding gift for my friends. Everything on it. No, really,' I added when Cassie and Cody demurred. 'Take the cheese pizza home for later.' I packaged it up, and gave it to them with a smile.

While the Supremo baked, I heard all about their apartment in dreary suburban Lynwood, all they could afford, but they wanted jobs here, in Seattle. Good jobs so they could afford to move. Cody worked part-time in the produce department at the QFC grocery store nearby. Cassie was doing temp work. I told them my parents owned this building, and I would put word out among the various merchants. They wrote down their phone numbers and emails on a napkin.

They took the Supremo to their table, Dean Martin on the muzak crooning about love. I smiled, sang along with Dean, my heart full of happiness for Cody and Cassie while I washed out glassware at the little sink behind the counter. I heard the bell over the door, and turned around to see Ethan James there. Thinner, his hair much shorter, looking older, and very Northwest Gortex, carrying his bike helmet, his bike shoes clicking on the floor.

'I'll have the Tosca,' he said, 'small.'

'For here or to go.'

He seemed to think. 'Can we talk?'

'For here or to go?'

'Tosca.'

I looked over at Cassie and Cody, beatifically in love, and here I was, facing Ethan James who had screwed me. Personally and professionally. 'What do you want?'

'I want to talk.'

'Go ahead. Talk.'

'This is a nice place. Unpretentious.' He looked around the restaurant appraisingly, resting his gaze briefly on Cassie and Cody. 'And I hear the food is good. As long as you don't want pineapple on your pizza.'

If he thought he was going to jolly a laugh out of me, he was much mistaken.

'I learned to sail, Tosca. Last summer. I motored that boat out of Friday Harbor, and then I spent three months learning how to sail. You were right about sailing. It's a wonderful sensation and uses all your faculties and all your senses, and you're testing yourself against yourself and the elements.'

'Competitive as ever, I see.' I toyed with my pencil.

'I suppose, but what I like about sailing is that you can excel at it without competing.'

'Fascinating. For here or to go?'

'To go.'

'Tosca! To go,' I called out to the cook. To Ethan I said, 'Here's your number.'

'I have a job. Part-time, but a real job. An old friend from Dartmouth, his brother makes video games, he has a studio over in Kirkland. I work for him, mornings. I'm learning the ropes.'

'The ropes of video games?'

'I'm sitting in on development meetings, but right now they only pay me to test them.'

'You play video games. That's your job?'

'Someone has to test them. It's not a career, Tosca. I'm looking at law schools. I studied for the LSAT all fall, and took it just last week.'

'Well, you have the nasty instincts of a lawyer.'

'I'm house-sitting their friend's houseboat on Lake Washington through the winter.'

'And then you'll be homeless.'

He ignored my jibe. 'I figured I'd find you here.'

'I only work part-time here to help out my dad. My own business, Tonnino Associates, is going just great. I have a lot of clients, and a lot of contacts, and a lot of friends here in Seattle. I have a boyfriend for your information.' I could feel my heart pounding, and sweat breaking out on my brow.

'I'm happy for you. You deserve to be happy and loved and successful.'

'Thank you. Go on and take your number. Wait over there.'

'What time do you get off?'

'I don't. I don't get off anymore. Ever. With anyone.'

Ethan put his bike helmet on the counter. 'It's December 12th.'

'What of it?'

'It's been six months exactly. I promised myself I wouldn't find you until it had been six months, and until I could prove myself to you. I've been absolutely clean for a year, not so much as a toke, except for that lapse, in June when Win came up.'

'Then it hasn't been a year, has it?'

'I'm not blaming Win. It was my own bad judgment. I really am sorry, Tosca. It was all my bad judgment. Win called and said he'd come up and do a reading, and we got to talking, and I told him about the Lucy Lamont thing, and he thought it would be funny.'

'And you went along with him like the tool that you are.'

'Was.'

'The reformed tool. So inspiring.'

'I should have stopped him, and I didn't. I didn't think it would turn out like that. But I still should have stopped him. I take full responsibility for everything that went wrong.'

'I'm sure Miss Carter forgave you for everything.'

'No. She didn't. I tried to apologize. I called, and Nan hung up on me. I wrote her a letter of apology, but Nan wrote back and told me never to write again. I don't blame her. It was terrible. Edith could be pretty silly, but she didn't deserve that.'

'You're right. She didn't.'

'And what happened in February. That was my fault too. It shouldn't have been a one night stand. Everything between us—'

'Nothing happened between us. In February. Or ever,' I said coloring, and keeping my gaze on Ethan so I wouldn't have to look at Cassie and Cody.

'But it did happen. Look at me, Tosca, I still have the scar to prove it. I know I walked out on you like schmuck, or a shithead—'

'Please, you're being too kind to yourself.'

'Tosca, I knew you were going to screw with my head. Please don't make a face. I don't mean that way. I mean, I laid in that bed after you got up, and I thought about what we'd just shared, and how rare that was and how much it meant to me.'

'Just stop right there.'

'And I asked myself, are you really ready to actually try and love someone? To let her love you? To be Tosca's lover, the man who will—'

'Don't.'

'And the answer was no. I wasn't ready. I didn't know how. I didn't want to know how.'

I applied the towel to the counter, scouring in energetic circles.

'And I knew you wouldn't settle for anything less.'

'You overestimate yourself, buster. What would make you think I'd want a long term love affair with someone like you?' I said, not giving a shit if Cassie and Cody heard the whole damn thing. 'If I were looking for grand passion, and I'm not, you can damn well bet you wouldn't be the man I'd choose.' Then, against my better judgment, I blurted out, 'Is that why you took up with Jessie?'

'Jessie was a lapse. Jessie and I had a flingette. That's all. You and I had a chance at something larger, better, richer.'

'Oh God! You are *so* full of bullshit!'

'I'm telling the truth. That night, I knew you could have loved me, and I could have loved you. I knew from the way you made love to me when I was so busted up, the way you—'

'Will you stop it? We did not make love!' I was looking for the slipper to beat myself with, when, to my surprise, Lucy Lamont came to my rescue, and I blurted out proudly, 'To make love is a lifelong act, not a mere night's dalliance.'

'Wow!' said Cody to Cassie. 'That's awesome! I'm going to remember that.'

But Ethan would not be stopped 'You could have loved me, and I threw it away. You could have loved me the way you love Astor Piazzolla.'

'Will you fucking leave Astor out of it! This isn't about tango! It's about you and me. No, wait, I take that back. Leave me out of it too.'

'You were so intense and alive and vivid, and warm and caring, and I was so beat up physically, that night, but I'd been beat up mentally and emotionally, for years, and before that night, I didn't even know it—'

'Dude, tell it to Oprah. Not to me.'

'With you, that night, it's like I could see beyond all that. No one's ever—'

'Just stop. Just shut the fuck up. That's bullshit. I hate bullshit. '

Ethan glanced over at the newlyweds, their young faces rapt with attention, the Supremo cooling between them, the ice melting in their Cokes.

'All right. I don't blame you. I fucked up big time.'

I should have pinned my lips shut right then, but I didn't. 'You fucked up, all right. For years and years! Your own grandmother had to bail you out. Again. You said those pederasts at St. George taught you money can buy anything, and then you went out and lived it! Money *can* buy everything, respect, love, loyalty. You are one big success story, aren't you? Don't make waves. Don't make ripples. Just follow along behind Win Jefferies, like the tool, like the weenie that you are. You did what Win wanted, followed his every stupid lead, probably for years! You took the path of least resistance and ended up in rehab. You let your awful father turn you into a sniveling coward. You went to all those hot shot schools and graduated to a padded cell. Brav-fucking-o. You couldn't even be an ordinary schmuck and hold down an ordinary job without fucking up. You couldn't….' I was trembling, and I glanced at Cody and Cassie with their great round eyes and dropped jaws. 'Just pay for your pizza and get out of here, will you?'

'Before I leave I'm going to say what I came here to say. I've waited six months to tell you. I've broken with Win. I haven't had any contact with him since that day, since … since I left Friday Harbor on the *French Letter*. He's called a couple of times, texted, all that, and when I didn't reply, he quit. That friendship is over, maybe it was never a friendship, but a kind of co-dependency.'

'God! Save it for the self-help gurus!'

'You were right, Tosca. I was Roger in *The Body Electric*, and Roger was an asshole, but even an asshole deserves to be mourned. Roger kills himself and the Unnamed Narrator feels nothing. That's the way we were. We thought we were cool. I'm tired of feeling nothing. I'd rather feel pain. I'm free of Win, and I'm done with drugs forever. I don't even drink, except wine with food. I couldn't give that up.'

'What is this, some kind of twelve-step confession fest? Go to church, Ethan.'

'I need to tell you this.'

'You don't owe me anything.'

'I didn't come here because I owe you. This is personal.'

'Yeah, well *this* is a fucking pizza parlor.' Actually, this was like one of those bad dreams where you're naked in the workplace, and you can't find your clothes, and though you tell yourself you can wake up, you can't. The cooks behind me, Cassie and Cody out front, everyone immobile with shock. 'Listen, Ethan, I'm happy that you've found … whatever it is you've found. I'm glad you've made apologies, and got yourself off the sauce, and now you can just congratulate yourself, and be happy and positive, and keep your spirits up and your gluten down, and fondle your crystals and practice deep breathing. Just like Jessie was always saying she was really happy, though she was always really miserable because she lived with an oaf like Murph, and it wasn't Jessie who needed the help, it was Murph. And then he dumped her, and she should have been happy, but no, she was miserable, that is till she took up with you, which, by the way, I don't care about. No. I don't.' I slapped the towel on the counter. 'But if you think you can come in here now, and mealy-mouth boo hoo, apologize, and add me to your list of mea culpas, well fuck you. Maybe your grandmother forgave you, but I don't. I won't. I won't even waste my time listening to your bullshit. So leave me the fuck alone, and don't come back!'

Two new customers came in, and stood in line behind Ethan.

'Small Tosca to go!' cried out the cook, putting the pizza on the window. I got the box, and turned back to the cash register, but Ethan had gone. I was trembling. I took the two orders from the customers, and then I went over to collect Cassie and Cody's plates. Cassie put her hand on mine. She gave me a sad smile, moved by … what? Pity? Fellow feeling? I didn't know, but I feared I might cry.

I didn't of course. Not me. No tragic heroine stuff for Tosca Tonnino. No grand opera theatrics for Tosca. I went back behind the counter and swallowed my tears and my anger, and pain, and confusion and uncertainty and anxiety. I swallowed them one after the other. All night long.

Chapter Twenty-Two

NEXT AFTERNOON, SAME time of day, Ethan rode his bike to Tonnino's pizza, got off, and pushed it into through the door. He didn't take off his helmet. He said he wanted to pay for yesterday's pizza. I took his money, gave him his change and a receipt, he nodded, and left. I watched him through the window on his gleaming, spindly bike, and his beetle-ish yellow helmet. Day after that he came back too. Ordered a small Aida, and a Coke.

'For here or to go?' I asked.

'For here.'

'Here's your number.'

He sat at a small table by the window, and got out a book. Read it while he ate the pizza. He bussed the dishes up to the counter himself.

'Thanks, Tosca,' he said.

'Sure.' I turned around toward the cooks.

This went on for another four or five days, talking a little more every day. Just small stuff. I didn't trust him, and I wouldn't give him more than just the ordinary, boring courtesies. Then one afternoon, he didn't show.

The next morning at breakfast, my dad said that some kid had come in on a bicycle and asked Dad if he ever thought of delivering local pizzas by bicycle, that in traffic, and certainly over short distances, a good cyclist could be every bit as fast as a car. Faster. And a bike didn't need parking. Parking on Capitol Hill was terrible. My father said he knew that. The guy also rattled on about bicycle delivery saving money on gas and being green.

'Wait,' I said, looking up from reading the Cheerios box. 'Was this a guy my age, sort of six foot, a strong jaw and dark eyes. Well-dressed, a scar at the mouth? Yellow bike helmet?'

'Yes. You know him?'

'Sort of. He worked at the bookstore for a while.'

Dad, Mom and Aunt Clara, shot glances to one another. Their collective Nice Young Man antennae all quivered.

'He seems to know his Astor Piazzolla,' said Dad. 'He asked me why I didn't play Astor in the restaurant.'

'No one can eat to Astor,' said my mother. 'Heartburn.'

'Heartburn,' said Clara sagely.

My dad said, 'Astor is not muzak. That's what I told him.'

'Great, Dad.' I returned to my Cheerios.

'He commented that maybe I should use some other music, besides Dean Martin. He says there's a group called Quartetto Gelato, that they have a nice light sound. I never heard of them. Have you? He said Hank Jones and Charlie Haden? Have you ever heard of them?'

'Yes.'

'What do you think?'

'I think he should keep his nose out of other people's muzak.'

'He seems very thoughtful, Tosca.'

'He plays video games all day.'

'He does?'

'Part-time. He tests them. Great, huh? A grown man playing video games for a living.'

'Well,' my father's heavy shoulders shrugged, 'someone has to test them.'

On that unsettling note, I excused myself and went upstairs. I had work to do.

Ethan became a regular late afternoon customer at Tonnino's. Before the Working-Mom onslaught at five, maybe, three-thirty or four, dusk in winter, he'd come in, make small talk, stuff like the weather, order a small pie, take it to a table with a book. He'd finish, bus his own dishes and leave with a nod to me.

One day, he was paying for his pie, and I asked what he was reading. I couldn't help myself.

He showed me a tattered James Patterson paperback. 'Not the late David Foster Wallace,' he said, 'but more content than *The Book of Bunny Suicides*.' He waited for me to smile, and I did. I couldn't help myself. He said, 'I carry this book with me because it's beat up, and if it got lost, I could replace it easily. The books I really care about I leave at home.'

'You have books you care about?'

'The guy whose houseboat I'm living in, he's a great reader. Tons of books. You should come and see it sometime. Lake Union. It's especially beautiful at night.'

'No, thanks.'

'You can see the lights of the city, and the Space Needle. You can hear music and laughter from your neighbors, and see the lights on the water. I love Seattle. I'd never live any place else. My two top law school choices are UW and Seattle University, Gonzaga third.

I'm never going back east again. Miss Carter was right about the Northwest. I've joined a Seattle cycling club, not to race, but to tour. You still ride, Tosca?'

'No.' And of course, I wondered if he noticed the seven pounds I'd put on in these months. 'No time.'

'You should make time. You must get a day off now and then. We could cycle somewhere.'

'Hey,' said the guy behind him in line, 'get a room, willya? I'm starving.'

The next day I had another afternoon appointment with Mary Hill, and this time she committed what to me was the Unpardonable Sin; not only was she incredibly late, but she wanted to linger, and talk, just as if she'd been on time. I watched her jaws flapping. I remembered Lucy Lamont at the PNBA blithely taking up all that precious time that Frances McTeer needed. Finally I said, 'Mary, let's continue this tomorrow, by phone. Phone works, yes? I really have to go. I have another appointment.'

This was a lie. I beat myself with the proverbial slipper, all the way out to the parking lot, but if I were honest with myself, the truth is, I didn't want to miss Ethan James. I put the key in the ignition and the Subaru would not start.

By the time Mom let me out in front of Tonnino's on Capitol Hill (and AAA had come to tow the Subaru) I was more than an hour late. I recognized Ethan's bike out front by the window, and I saw him in the warm glow of the restaurant, but I flew through the door, ducked under the bar, and stashed my purse and laptop under the counter. Greg glowered at me.

'So sorry, Greg. Really, it wasn't my fault,' I blithered and spewed. 'My car wouldn't start. I came as fast as I could. I'm so sorry.'

'You think you're such hot shit,' said Greg, never minding the customers lined up, a couple of moms with youngsters, a gaggle of teens. His face was purple. 'I've had just about enough of this shit.'

'Look, I'm sorry. It won't happen again. Please.' I nodded to the customers. 'I'm really sorry, Greg.'

'Too little too late, bitch. I quit.'

'You can't quit. It's the Christmas rush.' The teens giggled. One mom bolted, kid in tow.

'So, Boss's Daughter, watch me.' Greg took off his apron, threw it on the floor, and left.

'A spat,' I said to no one in particular. I was shaking. 'A silly spat. Can I help someone. Please, can I help someone?'

No one moved until Ethan rose, ducked under the counter, tied Greg's apron around his waist, picked up a pencil and a pad, and said, 'Next in line, please.'

That night, as we closed up, the cooks left in what seemed to me an undue hurry. Greg's bad juju hung in the air like the smell of old pizza.

'How will you get home?' asked Ethan. 'Without your car?'

'Walk. I don't live too far from here. I walk home all the time. I've walked home from Tonnino's since before I could walk.'

'I'll walk with you.'

'The last time a boy walked me home from the pizza parlor, I was sixteen.'

'That was the next to the last time.'

The bike between us, we walked to East Valley Street through the damp fog. He told amusing stories of his video game job, how nerdy the other guys were (and all a lot younger than he was) and how their joy in playing these video games surpassed all else. It was a closed world, really, 'But I've learned a whole new lingo from them. Have you ever heard of a nerdgasm?'

'No.'

'That's the highest possible score on the comment chart. If the game gives you a nerdgasm, it must be great.'

'Do they give you nerdgasms? The games I mean.'

'No, I'm in it for the chicks.' He gave his old sly smile which I recognized, though did not deign to acknowledge. We walked a while further. The sidewalk was slick with frost and moss and wet leaves.

'Well, here we are,' I said stopping in front of my parents' gate.

'This is your place, huh?'

'My parents bought this house in the Sixties. They've lived here ever since. My Aunt Clara lives here too.'

He regarded the house with all its Edwardian era solidity. The deep porch, and broad windows; the Tiffany glass chandelier visible through the transom above the door. The light was on in my room. A belief of my mother's: you need a light on in your room to welcome you home at night.

'Nice place to grow up,' he remarked.

'It was.'

'But you still live here.'

'For the moment.'

'So are you still growing up?'

'Don't be an asshole,' I said, knowing full well that such a retort means you've lost this round.

'Which room is yours?

'The one with the light on upstairs.'

'I don't see the poster with Ginger Roger and Fred Astaire on the wall.'

'I didn't bring it with me,' I said crisply. 'I left it there in the bedroom of my old apartment.'

'And the opera singer?'

'Emma Calvé. I brought her with me.'

'But not Ginger Rogers? I thought you loved all those old musicals where they danced and sparred.'

This would be the test of my new resolve, wouldn't it? 'I don't live in a Thirties musical. I have my own life. I have to ask myself what would Tosca Tonnino do? I have to trust myself.'

'So you are still growing up,' he observed with something of his old inherent cool.

'Goodnight, Ethan.'

'There's two guys playing tango at this club in Belltown. Wanna go? Have a drink. Listen.'

'No. I have plans.'

'I didn't specify a night, Tosca.'

'I'm sure I'm busy.'

'What's your day off?'

'Wednesday.'

'How about Wednesday night? You want to get out your phone and see if you're busy that night?'

'I suppose I could. I might be free. Give me your number.' If I changed my mind, I'd simply call him, and say I couldn't go. 'I'll meet you there. The Subaru will be fixed.' I did not want to go to that houseboat on Lake Union. I did not want to see the lights of the city against the dark sky. I did not want to hear the lake waters lapping at the hull, nor the music and laughter from other houseboats. I did not want to be alone with Ethan James.

'Great. Can you ask if I can have Wednesday night off too?'

'What?'

'Well, I assume I'm hired. You need another hand at the restaurant, and it's too late to hire someone else, and I'm free in the afternoons. So, I'll see you tomorrow afternoon at the pizza parlor.' And with that he put his helmet on, got on his spindly bike and rode away.

I went up the steps, opened the door, and from the living room I heard the comforting soundtrack of *Hawaii Five-O*. I came in and flopped down beside Aunt Clara, my arms folded over my chest.

'Don't those Bad Guys know they're going to get caught?' she said in her woeful fashion.

I kissed her dry old cheek, said goodnight and went upstairs.

At breakfast the next morning, I told my dad what had happened with Greg. I didn't let Greg off the hook (though I certainly did not add that he had said shit in front the customers) but it was my fault. I was late. 'Greg just walked out, and then there was this guy, a regular customer, who just sort of rose to the occasion, put on Greg's apron and started taking orders. I think he wants the job. He said he'd like to go on working for us. Part-time. He works in the mornings. Elsewhere.'

My dad pondered this. 'Is this the guy with the yellow bike helmet and the scar on his lip? The guy who watches video games and wants to go to law school? The guy who thought it would be a good idea to deliver pizzas on a bicycle, who thinks the muzak—'

'Yes! That guy. His name is Ethan. Ethan James. Do you want to hire him, or look for someone else?'

'Well, what's he like, Tosca?'

Mom and Aunt Clara all but Morse-coded with their eyelashes.

'What do you mean, what's he like?'

'Retail, of course. Did you tell me he used to work

with you at the bookstore?'

'Yes. He was very good at retail when he was excited about the product.'

My dad ran a hand through his gray hair. 'Does he like pizza? Does he get excited about pizza?'

'He likes Tonnino's pizza.'

'I'll hire him,' said my dad. 'He seems like a smart guy.'

'He's going to wield a broom and a pen in a pizza parlor, Dad. It's not astrophysics.'

'It's the Christmas rush,' said Mom. 'No time to train someone else.'

My father returned to the sports section of the *Seattle Times*. My mother asked what was a four letter word for exorbitant. My Aunt Clara read the front page, clucking over the state of the city, the state of the world, the sorry mess of the entire universe. No one said another word about Ethan James.

For days I worked the same shift with Ethan while I braced for someone – Carmen, Aida, Norma, Aunt Clara, Mom, even Dad – to say, 'Why not invite him for Christmas dinner? He's such a Nice Young Man.' But no one did.

When Carmen came in to Tonnino's for a quick coffee, I asked her outright. 'Why hasn't anyone said let's invite Ethan for Christmas?'

'Who?'

'Ethan James. The new hire.'

'That Greg,' Carmen tutted, 'that was just awful what he did, scaring away customers. No excuse for that. I'm sure the new guy will work out fine.'

'That's who I'm talking about!'

'Is he the new guy?'

'He is.'

'Didn't he used to work at Carter & Co. with you?'

'God, Carmen, I can't stand it when you play stupid.'

'What? Oh, wait … he's the one who brought Win Jefferies up there, wasn't he? What a terrible day, but you know, Prune, that whole fiasco was a blessing in disguise. Really, you needed to get off that island. Too bad about Miss Carter, of course, but really, ask yourself, would Ginger Rogers be weeping in her beer over that job?'

'Carmen! Jesus! I'm not weeping in my beer and I'm not talking about Ginger Rogers. I'm not even talking about my old job.'

I heard Ethan's voice as he came in through the kitchen and said hello to the cooks. (Who I knew, to a man, were still sniggering over the blow up that first day he came in, and the fact that he now worked here.)

'Hello, Tosca,' he said as he came to the counter. He wore his Tonnino's shirt and the apron, carried the Windex bottle and a towel, and he went to work on an empty table.

I was going to introduce him to Carmen, but she kissed my cheek, said she had to run.

'See you soon, Prune!' Nothing more.

Now, I was worried.

Chapter Twenty-Three

I HAD DIFFICULTY finding the place where I was supposed to meet Ethan, and parking was impossible in Belltown, so I was running late. My high heels clicked percussively on the pavement, as I hurried toward the bar.

'Hey, baby,' said a grungy, grinning panhandler, rubbing his nicotine-stained fingers together, 'you need some directions?'

'I know exactly where I'm going.'

I stepped into the badly lit bar. No Ethan. I remembered with a pang, worse than that, a tiny little seizure of the heart, the night Vince stood me up, the karaoke bar in Portland, and I wondered if Ethan would pull a Vince. I braced for the worst, but I put a look of Gingery insouciance upon my face and waded in. The tables were all postage stamp small, maybe fifteen of them, only half with customers, all couples, or groups of friends. I was the sole solo. A small stage with two high stools fronted a tiny dance floor. A guitar leaned against one stool, an accordion leaned against the other. At the bar there were half a dozen swarthy looking men, and the waitress, with her nose stud and lip ring, looked world weary. Washington law prohibits smoking in public places, but this place didn't need cigarettes. You felt the smoky ambience in any event. At long last the waitress came and asked what I wanted.

'I'll have a sidecar.'

'A what?'

'A sidecar. Ask the bartender. He'll know. When does the music start?'

'They're on break. You meeting someone?'

'Yes,' I said with more conviction than I felt.

She shrugged, went to the bar and returned with the worst sidecar in the history of alcohol.

Perhaps ten minutes later, Ethan wheeled his bike in with him, and the bartender waved, nodding his head, pointing to a door that said Employees Only. Ethan pushed the bike through the door, left it with this helmet, pulled a fiver out of his pocket and dropped it in the tip jar. Evidently this had happened before.

He took the pant clips off his ankles. 'Tosca, I'm so sorry I'm late. I know women hate to wait alone in bars. Please forgive me.' The waitress (smiling by the way) showed up instantly, and brought him a tonic with lime. He lifted his glass to mine just as the musicians left the bar, and ambled to the stage.

They were two brothers, one guitarist and one on accordion. They weren't Astor Piazzolla, but they were intent upon the music, rapt and intense. Their music washed out and over the place, filling it up. But they made no banter with the audience. They played for themselves, communicating through their instruments, and though they got applause, that clearly wasn't the reward they truly valued. Their music insisted on respect, so we were silent while they played, and I was just as glad not to have to talk.

'I like this place because people come here for the

music, or they just don't come,' said Ethan when the musicians took another break. They went outside to smoke.

The waitress came again, carrying another tonic with lime for Ethan. This time I ordered Campari and soda.

'I come here whenever they're playing,' Ethan explained after she left.

'How did you find this place?'

'It took me months after I moved here. I went to every Argentine restaurant, ordered the cheapest thing on the menu, and asked a lot of questions.'

'I've never been to any place like this in Seattle. My high school friends hang out at the old local watering holes, and my college friends who've made it hang out at upscale, high-priced bars.'

The musicians came back, and took their places on the little dais in a pool of milky light. They played another set, sparing me having to talk further.

At their next break, a semi-strained silence reigned between us, and then Ethan said, 'A year ago, I would never have guessed things could be so different. Last year I endured Christmas day with Edith and Nan. This Christmas I'm doing the all day marathon, maybe all night too. I'm playing in the Call of Duty marathon. One of the nerds invited me.'

That's the end of Nice Young Man dilemma, I thought, pleased. 'What's that?'

'People play Call of Duty non-stop. They do it in shifts, taking breaks to sleep and eat and pee. They're trying to break last Christmas's record of a hundred and thirty-six hours.'

'Fascinating,' I said, sipping my drink. 'Actually that sounds like the most boring thing I can imagine.'

'It's not chess.'

'Do the nerds play chess?'

'Not really. I miss Statler and Waldorf a lot. I don't like online chess games. I like to see the competition. What is it they always say? The thrill of victory, the agony of defeat? How can you do that on a computer?'

'Sometimes the computer feels like a substitute for living.'

'You must be on it night and day with your PR business.'

What I told him of Tonnino Associates was not outright lies, just truth enhanced. Photo-shopped, you might say, and this would have been fine with the old Ethan James, Mr Sarcastic Irony who invited and returned, even rewarded a cutting barb. But I felt increasingly, if not altogether false, at least, disgustingly shallow. Finally, I just said, 'Having my own PR firm hasn't been everything I'd hoped for. I just got a new client today, a novelist who's written a cookbook-memoir, but I can't get excited about working with her. It's not her fault. None of it is as fulfilling as I thought it would be. I'm creating buzz, I guess, but I'm not part of anything. At the bookstore, when authors came, I'd read their books, and meet them, and customers would respond, and talk afterwards. There was a wonderful sense of connecting readers and writers, but now, what do I have to show for all my work? I can't point to any one thing, and say I did that, or I made that. Who cares? It all dissipates.'

'Maybe you should write a book instead. Then you'd have something to show.'

'I couldn't write a book.'

'You don't know that. You have to try. I would never have thought I'd be any good at developing a story, and graphics, and all that, but I really love working in video game development. The concepts, not the testing. I like the work.'

'What about law school?'

'I did pretty well on the test, but honestly, I don't think I'll get into the schools I want. My grades at Dartmouth weren't very, well, you can imagine what they were like. I don't have anything to show for the years after college, a few cycling championships, skiing competitions, working at the bookstore. And I don't have any references.'

'What about Win Jefferies? He's pretty impressive,' I said sarcastically.

'Why would a law school trust a novelist's reference? Anyway, that friendship is over. He and I screwed up big time, and at least Win was able to do something with it, make something out of it. He wrote a book. What did I do?'

His candor made me feel bad for being such a snot. 'If you don't get into law school, what will you do?'

'I'll design video games. Actually, I might do that anyway, and never mind law school. I work with a good bunch of people, and I like the place, the ambience. They're intense and creative, but it's video games, so it's fun too.'

The musicians returned to the stage and began playing again. With each set, their music had grown more fervid, filling the small place with tango, the music of pain and pleasure, love and heartbreak, sex and sweat, hands and haunches, the fleshy satisfactions of having a body at all.

'I watched all those old Fred and Ginger movies,' Ethan offered when they next stepped outside for a cigarette. 'I thought if you liked them, they must be entertaining.'

I shrugged. 'They're fun.'

'They're more than that. The stories are silly, but the dance numbers, they're masterpieces. And they make it look easy, when you know it's not. You know that hours and hours of work went into each step, but they still look like they're having the most wonderful time of their lives when they're dancing.'

Unbidden, there came to me the lyrics of *The Continental*, something about … you kiss while you're dancing. I thought about beating myself with my slipper.

'You wonder, though, don't you, if they knew.'

'If they knew what?' I asked.

'That, those few films together, that was the best they would ever be. They both went on and had long careers afterward, but neither one would ever reach such heights again. They were better together than they ever would be apart. Do you think they knew it then?'

'Oh, probably not,' I replied, trying to sound airy and uninterested.

'No matter what they did with anyone else, they would never be as perfect as they were in those few years, 1934 to 1938. Kind of sad, really. That was all they had.'

'Oh, I don't know. Ginger won an Oscar. For *Kitty Foyle* in 1940. She beat out Joan Fontaine and Katherine Hepburn to win it.'

'Yes, and when you think of Ginger Rogers, is it *Kitty Foyle* you remember?'

'No,' I conceded, 'when you think of Ginger Rogers, you think of Fred Astaire, and their dancing. They were better together than they ever would be with anyone else.'

The brothers returned to their small dais and picked

up their instruments and began again.

'You want to dance?' asked Ethan. I looked at the tiny, empty dance floor. 'I've forgotten everything I ever knew about tango.'

'It's like riding a bicycle.'

'How do you know?'

'Because I ride a bicycle.'

'You said you never learned to tango.'

'I said I wasn't that good.'

'Really? Something Ethan James isn't good at?'

'I'm willing to try.' He stood and offered me his hand, and I took it. We moved to the small space in front of the musicians; the light was poor, but you don't need light for what we were doing, tango, yes, though without those fancy moves that turn tango into narrative, literally love stories in motion, the moves that take emotional narratives and give them flesh. I had not forgotten everything I knew about tango, and though he wasn't that great of a dancer, certainly not Fred Astaire, Ethan had the feeling for it. He had that.

We got a round of light applause from other customers whose faces I could not see, and a smile from the musicians. We walked back to the table.

'Your boyfriend must be really understanding,' he said.

'What?'

'If he doesn't care that you go out with me.'

'I go out with whomever I wish. I don't have to ask permission.'

'If you were my girl, I wouldn't want you going out dancing with some dude.'

'Is that you? Some dude?'

'I suppose that's what you can tell your boyfriend.'

At the end of that set I had to leave. Tomorrow, 23

281

December, would be a busy day. He walked me to my car while he balanced his bike. I opened the door, and was about to remark on the bun-biting cold, to say something clever and flip, but he kissed me. Not a great ardent kiss, but a kiss just the same. It reminded me of being a kid at the beach, and putting my toe in the icy Sound, and shivering so, I had to run back up the rocky beach. Or maybe it's that his nose was cold on my cheek. Or maybe it was the three drinks. I did not kiss him back, but before I closed the Subaru door, I said, 'I don't have a boyfriend.'

On 23 December, Tonnino's Pizza did three times our usual Thursday business. Ethan and I worked the counter non-stop; we had three cooks in the back, and two guys washing dishes, and the delivery guy just left the motor running as he dashed in and out with the pies. On top of all that business, we probably sold two dozen Gift Certificates. People would come in, gray-faced with shopping fatigue, hoisting huge, heavy bags, and stare at our big sign by the cash register.

'A Tonnino's Gift Certificate is the best present in Seattle,' Ethan advised them as he was ringing up their pizzas. 'No need to gift wrap.'

In the days he'd worked here, he had proved he was good with the customers. Just like at the bookstore, he put people at ease; he treated the teens and the old folks with respect, two groups of people who generally got no respect at all. He no longer assumed masculine superiority; he had no complaints about cleaning up, stocking shelves, scouring down the sinks and the long wooden paddles we used for the pies.

We worked our butts off that day, and closing up at ten, I reminded everyone that tomorrow, Christmas Eve was only a half day.

'No rest for the wicked,' said one of the busboys.

I was locking up when Ethan asked me where my car was. Had it quit running again?

'No, my mom said she needed it for some last minute shopping. My niece borrowed her car, and my dad's is in the shop,' I added, wondering momentarily why Maddie needed Mom's car. She had Carmen's. 'Anyway, Mom dropped me off at work.'

'So you're walking home.'

'Yes. I guess I am.'

'I'll walk you home if that's all right.'

'Sure.'

I knew that route from Tonnino's to East Valley Street like the back of my hand: every crack in the sidewalk and uneven bit of pavement, every root that knobbed up like a knuckle through the sidewalk. But the light snowfall changed everything, softened it and sharpened it in the same minute. The Christmas decorations up on many houses blinked and shone in the snow, and the streetlamps cast odd shadows. Many front windows framed Christmas trees, and I got rather nostalgic, thinking of Miss Carter's famous party. There would be no more of those. Suddenly I realized that Ethan was the only person in Seattle, in my present, who shared, who knew any part of my island past. He must have been thinking the same thing because he mentioned Miss Carter with affection and regret.

'I had a lot to explain to my grandmother,' he added, 'but at least I made it clear that the whole fiasco was my own doing, and didn't reflect on her friend.'

'What about your dad? He had a hand in it.'

'I didn't mention him. I could have stopped it, and I didn't. I took responsibility.'

I let that pass in silence for a bit. 'So they're still friends, Marjorie and Miss Carter?'

'As far as I know.'

At my parents' house, the Christmas tree filled up the whole front window. I opened the gate, and he pushed his bike inside and leaned it against the copper beech in our front yard.

'Merry Christmas, Tosca.'

'Thanks. Same to you.'

'I'm not working tomorrow, so I'll see you at Tonnino's on December 26th.'

'Sure. See you then. Have fun with the Call of Duty nerds.'

He brought his lips to mine and kissed me. I responded. Against my better judgment, yes, but not against my will. Resolutely, I said goodnight, went up the porch steps and into the house. As I closed the door, I saw he was kneeling down by the bike, adjusting a spoke or a pedal, or something.

'Tosca?' Aunt Clara called from the living room. A *Hawaii Five-O* re-run blared from the TV. 'Is that you?'

'Who else would it be at eleven o'clock at night?'

'Come in here.'

'I can't. I'm exhausted.'

'*I'm* exhausted! Who do you think keeps this whole house running? Me.'

'Oh, Clara,' said my mother, 'quit complaining.'

I went into the living room. They sat there bathed in the blue glow of the television.

'I'm eighty-five years old. Am I complaining?' Clara demanded. 'No. I do all the cooking. I'm on my feet all day, and what thanks do I get for it? None. At least let me be exhausted in peace.'

I sagged onto the couch and sighed.

Clara began to cluck, and wagged her finger at the TV. 'Why do they do it?'

'Who?' I asked, super-sick of this same conversation.

'The Bad Guys! Don't those Bad Guys know they're going to get caught? Steve McGarrett and Danno are going to catch them. They're going to prison! I ask you, why do they even try?'

'Oh God, Aunt Clara!' I stood up and started for the stairwell. 'You ask that all the time!'

'You never answer,' she said. 'No one answers me. Everyone ignores—'

'Because if they didn't try, there wouldn't be any story!' I shouted. 'See? Get it? If they didn't actually take some action, rob the bank, or steal the plane, or whatever they do, there'd be no one for McGarrett to catch. If they didn't actually *do* something bad, they wouldn't be Bad Guys! If they didn't *do something*, there wouldn't be any story to tell!'

Aunt Clara grunted. 'No need to yell.'

Grumbling, I started up the stairwell, trudging, when unmistakably, and unbidden there came the voice of Ginger Rogers, from one of the classic films, and it probably didn't matter which one because Fred was the one always pursuing her, and she was always just as cool as could be. She always gave him a sophisticated glance, and judged him wanting, but somewhere in there, Ginger always reversed herself, and fell completely in love, capitulated. She loved him, and she knew she loved him, and she knew he loved her. Though they did their love scenes (sex scenes, really) in dance numbers, you knew that Ginger had thrown caution to the winds. Okay, my life wasn't one of those frothy films, but I suddenly saw the hard truth of what I'd just told Aunt Clara: *If you don't risk the pain of love, you will never know the pleasure. You must act, or risk having no story to tell at all.*

I bolted down the stairs, to the front door, and out to the porch. Ethan and the bike were gone. The gate was closed. I dashed out to the sidewalk.

'Ethan!' I called into the cold air. 'Ethan! Ethan!'

No answer, no sound even, save for the slight crinkle of falling snow. I could see the thin track of his bicycle tire in the snow, all the way down the sidewalk, and then, I saw a fleeting shadow in the distance, at the end of the block.

'Ethan!' He stopped, and I could see him poised there in the light cast by the street lamp, his yellow helmet glowing. He got off the bicycle and turned it around. 'Ethan!'

He got back on the bike, and raced up East Valley, bouncing back up the uneven sidewalk to where I stood. He took off his helmet. 'Tosca.'

'Would you like to come for Christmas?' I asked. 'I just thought, maybe instead of Call of Duty marathon, and the nerds ... I mean, it's the whole family, I'm afraid, and they can be a little overwhelming, but if you'd like to—'

He pulled me close up against him, dropped his helmet into the snow, and wound his arms through my open coat, up my sides, his hands splaying over my back as though he was the maestro, and I was a musical instrument. I wrapped my arms around his neck and brought my lips to his. He kissed me with what I can only describe as Great Expectations, and I knew, Reader, I would not be parted from him again.